THE MEMOIRS OF DOLLY MORTON

'One afternoon, about five o'clock, I had strolled into Central Park, where I seated myself on a bench under the shade of a tree to smoke a cigar. There my eyes turned upon a lady who was sitting on the adjoining bench, reading a book. She was a very pretty little woman with, as far as I could see, a shapely, well-rounded figure. She was neatly gloved, and handsomely but quietly dressed; everything she wore being in good taste, from the little hat on her head, to the neat boots on her small, well-shaped feet, which peeped from under the hem of her wide skirt. I stared at her harder than was polite, thinking she was quite the type of a pretty American lady of the upper class.

She looked steadily at me for a short time; then, apparently satisfied with my appearance, a bright smile came to her face, and she shot a saucy glance at me, at the same time making a motion with her hand inviting me to come and sit beside her. I was rather astonished, as I had not thought from her appearance that she was one of the *demi-monde*; but I was quite willing to have a chat with her, and also to poke her, if her conversation pleased me as much as her looks …'

THE MEMOIRS OF DOLLY MORTON

Anonymous

A STAR BOOK

published by
the Paperback Division of
W.H. ALLEN & Co. PLC

A Star Book
Published in 1984
by the Paperback Division of
W.H. Allen & Co. Ltd
A Howard and Wyndham Company
44 Hill Street, London W1X 8LB

Preface copyright © Star Books 1984

Printed in Great Britain by
Anchor Brendon Ltd, Tiptree, Essex

ISBN 0 352 31482 6

PREFACE
by
Alexis Lykiard

i.

The likely author of *The Memoirs of Dolly Morton*, Georges
Joseph Grassal (1867–1905), scarcely better known as
'Hugues Rebell' (the most frequently used of his various
pseudonyms) rates one tantalizing paragraph in the 1959
Oxford Companion to French Literature. His poetry is
mentioned alongside 'novels, usually with elaborate
historical settings and said to be reminiscent of those of Pierre
Louÿs.' Coincidentally, Louÿs (1870–1925) was also one of
the finest French writers of erotica – something else he had in
common with Grassal.

Grassal, however, became virtually bi-lingual. He not only
translated books into both English and French but wrote
several, including *Dolly Morton*, in English first. He may
have owed this linguistic facility to his education at the Jesuit
College, Jersey. One cannot resist the guess that he there
acquired both his taste for the English tongue and 'the
English vice' – for he certainly wrote often about flagellation
(see *Bibliography*). This particular interest, though, was
reflected in only part of a considerable literary output.

Grassal proved amazingly prolific during his short life, producing books of poetry, novels, essays, stories, art criticism, philosophy and literary criticism, as well as translating into French both Oscar Wilde and various run-of-the-mill English erotic works.

Little is known of Grassal's life: he was born in Nantes, wrote from necessity as well as choice, and lived in Paris, where he pursued his profession of *homme de lettres* and where he died. He used to stay at the Château de la Pervenchère, Casson, near his birthplace, and some of his novels (including *La Femme qui a connu l'Empéreur*) are set in the Nantais region. He is buried at La Chapelle-sur-Erdre, near Nantes.

The young Grassal was associated with the Symbolist poets (the 1933 Larousse praises his 'sensuous imagination' and 'warm and vivid style') but then joined the 'École Romane' group founded by the Greek-born poet Jean Moréas (Iannis Papadiamantopoulos). The École Romane admired the Troubadours, Ronsard, Racine and La Fontaine, repudiated Romanticism, and tried to emulate classical literature, reverting to regular verse forms and the elegiac tone.

At some point early in his promising literary career it seems Grassal lost all his money and/or accumulated considerable debts. He therefore began working as a hack (albeit a superior one) for the shady Paris-based publisher Charles Carrington. Carrington, a Portuguese whose real name was Paul Ferdinando, 'issued both in English and French, in excellent editions provided with prefaces, the most famous erotica of the world,' wrote Henry L. Marchand in *The Erotic History of France* (1933). 'True bibliophile that he was, no erotic product was outside his domain: anthropology, chronicles of scandal, flagellation, original gallant literature, scientific works on sex, etc.' The portrait of Carrington in Alec Craig's *The Banned Books of England* (1962) is an extraordinary one: 'Carrington started life as an errand boy, vanboy, and then lavatory attendant. At sixteen he was keeping a book barrow in Farringdon Market. By reading his wares he graduated into the company of men like Dowson, Beardsley and Wilde. In the Paris of the early Twenties he was a pathetic figure not without a little dignity of tragedy. Blind as the result of syphilis, he was no match for his predatory mistress and was helpless before the follies of his five children. They and their hangers-on swarmed over his house and stole his books. A shop was even opened specially to dispose of the thefts. He endured five years of this misery before perishing in a lunatic asylum at the age of sixty-five. His mistress provided a magnificent funeral and his tortured body was consigned to earth by the Catholic Church.'

But between 1895 and 1917 Carrington was riding high and as Craig also confirms, Carrington's 'publications were well edited and printed and many of them of legitimate literary or scientific interest.' When Carrington published Grassal's *Memoirs of Dolly Morton*, which H. Montgomery Hyde in his *History of Pornography* (1964) calls 'an interesting and moving book, which certainly recaptures the plantation atmosphere, even more graphically than *Uncle Tom's Cabin*', it was with his customary dealer's hype. '*The Memoirs of Dolly Morton*, the Story of a Woman's Part in the Struggle to free the Slaves,' ran the full original title, continuing: 'An Account of the Whippings, Rapes and Violences that preceded the Civil War in America, with curious Anthropological Observations on the radical diversities in the conformation of the Female Bottom and the way different Women endure Chastisement.'

Certainly Carrington knew his market, for as the Frenchman Taine commented in his *History of English Literature* (1878): 'All tender considerations of modern humanity have failed to abolish boxing-matches and the use of the rod among this people [ie the British]', and most of Carrington's customers were British and American. Yet as Peter Fryer has written, *Dolly Morton* is 'virtually the only flagellation fantasy of the period that sustains, for any length of time, the interest of readers who do not share the predilection.' This is because of 'the unusual feature that its characters are, for the most part, credible human beings in credible situations and not merely disembodied sex organs' – and also because Grassal was a good writer. For C.R. Dawes,

vii

another authority on Victorian erotica, *Dolly Morton* was 'by far the best of all the books whose main theme is Flagellation', since 'there is an intensity about it that is arresting and places it as being among the very few good erotic books of the period.'

It seems likely that Grassal was interested in and convinced by his subject and therefore wrote with conviction and passion. This is no tongue-in-cheek piece of hackery, although his contemporary, the very shrewd observer and more famous writer Jules Renard (1864–1910), hints that he possessed a deadpan sense of humour. 'Rebell,' wrote Renard in his *Journal* for 1898, 'whose lips take pains to convey the Mona Lisa smile. They say da Vinci worked on it for four years. Rebell works on it all his life.' At a funeral in 1899 Renard notes Rebell, 'clean shaven as a priest's arse', in the company of Moréas and other Bohemian types with the 'hairless faces and slicked-down hair' unusual in that sober, luxuriantly bewhiskered age. Our last view of him, via Renard, is in the *Journal* entry for April Fool's Day 1905, when, perhaps appropriately enough, Renard hears that 'Rebell has died destitute, surrounded by 40,000 francs' worth of fine editions he did not want to part with. He was, remarks the ever-satirical family man Renard, 'the celebrant of a lustful faith.'

With recent reprints of some of Grassal's books in France (among them novels set in Renaissance Venice and in Haiti: see *Bibliography*) and now in the UK (the offbeat and rather charming *'Frank' and I*, also published by Star, 1983) there is a good chance that the enigmatic Grassal/Rebell will not be forgotten. A minor writer he remains, but he had more than sheer industry to commend him: his books are often surprizingly lively and intelligent – worth more than a passing mention in the literary reference books.

ii

G. Legman, that erudite and illuminating writer on social, sexual and literary topics, has called *Dolly Morton* 'a curious novel' and so it is, in almost every sense *except* the booksellers' tired euphemism. Indeed, as Patrick J. Kearney aptly notes (in *A History of Erotic Literature*, 1982) *Dolly Morton* is 'not a typical piece of hardcore pornography, and possesses points of interest that are unrelated to its sexual content.'

What seems initially a conventional genre novel soon reveals additional levels of meaning: unexpected perceptions abound and a passionate indignation rises to the surface. Dolly – by a nice authorial irony born in Philadelphia, city of brotherly love – is motherless at the age of two and absolutely dependent upon and subservient to her disciplinarian bank-clerk father. Her relationship with this tyrant is neither 'normal' nor loving. He is, in her own phrase, 'utterly unsympathetic', and beats her regularly throughout her childhood. He continues to inflict corporal punishment well past her adolescence (thereby perhaps expiating, it is hinted, his murkily incestuous desires), until Dolly is made to feel helpless, frightened and inferior. She is never allowed to grow up into the fond companion and friend to her father she yearns to become: in short she is less a daughter than a slave. And male domination outlives even death: her father finally bequeathes her not the convenient legacy of so many Victorian novels but crippling debts instead, thus dooming her to further dependence on that very patriarchy which has so far given her nothing but pain.

Dolly is eighteen, penniless and homeless, but she remains idealistic. It is just before the US Civil War. Taking a chance, she joins Miss Dean, a Quaker philanthropist, and they journey South to Virginia, their mission to strengthen the network helping runaway Negro slaves escape to the Northern states. Their activities within this organization, the Abolitionist 'underground railway', will, ironically, plunge Dolly herself into abject servitude. 'There had never been,' she remarks, 'an instance known of an "underground station" run by women.' True or false, this is a deft invention of Grassal's, enabling him to link and emphasize his main themes: slavery (in the widest sense) and its effects of coarse

ix

brutalization and the painful, inevitable struggle for liberation. In the North Dolly, through circumstances beyond her control, was a slave to convention – symbolized by the authoritarian paterfamilias. Now, indirectly yet by her own *unconventional* choice, she falls into still worse slavery, inflicted by the racist (hence also sexist) White Southern male.

She and Miss Dean – peaceable, fairminded, loving women – endure virtual martyrdom for their pains. Only when Dolly meets the gallant yet tender Northern soldier Captain Franklin can she know mutual love. He is killed, fighting the good fight to free the slaves and she survives humiliation, rape and torture, changing inevitably in the process. After this one 'normal' relationship (shared love with Franklin), when she finally returns North it is back to slavery once again – this time the financial and physical servitude of prostitution.

Despite her appalling past experiences she does not hate *all* men, and when she has sex with the narrator (to whom, according to a convention more literary than realistic, she in turn tells her story) she herself at first appears to be that plump, reassuring Victorian stereotype, the tart with a heart. Still only 22, she maintains: 'I did not like having to adopt the life, for notwithstanding all I had gone through, I was still a modest woman to a certain extent … I hated the life at first, and I dislike it still, but I have got accustomed to it – like other women in the same positon. Nearly four years have passed since that time, and I have done well in the "profession" … although I am what I am, I will never marry a man unless I love him.'

The narrator wishes her well, he hears later that this is indeed what has happened, and there is thus a happy ending – itself undercut by the narrator's rather patronizing concluding comments. But then he *is*, after all, a Briton – Dolly a mere colonial and a reformed prostitute at that! His somewhat bland, smugly benevolent tone, Grassal may be implying, perpetuates yet another variety of masculine domination …

For Dolly, like so many other young women in the last century, scarcely any alternative existed: marriage was the aim of life; even an unhappy union was not necessarily regarded as either compromise or disaster. Opportunities for escaping the twin yoke of economic serfdom and male despotism were rare. When Dolly first meets the novel's villain Randolph, the wealthy Southern plantation owner who will soon be her tormentor, father-substitute and keeper, he reminds her: 'I am your landlord, as the house you are living in belongs to me.' She finds out that 'Randolph was a clever man, and well read, but he was a thorough libertine who considered women merely toys to be used for the gratification of his sensual desires.'

Infatuated, Randolph soon abandons his gentleman's manners. The charming mask drops: he stops reading poetry to her and instead attempts a more direct approach – rape. When Dolly resists, he resorts to bribery (psychologically appropriate, in his case) and finally leaves, mouthing ominous angry threats. As G. Legman wrote in his pioneering *Love and Death* (1949): '[men] ... are afraid to acknowledge that even after ten thousand years of enslavement, woman – through the naked physical fact of man's need of her – is still strong enough to get her master down'. The thwarted Randolph duly takes his vicious revenge.

The 'underground station' is exposed and for their subversive activities Miss Dean and Dolly are cruelly punished. Their ironically-named punishment is 'riding the rail', and Randolph arrives to gloat and mock: 'I must say Dolly, that you squealed just like a pig being killed.' The book grows progressively grimmer. By the time Dolly – an eighteen-year-old female, alone, friendless and disgraced in unfamiliar, hostile territory – is compelled to go along with the appalling Randolph, becoming his mistress and also mistress of his plantation 'Woodlands', she has realized the true enormity of the system in which she is trapped.

Although privileged compared to the plantation blacks, she remains a chattel herself, 'at the beck and call of a master; for such Randolph was to all intents and purposes ... I was always more or less afraid of him.' And with good reason! After flogging a female slave, Randolph explains to the distraught Dolly: 'You are a Northern girl, so you don't understand how we Southerners look upon our slave women ... Their bodies belong to us, so we can use them in any way we please.' They are, he continues, on a par with his dogs and horses. Finance, possessions, sex, all are inextricably linked: a young female slave is worth 2000 dollars (then a considerable sum) and towards the end of the book when the runaway Sophy is recaptured, Randolph is furious at having to pay 400 dollars reward money and 'paddles' the luckless girl mercilessly. By then Dolly is 'well aware that whipping a woman excited him' and soon afterwards, significantly, she notes that he 'gave me a strong poke from behind'. This is a man who 'used to say that a woman should never be "had" twice in succession the same way,' and who maintains to Dolly 'that if a man always poked a woman in the same position, he would get tired of her sooner than if he varied the embraces'; he is a man corrupted by his absolute power.

The description of his 'lovemaking' is acute and sardonic: '"Now my dear little girl, I've got you at last!"' 'It was,' (continues Dolly) 'the first time he had made use of a tender word to me that night. While stripping me, he had not spoken a word but he had treated me as if I had been merely a lay figure.' Later, he sharply orders: 'Keep still, whatever I do.' She must remain his slave, passive and obedient. The poison of slavery has completely tainted him. To him sex has become a sort of uncontrollable illness, a demanding fever: 'My tool is aching from its prolonged erection' he informs Dolly, 'so I must take the stiffness out of it at once.' Dolly, the eternal optimist, fleetingly thinks 'that if he would only treat me more as a woman and less as a subject for the gratification of his passions, I might get to like him a little,' but it is too late – the corruption is total.

Dolly experiences the whole debased hierarchy of slavery. The slave Dinah talks to her 'freely, but always with perfect respect. The fact of my having been indecently whipped by a band of men had not lowered me the least in her estimation. To her I was still a white lady from the North, while she was only a slave.' And yet Dolly is surprised by 'the contemptuous way Dinah spoke about nigger wenches. Although she was a slave herself, and liable at any moment to be whipped if she committed an offence, she had a great idea of her own importance as housekeeper of Woodlands.' Later, Dinah 'evidently did not think it strange that a woman of her age should have been whipped in such an ignominious way, and did not appear to bear her master the least malice. She was his slave; her body belonged to him, therefore he could do what he liked with it. Such,' (Dolly concludes) 'was the degrading effect of slavery on the minds of the human chattels.' But when Dolly is insulted by the younger, more rebellious octoroon Rosa: 'The tears came into my eyes, my heart swelled, and I felt a deep sense of degradation. It was hard that owing to a series of misfortunes, I should have come to be spoken to in such a coarse way by a slave girl. But, alas! what she had said was the truth. I really was no better than her.' Dolly knows all too well that Randolph 'certainly had given me plenty of fine clothes, and a quantity of jewellery, but then – as he would probably have said himself – he had taken the value out of my body.'

The relentless cruelty and exploitation inexorably leads to general callousness among black and white, male and female, young and old. Dolly herself spanks two black children for torturing and killing a kitten. She notices she has 'grown somewhat callous', and 'accustomed to seeing women whipped. . . Moreover, since my own shameful whipping. . . my nature had become hardened.' However, she never adopts the questionable nineteenth century opinions expressed by, for instance, John Davenport: 'As an erotic stimulant. . . considering the many intimate and sympathetic relations existing between the nervous branches of the extremity of the spinal marrow, it is impossible to doubt that flagellation exercised upon the buttocks and the adjacent parts has a powerful effect upon the organs of generation.' (Davenport: *Aphrodisiacs and Anti-Aphrodisiacs*, London 1869). Women can of course be quite as cruel as men: a woman, Theresa Berkley, was the notorious inventor of the 'chevalet' or 'Berkley horse', a nastily ingenious whipping contrivance. But Dolly is neither impassive observer nor passive victim: she is invariably intelligent and in search of love, not cruelty.

She finds this love with the Northerner, Captain Franklin. Although brief, it is genuine, ecstatic and uncorrupted. Her view is clearly stated: 'I think that a man always enjoys poking a woman whether he loves her or not: but I am sure that a woman never really enjoys a man's embrace unless she loves him.' The key and moral to the whole book – the only sentence printed in bold type – is supplied by Dolly herself: '**I think a man copulates with the woman he loves differently to the way he pokes the woman he merely lusts for.**' This is proper discrimination, significant not only because it is an unusual sentiment in a supposedly 'pornographic' novel, but also because it is true.

It is, too, a clue to the author's foreign-ness: an American would have written *differently than*, an Englishman *differently from*. Yet throughout the book no one could doubt the author's power and ability. *Dolly Morton* is full of telling perceptions, its use of language often extraordinarily forceful and flexible. Specific, too. There are scarcely any four letter words, though: Dolly uses *thing*, *spot* and *poke*, and often in inverted commas as if to emphasize her own and the Victorians' genteel ambivalence towards sexual matters. The word *fuck* is used only when she is raped, and 'a dirty pack of cards. . . produced, and cut by the men in turn.' Converted ignominiously into an object to be played for, she can then be target for her aggressors' scorn. If there is no equality, language can be reduced to the coarse blunt instrument such men make of it. Their 'We are going to fuck you' carries here the full brutal menace the author wants to convey. The rape of the young slave Peachie is described with even more horrific disgust: surely no one could find this grim extension of a collective, persistent macho fantasy in the least stimulating. For Peachie is literally 'fucked to death': the author intended readers to be aroused – but to anger and protest. Grassal is always provocative in one way or another: for instance, unexpectedly perhaps, the book contains no oral sex. This is intentional and logical, since trust and tenderness are crucial in oragenital relations: when power and cruelty distort relationships there can be no room for tenderness, nor for mutual respect and pleasure.

Clearly *Dolly Morton* is an unusual and multi-layered psychological fiction. By a mixture of design and accident, writing in an adopted language, probably at speed to a deadline, in a genre that can so easily remain stale and unconvincing, Grassal achieved a curious book indeed – and a moral one. Dolly endures, survives, and triumphs. She lingers in the mind, as do some prophetic remarks from G. Legman's *Love and Death*: 'Men will always be afraid of women, so long as patriarchy lasts, for the same reason that millionaires will always tremble at the thought of revolution. The master fears the slave. The slave might revolt. There does not seem to be any reason why women should not enslave men. Men have enslaved women for ten thousand years. If it is woman's turn now, who can have the gall to object?'

G.J. GRASSAL: SELECT BIBLIOGRAPHY

NOVELS IN FRENCH:

Baisers d'Ennemis (Paris 1892)
La Nichina (Paris 1897; reissued, 2 vols., in the series 'Les Classiques Interdits' by J-C. Lattès, Paris 1980)
La Camorra, la Câlineuse (Paris 1900)
Les Nuits Chaudes du Cap Français (Paris 1900; reissued, Editions G. Raoult, Paris 1953; 'Les Classiques Interdits', Lattès, Paris 1980)
La Femme qui a connu l'Empéreur (*L'Espionne Impériale*) (Paris 1901)

La Saison à Baïa (Paris 1901)
La Brocanteuse d'amours (Paris 1901)
Journal d'une enfant vicieuse by 'Mme de Morency', preface by H. Rebell (Carrington, Paris 1903; reissued, 'Les Classiques Interdits', Lattès, Paris 1980)

NOVELS IN ENGLISH:

The Memoirs of Dolly Morton (Carrington, Paris 1899)
(The later French edition purported to be by 'Donovan Kipps' translated by 'Augustin Sarcel', i.e. Grassal in both instances)
'Frank' and I by 'Anon' (Carrington, Paris 1902; Grove Press, New York 1968; Star Books, London 1983)

SHORT STORIES:

Le Magazin d'auréoles (Paris 1896)

ESSAYS AND NON-FICTION:

Les Jeudis Saints (1886)
Les Méprisants (1886)
Les Etourdissements (1888)
Athlètes et Psychologues (1890)
La Méthode Scientifique de l'histoire littéraire (1900)
Trois Artistes Etrangers: Robert Sherard, Sattler, Félicien Rops (Paris 1901)
Les Inspiratrices de Balzac, Stendhal, Merimée (Paris 1902)
Le diable est à table (1905)

ON FLAGELLATION:

Etudes sur la Flagellation (as 'Jean de Villiot' – Paris 1899)
Femmes Châtiées (no date given)

TRANSLATIONS FROM ENGLISH TO FRENCH:

The Merry Order of St Bridget by James G. Bertram (Hotten, London 1868) [as *Une Societé de Flagellants* by 'Jean de

Villiot' (Carrington, Paris 1902)]
The Romance of Chastisement, or the Revelations of Miss Darcy
by St. George H. Stock (Dugdale, London 1866) [as *Le
Magnétisme du Fouet, ou Les Indiscretions de Miss Darcy* by
'Jean de Villiot' (Carrington, Paris 1902)]
(Originals listed and discussed in H.S. Ashbee's extraordinary
Index Librorum Prohibitorum, 1877)
Intentions (essays) by Oscar Wilde (Carrington, Paris 1905)

POETRY:

Chants de la pluie et du soleil (Paris 1894)

BOOKS ON GRASSAL:

J. Brueckmann: *Hugues Rebell ein Vorkämpfer der französischen
Nationalismus* (1937)

The Memoirs
of Dolly Morton

INTRODUCTION

How I made the acquaintance of Dolly Morton, with a faithful account of the circumstances under which she felt impelled to tell me the story of her life.

In the summer of the year 1866, shortly after the conclusion of the civil war between the North and South, in America, I was in New York, to which city I had gone for the purpose of taking my passage in a Cunard Steamer to Liverpool, on my way back to my home in one of the midland counties of England, after a shooting and fishing trip I had been making in the province of Nova Scotia.

My age at that period was thirty years, I stood six feet in my socks, and I was strong and healthy; my disposition was adventurous; I was fond of women and rather reckless in my pursuit of them; so, during my stay in New York, I went about the city very much at night, seeing many queer sights, and also various strange phases of life in the tenement houses. However, I do not intend to relate my experiences in the slums of New York City.

One afternoon, about five o'clock, I had strolled into

1

Central Park, where I seated myself on a bench under the shade of a tree to smoke a cigar. It was a beautiful day in August, and the sun, sloping to the west, was shining brightly in a cloudless sky. A light breeze was blowing, tempering the heat and making the leaves of the trees rustle with a soothing sound, and I leant lazily back in my seat, looking at the trim, and often pretty nurse-maids of various nationalities, in charge of the smartly dressed American children. Then my eyes turned upon a lady who was sitting on the adjoining bench, reading a book.

She was apparently twenty-five years of age, a very pretty little woman with, as far as I could see, a shapely, well-rounded figure. Her hair was a light golden brown, coiled in a big chignon at the back of her head – it was the day of chignons and crinolines. She was neatly gloved, and handsomely but quietly dressed; everything she wore being in good taste, from the little hat on her head to the neat boots on her small, well-shaped feet, which peeped from under the hem of her wide skirt. I stared at her harder than was polite, thinking she was quite the type of a pretty American lady of the upper class. After a moment or two, she became conscious of my fixed gaze, and raising her eyes from her book, she looked steadily at me for a short time; then, apparently satisfied with my appearance, a bright smile came to her face, and she shot a saucy glance at me, at the same time making a motion with her hand inviting me to come and sit beside her. I was rather astonished, as I had not thought from her appearance that she was one of the *demi-monde*; but I was quite willing to have a chat with her, and also to poke her, if her conversation pleased me as much as her looks.

Rising from my seat, I went over to her, and she at once drew aside her voluminous skirts so as to make room for me on the bench beside her. I seated myself, and we began to talk. She spoke grammatically and in an educated manner, and, although she had the American accent, her voice was low and musical – I do not dislike the American accent when I hear it on the lips of a pretty woman – and she certainly was a pretty woman; her eyes were large, clear and blue, her complexion was extremely good, her teeth were white and regular, her nose well shaped, and she had a small mouth with red lips.

She had plenty to say for herself, chatting away merrily, and using quaint expressions that made me laugh. I took quite a fancy to the lively little woman, so I made up my mind to see her home and spend the night with her. She had at once noticed by my accent that I was an Englishman, and she informed me that she had never before spoken to a man of my nationality. After we had chatted for some time, I asked her to dine with me. She seemed pleased at my invitation, and at once accepted it; so we strolled quietly out of the park to a restaurant, where I ordered a good dinner with champagne.

When the meal was over, and I had smoked a cigar, I took my companion, who told me her name was 'Dolly,' to a theatre; and at the end of the performance I engaged a 'hack', as the conveyance is called in New York, and drove the woman to her home, which was in the suburbs, about three miles from the theatre. As it was a bright moonlight night, I was able to see that the house was a pretty little one-storied building, with a creeper-covered verandah, standing in a small garden, surrounded by iron railings. The door was opened by a neatly dressed quadroon woman, who ushered us into the drawing-room; then after drawing the curtains and turning up the jets in the gaselier, she went away. The room, which had folding doors at one end, was prettily furnished; there was nothing the least suggestive about it, everything being in good style. The floor was covered with a handsome Oriental carpet, the curtains were velvet; some good engravings were on the walls, and a cabinet contained some choice specimens of old china.

My companion told me to sit down and make myself comfortable, then begging me to excuse her for a moment or two, she passed through the folding doors into the adjoining apartment, which I saw was a bedroom. In a short time she returned, dressed in a white wrapper trimmed with blue ribbons. She had taken off her boots, and put on dainty little French slippers, while her hair was flowing loose over her

3

shoulders nearly down to her waist. She looked so 'fetching,' that I at once took her on my knees, and gave her a kiss on the lips, which she returned, at the same time inserting the tip of her tongue in my mouth. Then I put my hand up her clothes, finding that she had nothing on under the wrapper but a fine lace-trimmed chemise and black silk stockings, which were fastened high above the knees with scarlet satin garters, so I was able to feel her whole body with perfect ease.

She was as plump as a partridge; there was not a single angle about her figure. Her skin was as smooth as satin; her bubbies were rather small, but they were as round as apples, quite firm, and tipped with tiny, erect, pink nipples. She had a very good bottom with plump firm cheeks, and the hair on the Mons Veneris was silky to the touch.

She gave me a brandy and soda, and we chatted while I smoked a cigar; then we went into the bedroom, where everything was exquisitely clean and sweet. In a short time we were between the sheets; my breast on her bosom, my mouth on her lips, my amatory organ up to the roots in her den of love, my hands grasping the cheeks of her bottom, and I was riding her vigorously, while she was sighing, squeaking, and bucking up under my powerful digs. My member was big, her fissure was small and wonderfully tight, moreover she was a good mount, so I enjoyed the 'flutter' very much, especially as I had not 'had' a woman for a month. But I had knocked all the breath out of the little woman, and when all was over she lay panting in my arms. However, when she had recovered her wind, she said with a little laugh:

'My gracious! you are very big and very strong. I don't think I've ever had such a vigorous embrace in all my life. You seemed to go right through me. But I liked it.'

I laughed, making no remark, but lying quietly resting, still holding her in my arms, and stroking her cool velvety skin until I was ready for action again.

Then making her kneel on all fours outside the bed, I poked her from behind *en levrette*, again making her wince, squeak, and wriggle her bottom. We then got between the sheets again, and I made her turn on her side with her back

4

towards me, while I lay behind her with my belly and thighs pressed against the cool plump cheeks of her bottom, and with my half stiff tool resting in the cleft of her thighs. In this position we fell asleep.

I slept soundly, not once waking till half-past eight next morning. Sitting up in bed, I looked at my companion, who was still fast asleep, lying on her back with her long hair streaming over the pillow, and her arms stretched above her head. She looked quite young and pretty; and there was a faint pink tint on her round cheeks. I gently pulled the bedclothes down to her feet, and rolled up her night-dress to her chin without waking her; then I took a good look at her naked charms. And they were worth looking at. Her skin was as white as milk and without a blemish; she was really very well-made, and perfectly proportioned. Her little bubbies stood out from her bosom in high relief; her plump, well-rounded thighs were shapely, she had good legs, her ankles were slender, and her belly was without a line or a wrinkle. She evidently had never had a child, and her rose-bud was shaded with fine curly, golden hair. My pintle was as stiff as a poker, so I woke her by gently tickling the edge of her grotto with my fore-finger. She looked smilingly up in my face, her big blue eyes twinkling with fun, saying:

'So you have prepared me for the morning sacrifice. Well, I am ready to receive the stroke.'

She then stretched out her legs, and in a few seconds I had given her a strong morning poke, which pleased me more than the ones I had had over night, for while I was working at her, the little woman bucked up more briskly, and wriggled her bottom in the spasm even more lasciviously than on the two other occasions. She really seemed to like the digging I gave her, and I don't think she had pretended to be voluptuously excited merely to please me – women of her profession often simulating passion. Presently we began to chat on various subjects, her conversation showing that she took an intelligent interest in the affairs of the day. Our talk eventually turned to what was at that period a burning topic, the late civil war, and I asked her which side had had her sympathies.

'I am a Northern woman,' she replied, 'so I was always for the union, and am exceedingly glad that the Southerners were beaten, and the slaves set free. Slavery was a horrible thing, and a disgrace to the country.'

'But,' said I, 'from all the accounts one hears, it seems that the negroes in the South were better off before the war as slaves, than they are now as free people.'

'Oh, but they are free now, and that is the great point. No doubt things are bad at present, but they will improve in time.'

'I thought that, as a rule, the slaves were well treated by their owners.'

'So they were in many cases,' she replied, 'but there was no security for them; there was always the chance of their being sold to strange people; and then wives were separated from their husbands, and children from their parents. Besides, there were many owners who treated their slaves badly; working them hard, feeding them scantily, and whipping them cruelly for the least offence. Then again, slaves had no rights of any sort. The girls and women, if light coloured and pretty were not allowed to be virtuous, even if they wished to be. They were obliged to give themselves up to the embraces of their masters, and if a woman dared to object, she was severely whipped.'

'Oh! surely you must be mistaken,' I observed.

'No, I am not. I know what I am talking about, for I lived in a Slave State before the war, and I had special opportunities for finding out all about slavery and the distressing things connected with it.'

'Was it a common thing for women to be whipped?' I asked.

'Yes; I do not suppose there was a single plantation in the whole of the South where the female slaves were not whipped. Of course, on some plantations there was more whipping than on others. And what made the thing more horrid was the fact that the whippings were always inflicted by men, and very often in the most public way.'

'On what part of the body were the slave women whipped; and what instruments of punishment were used?' I inquired.

'Sometimes they were flogged on the back, but most frequently on the bottom; the instruments used were various; there was the hickory switch, the strap and the paddle.'

'What is the paddle?'

'It is a round, flat piece of wood fixed to a long handle, and it was always used on the bottom. It does not draw blood, but each stroke raises a blister on the skin and bruises the flesh. The hickory switch, with any degree of force, will cut the skin and draw blood. There was another terrible instrument of punishment called the cowhide, but it was very seldom used on women.'

'You seem to know all about whipping. Now tell me how it was you came to be living in a Slave State,' said I.

'I was helping to run a station on the "underground railroad;" – but I suppose you don't know what an underground station is.'

'No, I do not. What is it?'

'"Underground railroad stations" were houses in which the abolitionists used to conceal the runaway slaves. There were a number of these stations in various parts of the South, and the runaway was forwarded secretly by night from one station to another, until he or she finally got to a free State. It was dangerous work, as assisting a slave to escape was against the laws of the South, and to do so was considered a very great crime. Any man or woman caught at such a work was sure of getting a long term of imprisonment with hard labour in the State prison. Besides, everyone's hand was against the abolitionist; not only the slave-owners, but also the ordinary white people who did not own a single slave, and it often happened that abolitionists were lynched. They were tarred and feathered, or ridden on a rail, or made to suffer in some other way, by bands of lawless men.'

'Did you ever get into trouble while you were at the underground station?' I asked.

'Yes, I did. I got into bitter trouble, and went through dreadful sufferings. In fact, what happened to me changed the whole course of my life, and was the cause of my being what I am now. Oh! how I hate the Southerners. The cruel wretches!' she exclaimed fiercely, her eyes flashing, her bosom heaving, and her cheeks reddening.

I was surprised at her sudden outburst of anger, and it at once struck me that the little woman had a story. I was curious to hear it, so I said:

'I should very much like to hear what happened to you in the South. Will you tell me?'

After a moment's hesitation, she replied:

'I have never told my story to a man yet; but I will let you hear it, as you are an Englishman, and I think you have a sympathetic nature. The story is a very long one, and there is not time to tell it to you now, but if you will come here to-night at seven o'clock and dine quietly with me, I will give you a full account of my life.'

I replied that I should be delighted to dine with her, and that it would give me great pleasure to hear her story.

Just then there was a knock at the door, and the quadroon woman, neatly dressed, and wearing a smart cap on her head, came into the room with tea and buttered toast on a tray, which she placed on a table beside the bed.

My companion sat up, saying to the quadroon:

'Mary, give me my wrapper.'

The woman handed her mistress the garment, which she threw over her shoulders. Then turning to me, she said with a smile:

'Mary was a slave for twenty-five years; and if you like to ask her any questions about her life, she will answer you truthfully. She is not shy. Are you, Mary?'

The quadroon, who was a very buxom, rather good-looking woman, smiled broadly, showing a double row of white teeth between her full, red lips.

'No, Miss Dolly,' she replied, 'I isn't shy.'

I was quite ready to ask Mary to give me some information about herself, so to begin with, I said:

'Well Mary, how old are you, and what State do you come from?'

8

'I'se thirty years old, Sah, an' I was raised on ole Major Bascombe's plantation, in de state ob Alabama. Dere was one hundred an' fifty field hands on de plantation, an' twelve house-servants in de place. I was one ob de parlourmaids, Sah;' she added, with a sort of pride.

'Was your master a good one?' I next asked the woman.

'Well, Sah, he was a pretty good Massa on de whole; he fed us well, an' he didn't work us too hard; but he was bery strict, an' dere was plenty ob whipping on de plantation, an' in de house too.'

'Were you ever whipped?'

Mary looked at me with an expression of surprise on her face at being asked such a silly question.

'Ob course I was, Sah, many a time,' she replied. 'I got my fust whippin' when I was 'bout seven years old, an' I got my las' one when I was twenty-five; only a week 'fore we was all set free by de President ob de United States.'

'How were you whipped?'

'When I was a little girl I used to get spanked; when I grew big, dey whipped me on de bare back or bottom wid de strap or de hick'ry switch; an' I'se had de paddle on my bottom seberal times;' said Mary as coolly as possible.

'Who used to whip the women?'

'One ob de overseers gener'ly; but sometimes de massa himself used to whip de house-servants. Dere was a room kep' for de purpose, an' when a gal or a woman was whipped, she was tied face downwards on a long bench, den her close was turned up, an' she got her allowance.'

'Were the whippings severe?'

'Oh, dey always hurt us dreffle, an' made us squeal out loud an' wriggle; an' sometimes we was whipped till de blood come.'

Here Dolly broke in, saying: 'And when the skin of a woman's back or bottom has been broken by a whipping, the marks never entirely disappear. Mary has plenty of marks upon her body at this moment. Show your bottom to the English gentleman, Mary, and prove the truth of what you have told him.'

The woman, without the least hesitation, turned her back towards me, then she gathered all her clothes up under her arms, exposing the whole lower part of her person, as she was wearing no drawers.

It was a sight!! All women of negro blood have, naturally, big bottoms; and, as Mary was rather stout, her bottom was enormous; the plump hemispheres of flesh swelling out, and sweeping in great curves to the massive thighs, and sturdy legs cased in tight, white cotton stockings. Her skin was smooth, and of a light brown tint, and I at once noticed that both the fat cheeks of her bottom, as well as the upper part of her thighs, were marked with long, fine, white lines where the skin had been cut by the lash.

She seemed to like showing her opulent charms, for she was in no hurry to drop her petticoats, but stood looking over her shoulder at me, with a complacent smile on her face, till her mistress said:

'That will do, Mary.'

She then let her clothes fall, and left the room smiling.

'There,' said Dolly, 'you have seen the marks on her bottom, and I can tell you that her back is just as much marked.

'Moreover, she was seduced, or to speak more correctly had to give herself up to her master's eldest son when she was only fifteen. She afterwards passed through the hands of two younger sons; but the fact of her being the plaything of the three young men did not save her bottom from being blistered by the paddle, or striped with the switch whenever she committed an offence of any sort. She has told me that she had sometimes to go to the room of one or another of the young masters while her bottom was still bleeding from a whipping. I have another woman, about thirty-five years of age, in my service as cook; she comes from South Carolina, and her body is even more scarred than Mary's with the marks of the whip.'

Dolly paused for a moment or two while she sipped her tea, then she said:

'Now don't you think it is a good thing that slavery has

been abolished in the United States?'

'Yes, indeed I do. I had no idea that female slaves were ever treated in such a way,' I replied.

The details given me by Dolly and the quadroon surprised me very much, and also somewhat moved me; but at the same time I was feeling very randy. The sight of a woman's bottom always has an exciting effect upon me, therefore the full view I had just had of Mary's big posteriors had given me a tremendous cockstand. So taking hold of Dolly, I laid her on her back, pulled down the bedclothes, tucked up her drapery, and poked her again with great gusto. Then, after refreshing myself with a cup of tea and a piece of toast, I got up and had a cold bath in a small dressing-room adjoining the bedchamber. As soon as I had dressed myself, I bade Dolly goodbye, promising to be back again without fail at seven o'clock. Then giving her a kiss and a good present, I left the house and made my way back to the hotel where I was staying. After changing my clothes, I sat down to breakfast with a good appetite, feeling very well satisfied with my night's amusement.

The day passed rather slowly, and at seven sharp I was back at Dolly's house, curious to hear her story, and fully intending to stay with her all night again.

She seemed glad to see me, and was looking very nice in a pretty frock of some soft white material. She gave me a simple, but well-cooked little dinner, with a bottle of excellent Burgundy.

Mary, smartly dressed and beaming with smiles, but perfectly respectful, waited on us, and when the meal was over and we had gone into the drawing-room she brought some really well-made coffee.

Dolly leant back in an easy chair, with her feet, in smart velvet slippers, resting on a stool, and as her skirts were slightly raised, I was able to see her trim ankles cased in pale blue silk stockings.

I lit a cigar and settled myself down in another easy chair opposite her. She then began to tell me her story which turned out to be a very long one: so it was not nearly finished

11

when we went to bed after a little supper at midnight. But as I had got interested in the narrative, I wished to hear the end of it, so I paid Dolly three or four more visits, and she continued her story each time I saw her until at last she had related the whole of her adventures to me, and as I was able to write shorthand, I took down her narrative exactly as she related it, without a break, in her own words.

Chapter One

*A young girl's humiliating experiences – Death of my father –
How I made Miss Ruth Dean's acquaintance and what came of it
– Helping to free the slaves.*

My name is Dolly Morton, I am just twenty-six years of
age, and I was born in Philadelphia, where my father was a
clerk in a bank. I was his only child, and my mother died
when I was only two years old, so I have no remembrance of
her. My father's salary was a small one, but he gave me as
good an education as his means would allow: his intention
being that I should gain my living as a school-teacher. He was
a silent, stern, reserved man, who perhaps may have been
fond of me in his way: but he never showed any outward sign
of affection, and he always kept me under strict discipline.
Whenever I committed a fault, he would lay me across his
knees, turn up my short petticoats, take down my drawers
and spank me soundly with a broad piece of leather. I was a
plump, soft, thin-skinned girl who felt pain acutely, and I
used to shriek and kick up my heels and beg for mercy;
which, however, I never received, for he would calmly go on

13

spanking me until my poor little bottom was as red as fire and I was hoarse with screaming. Then, when the punishment was over, and my trembling fingers had buttoned up my drawers, I would slink away with smarting bottom and streaming eyes, to our old servant who had been my nurse, and she would sympathize with me, and comfort me until the smart of the spanking had passed off.

Our life was rather a lonely one; we had no relatives, my father did not care for society of any sort, and I had very few girl friends of my own age; but I was strong and healthy, my disposition was cheerful, and fortunately I was fond of reading, so although I often felt very dull, I was not absolutely unhappy when a child. And so the years rolled on quietly and uneventfully; my childhood passed, I was eighteen years old, and had grown to my full height of five feet four inches; my figure was well rounded, and I was quite a woman in appearance. I had begun to chafe at the monotony and repression of my life, and was sometimes very wilful and disobedient. But I always suffered on such occasions, as my father still continued to treat me as a child, taking me across his knees and spanking me whenever I offended him. Moreover, he informed me that he would spank me, every time I misbehaved, until I was twenty. This was very humiliating to a girl of my age, especially as I had become rather romantic and had begun to think of sweethearts. But I never dreamed of resisting my father's authority, so I took my spankings, which I must confess, were sometimes well deserved, with as much fortitude as I could muster up. But a change of my life was soon to come. My father was seized with an attack of pneumonia to which he succumbed after a few days illness.

I was stunned at first by the suddenness of the blow, but I cannot say that I felt much grief at my loss. My father had never made a companion of me, and whenever I had tried to interest him in my little affairs, he had invariably shown himself utterly unsympathetic.

However, I had not much time to think over the past; my position as it was at that moment had to be faced, and a most unfortunate one it was. My father had died in debt, and the creditors were pressing for payment. I had no money, so the furniture of the house was sold by auction, and when everything had been settled, I found myself without a cent, homeless, and quite alone in the world. I lived for a month with my old nurse, who would have kept me with her always, had she been able; but she had her own living to make, so was obliged to go into service again. Then I would have been compelled to seek shelter in the poor-house had it not been for the kindness of a lady, who hearing of my friendless and forlorn condition, took me into her house.

Her name was Miss Ruth Dean, and she was, at that period, thirty years of age. She belonged to the Quaker sect, or, as she called it: 'The Society of Friends.' She was a virgin, had no lovers, was her own mistress and lived in a large house about two miles from the city. She was well-off, and made good use of her money, spending most of it in charity. Her time was chiefly occupied in philanthropic work of all sorts, and she was always ready to give a helping hand to anyone who needed a start in life.

But before proceeding, I must give you a description of Miss Ruth Dean. She was a tall, slender, delicately-formed woman, with large earnest-looking brown eyes; her hair was also brown; it was long and soft, and she always wore it in plain bands. She had a lovely, clear complexion, but there was no colour in her cheeks, although she was in perfect health, and capable of going through a great amount of fatigue. She was a pretty woman, but there was always a rather prim expression on her face, and she rarely laughed, but was not the least morose. Miss Dean was as good a woman as ever lived, and she was the best friend I ever had in my life. From the first she treated me as a guest, and was most kind to me. I had a bed-sitting-room of my own, prettily furnished, and the servants, all of whom were devoted to their mistress, always treated me with respect. Miss Dean had a number of correspondents in all parts of the States, and now my education proved useful to me, for I was able to help my benefactress in answering her letters, and she, finding that I

15

was sharp and intelligent, appointed me her secretary, giving me a small salary for pocket-money, and also supplying me with clothes. I was very comfortable, and had never been so happy in all my life. There were no cross looks, or sharp scoldings, and above all, no horrid spankings. As time passed, Miss Dean became like an elder sister to me, while I grew very fond of her. She admired my face and figure, and always liked to see me nicely dressed, so she gave me lace-trimmed petticoats, drawers, and chemises, also several pretty frocks: although she herself was content with the plainest of underlinen and always wore the Quaker costume: a plain bodice with a straightcut skirt of drab, brown or dove-coloured material.

As a matter of course, Miss Dean hated the institution of slavery, and was an ardent member of the abolitionist party. She supplied funds to, and was in constant communication with 'Friends' in the Southern States who were in charge of 'underground stations,' and she frequently received into her house escaped slaves of both sexes whom she kept until they had got employment. She could openly harbour the fugitives as Pennsylvania was a free State.

I need not enter into the details of my life for two years, as nothing eventful happened. I was contented and happy; I had the society of young people of my own age, and I had plenty of innocent amusements. Miss Dean, being a Quakeress, did not patronize places of public amusement of any sort herself, nor would she allow me to go to one: neither did she approve of dancing; but she frequently gave quiet parties, and I was often invited to other houses. I was popular with members of my own sex, and had several male admirers; but as I did not care for any one of them I remained quite heart whole.

At the time of which I am speaking, the friction between North and South was becoming very great, and there were mutterings of the storm that was soon to break; although few people thought that things would end in a long and bloody civil war.

Towards the close of the year, the North was startled by the execution, or, as we called it: the murder of the great abolitionist John Brown, at Harper's Ferry. Miss Dean was particularly shocked and distressed at the news; she had known John Brown personally, and she considered that he had been quite right in getting up the insurrection which cost him his life. Any act, she averred, was justifiable that had for its object the emancipation of the slaves, and she declared that she would not hesitate to do the same thing herself if she thought it would forward the cause.

As the weeks passed, she became restless, and was not satisfied with merely sending money to the South, but wanted to do something personally to help the slaves, and finally she made up her mind to go South and take charge of an 'underground station.'

She told me one afternoon what she intended doing, and became quite enthusiastic about it.

'Oh!' she exclaimed, 'I am longing to begin the work of rescue. I am sure I could manage a station better than any man. Men are suspected, and constantly watched by the white loafers, but they would not suspect a woman of running a station, so if I live quietly and take all necessary precautions, I am not likely to be found out.'

My sympathies had always been with the slaves, and now Miss Dean's enthusiasm moved me greatly, so I at once made up my mind to go with her, and I told her of my determination.

At first she would not hear of my doing such a thing; she pointed out the risks of the undertaking and remarked that we might possibly be found out, and in that case we should be condemned to a long term of imprisonment.

'Not that I am afraid of imprisonment,' she exclaimed, getting up from her seat and walking up and down the room, her pale cheeks flushing, and her soft eyes sparkling, 'but for you, Dolly, it would be dreadful. You are a young, tender girl, and you could not bear the hard work and coarse fare as I could. Besides, they would cut off all your pretty hair. I have heard that the hair of female prisoners is cut in Southern goals. No, my dear, I can't let you go with me. For if I did, and anything was to happen to you, I should never forgive

17

myself.'

'I am not afraid of the work,' I said, 'and you have just as pretty hair as I have. If you choose to risk yours, I am ready to risk mine. Do you think, after all you have done for me, that I will let you go alone? I will not be left behind. Where you go, I go, and take my chance with you,' I exclaimed, clasping her hand and pressing it.

I saw that she was much touched by my fidelity to her, but still she tried her utmost to dissuade me from going South with her. But I was firm in my resolve to accompany her, so I met all her arguments, and wound up by saying that 'two heads were better than one,' and that I could be of great assistance to her.

So at last she consented to let me go with her. The point being settled, she kissed me, then sitting down, she wrote to 'Friends' in various parts of the South, asking them to let her know of a place where a new 'underground station' might be advantageously established. We then went to dinner, and when it was over we spent the evening in talking over our plans, and settling what we should do to the best of our ability.

In a few days time, Miss Dean received answers from all her correspondents, and they mentioned several places where an 'underground station' might be set up.

We discussed the advantages of the various sites, and after a long deliberation, determined to go to a place in Virginia, right in the middle of the Slave States.

The house which had been recommended to be used as a 'station' was situated near the small town of Hampton on the James river, and it was thirty-five miles from Richmond, the capital of the State. Miss Dean at once wrote to a local house-agent, telling him to take the house for her, and have it furnished as soon as possible for the reception of two ladies who wished to spend some time in Virginia.

In a short time she received a letter from the agent, saying that he had taken the house for her, and that it would be furnished and ready for occupation in a fortnight's time. I need hardly tell you that the agent had not the slightest idea that the house was going to be used as an 'underground station.'

Next day, we began leisurely to make preparations for our departure, and Miss Dean decided to take only one servant, a trustworthy, middle-aged, white woman named Martha. She was a Quakeress like her mistress, in whose service she had been for five years. She knew why we were going to Virginia, and was quite willing to accompany us. The other servants were to be left behind in charge of the house in Philadelphia. Miss Dean thought it would be safer not to let anyone in the city know the exact spot to which we were going, or what we intended to do, so she merely let it be known that we were going for a trip to the South.

A fortnight passed, and one fine morning at the beginning of May, we drove quietly to the Railway Depôt and took our tickets for Richmond. On arriving there we stayed at a hotel for a couple of days in order to get some stores we wanted.

Then on the third morning, at half-past eleven o'clock, we left the city in a two-horse buggy driven by a negro coachman, who deposited the three of us with our trunks at the house at six o'clock, after a long, but pleasant drive through a pretty country.

The agent to whom Miss Dean had written was waiting to receive us, with a couple of negro boys to carry in our baggage. He showed us over the house which we found to be in good repair, plainly but comfortably furnished, and everything in perfect readiness; supplies laid in, wood chopped, and the fire lighted in the kitchen.

The house was very secluded, as it was situated at the end of a lane about a quarter of a mile from the main road. It was a wooden structure on one storey, with a verandah back and front; it contained a parlour, kitchen, and four bedrooms; in the rear there was a barn, near which grew two hickory trees; and the whole place was surrounded by a rail fence.

When we had completed the inspection of our new home, the agent bade us good-bye and took his departure, accompanied by the two negro boys. Martha bustled about the kitchen, while Miss Dean and I unpacked our things in

19

our respective bedrooms.

In a short time, tea was ready and we sat down in the parlour to a good meal of ham and eggs, fried chicken, and hot cakes.

The parlour was a good-sized room with rather a low ceiling crossed by heavy beams; there were two bow windows with latticed panes, and on the sills were pots of sweet-smelling flowers. On one side of the room, stood a massive sideboard of polished mahogany, and there was an old-fashioned oval mirror with an ebony frame over the mantelpiece. These two bits of old furniture evidently belonged to the house, and they contrasted strangely with the bright coloured carpet and other modern furniture of the room.

When we had finished our meal Miss Dean wrote to the 'Friends' in charge of the 'underground stations' north and south of us, with which we were to be in communication. The station south of ours was thirty miles distant, and from it we would receive fugitives, whom we would pass on to the station north of us, which was twenty miles away.

Then we had a short chat, but as we were feeling tired after our journey, we soon went to bed.

I got up bright and early next morning, feeling in high spirits, and as soon as I had had my bath and dressed, I peeped into Miss Dean's room; but finding she was fast asleep, I did not disturb her.

Going quietly downstairs, I left the house and went for a morning walk along the tree-bordered road, and down lanes flanked with hedges of bright flowered shrubs of species quite unknown to me. I rambled about in all directions for an hour without meeting a single white person, though I came across several coloured people of both sexes who stared curiously at me, noticing that I was a stranger.

When I got back to the house, I found Miss Dean waiting for me in the parlour, and in a short time Martha brought in breakfast, to which I did full justice, as my walk had given me a good appetite. We soon settled down comfortably, and our new and risky life began, but neither of us had any forebodings of evil. Miss Dean was always cheerful, and I was quite charmed with the novelty of the whole affair. We stored supplies of bacon, flour and coffee in the cellar of the house, and hid a couple of mattresses and blankets under the floor of the barn, in readiness for the fugitives who might arrive at any moment from the station south of ours.

Chapter Two

My new style of life – Redeeming the slave – Our first runaways and how we passed them 'underground.'

The house we lived in was well adapted for our purpose owing to its isolated position. Our nearest neighbour lived three miles away, and the little town of Hampton whence we got our supplies was also three miles distant. The weather was fine but warm; however, it agreed with me, and I was in splendid health and condition. Dressed in a plain linen costume with a broad-brimmed straw hat on my head, I daily roamed about the country, soon making the acquaintance of a number of plantation slaves, who, seeing that I took an interest in them, were always glad to talk to me, and they used to bring me presents of bits of 'possum,' and 'coon,' two animals that the negroes are very fond of; but neither Miss Dean nor I could touch the meat. I sometimes visited the slaves' quarters on the plantations, and was always heartily welcomed, but I was obliged to pay my visits very secretly; for if the owners of the slaves, or the ordinary white folks in the neighbourhood had discovered that I was visiting the

22

quarters, my motives would at once have been suspected. Though the negroes whose acquaintance we had made never hinted at the subject, I felt pretty sure that they all guessed why we had taken up our abode in their midst.

Three months passed, and during the whole of that period the work at our station had gone on smoothly. Sometimes in one week we would have two or three fugitives: but often several days would pass without a single runaway arriving. They always came after dark, to the back of the house; and the first thing we did was to give them a good meal, then we put them in the barn for the night. Next day, we fed them well, and as soon as it was dark supplied them with a packet of provisions, and they started off for the next station, walking all night, and hiding in the woods during the day. If, as sometimes happened, the fugitive was a woman who was too tired to go on after only one night's rest, we kept her until she felt able to continue her journey. The runaways were of all sorts: old and young men, old women and girls, and sometimes a woman would arrive with a baby in her arms. Some of the fugitives were in good condition, and decently clothed, others were gaunt and ragged, having come long distances and been many days on the road. Some had even come from the extreme south of Florida. Many were scarred with the marks of the lash, some bore imprints of the branding-iron, and others had open, or half-healed wounds on their bodies. But all the poor creatures who passed through our hands were intensely grateful to us, and we often heard their stories, which were in many cases most pitiful. I need not enter further into details of our management of the station, but I will give you a short account of one of the cases that came under our notice.

One night, Miss Dean and I were sitting as usual in the parlour, chatting and sewing. The lamps had been lit, the curtains had been drawn, and everything was quiet and snug. There had been no arrivals for upwards of a week, and Miss Dean had just said: 'I wonder if anyone will come to-night,' when we heard a low tapping at one of the windows.

I ran to the door and opened it, and as I did so, a girl

staggered up to the threshold, then fell fainting at my feet. I called to Miss Dean, who at once came to my assistance with Martha, and we carried the girl into the parlour and laid her on the sofa.

She was a very light-coloured quadroon, with a pretty face and long, wavy, dark brown hair, which was flowing in disorder over her shoulders, as she had nothing on her head. Her age appeared to be about sixteen years, but her figure was fully developed, the rounded contours of her bosom showing plainly under her thin bodice – females of her race soon mature. She was evidently not a field slave, as her hands did not show signs of hard work, while her clothes were a good material, although they were draggled and torn to rags. She was wearing a neat pair of shoes, but they, as well as her stockings, were covered with mud. We soon brought her round, and she opened her great brown eyes which had a hunted look in them, while her face had an expression of pain and weariness. We gave her a bowl of soup, and some bread and meat, which she ate ravenously, telling us that she had had nothing for twenty-four hours.

As the girl was so weak and ill, we did not send her to the barn, but as soon as she had finished her supper I took her upstairs to the spare room, telling her to undress to go to bed. She looked bashfully at me, but after a moment's hesitation took off her frock and petticoats – she wore no drawers – and I then noticed that the back part of her chemise was plentifully stained with spots of dried blood. I knew what that meant! Going up to the girl, I raised her chemise and looked at her bottom, finding that the whole surface was covered with livid weals and that the skin was cut in a great many places.

I soon got her to tell me why she had been so severely whipped. It was the old story. She belonged to a planter, a married man with young children, who lived about twenty-five miles away. She was one of his wife's maids. Her master had taken a fancy to her and had ordered her to be in his dressing-room at a certain hour one evening. She was a virgin, and she disobeyed the command. Next day she was sent with a note to one of the overseers, who took her to the shed used as a place of punishment. He then informed her that her master had sent her to be whipped for disobedience. She was then stretched over the whipping-block, her wrists and ankles being held by two male slaves; then the overseer laid bare her bottom and whipped her with a hickory switch, regardless of her screams, until the blood trickled down her thighs. She was then allowed to go, after being told that if she did not obey her master she would find herself on the whipping-block again. She was a plucky girl, and determined not to surrender her maidenhead, so she ran away that night, sore and bleeding as she was, and made her way for twenty-five miles through the woods and byeways, until she reached our house. She had heard that we were kind to slaves, and she thought we would hide her from her master.

We did hide her, keeping her for a week, then we sent her on to the next station along with a man who happened to arrive just at the right time.

Now I will return to my own story, and that of Miss Dean, for our fates at this period became linked together even more closely than they had been.

Time passed and everything continued to go on quietly. Miss Dean was still full of enthusiasm for the work, but I had got rather sick of it; the stories of cruelty that I was constantly hearing, and the sights I sometimes saw, made my heart ache, moreover I was tired of the loneliness of my life. I wanted some companions with whom I could laugh and chatter freely and frivolously, for although Miss Dean was always sweet and amiable, her conversation was not of a light sort.

Occasionally too, a feeling of fear would come over me. We might be found out. I did not feel so brave as formerly; I dreaded being put in goal and having my hair cut, and I did not like the idea of the hard labour and the scanty fare. However, so far, I had had no cause for alarm. We had got to be well known by the people in the neighbourhood, but no one suspected that the two quiet women living by themselves in the lonely house were engaged in unlawful practices. There had never been an instance known of an 'underground station' being run by women. The ordinary white people –

and by that expression I mean the white folks who did not own slaves – were always civil to us whenever we had anything to do with them. Many of them were very rough-looking fellows, and there were some lazy loafers, but there was also a number of respectable, hard-working men with wives and families. Strange to say, all these whites, though not one of them owned a negro, were staunch upholders of slavery.

They sold us venison, wild turkeys, and fish, all of which were welcome additions to our usual homely fare.

Chapter Three

I am chased by a bull in the country and saved by an unknown gentleman who, in the sequel, proves a far more savage bull, differing only in the outward shape.

I still continued to amuse myself by wandering about the country; but it was dull work alone and I often wished for someone to talk to, and keep me company during my walks. At last my wishes were gratified.

One afternoon I was strolling along a road, when, on turning a corner, I came suddenly upon a small herd of cows, headed by a savage-looking bull which stopped on seeing me, and began to paw the ground, its head lowered in a threatening way and its eyes gleaming angrily. If I had stood still, the animal might have passed on: but as I was frightened I foolishly turned round and ran away as fast as I could.

The bull, bellowing hoarsely, at once pursued me, and I heard its breathing close behind me as I ran shrieking loudly, expecting every moment to be transfixed by the horns of the creature. Just in the very nick of time however, a gentleman on horseback leaped the hedge, and charging the bull, belaboured it with a heavy whip until the beast turned tail and dashed up the road followed by the cows. The gentleman dismounted and came to me. I was trembling all over and nearly fainting, and would have fallen to the ground had he not put his arm round my waist and held me up. He gave me a draught of wine from a flask which he took out of his pocket, then he made me sit down on the grass at the side of the road while he stood in front of me with the bridle of his horse over his arm, looking down at my face.

'Don't be frightened; the danger is past,' he said. 'It was lucky though that I happened to hear your cries and was able to get to you in time.'

I soon recovered myself, and thanked him warmly, at the same time taking a good look at him. He was a tall, handsome man about thirty-five years of age, with very dark hair and eyes; his face was clean shaven except for a long drooping moustache which hid his mouth, and he was dressed in a well-fitting riding suit. He fastened his horse's bridle to a tree, then sitting down beside me on the grass, began to talk in a lively and amusing way, putting me quite at my ease, so that I soon found myself chatting and laughing with him as freely as if I had known him for a long time. It was delightful to have a merry companion of the male sex to talk to. My spirits rose and I felt quite gay. I think we must have talked for an hour. He told me that his name was Randolph. I had often heard of him, as he was a bachelor, and the owner of one of the largest plantations in the neighbourhood; his place, called 'Woodlands,' being about three miles from our house, and I knew some of his slaves. But I did not tell him that. He asked me my name, and when I told him he smiled:

'I have heard of you and also of Miss Dean,' he said. 'In fact I am your landlord, as the house you are living in belongs to me.'

I was rather startled at hearing that, so I merely said:

'Oh, are you?'

'Yes,' he said laughing, 'and somehow I had got it into my head that my tenants were two ugly old Quaker ladies.'

I could not help smiling at the way he had spoken.

'Miss Dean is a Quakeress,' I said, 'but she is not ugly nor old. She is only thirty-two years of age. I am her companion, but I am not a Quakeress.'

'You are a very charming young lady, and I am glad to have made your acquaintance,' he said, looking hard in my face.

I blushed, feeling rather confused by his bold glances; but nevertheless I was pleased with his compliment. I was not accustomed to having compliments paid to me. The few young men I had known in Philadelphia were Quakers, not given to paying compliments.

He went on:

'You two ladies must find it very dull living all alone, especially in the evenings. What do you do with yourselves?'

This was an awkward question:

'We read and sew,' I replied.

'Well, I must give myself the pleasure of calling on you some night. I suppose you are always at home,' he observed.

My heart gave a little jump, and I felt hot and uncomfortable. It would never do to have him calling at the house, so I racked my brains to find something to say that would prevent him paying us a visit.

'I must beg you not to call. Miss Dean would not like it. She is peculiar in her ways, and I have to humour her,' I said, rising to my feet, and thinking I had better get home as soon as possible, so as to avoid being further questioned by him.

He also stood up, saying:

'If that is the case I will not intrude on Miss Dean, but I hope to have the pleasure of seeing you again. Will you meet me here to-morrow at three o'clock?'

I thought there would be no harm in meeting him, besides if I did not he would probably call at the house, and that was a thing to be prevented if possible. So I promised to meet him the following afternoon at the hour he had named. Then, shaking hands with him, I bade him good-bye.

He held my hand longer than was necessary and he also pressed it, at the same time fixing his gleaming black eyes upon mine with a look that made me feel rather uncomfortable again.

29

'Good-bye then, Miss Morton, till three o'clock to-morrow,' he said.

Then mounting his horse, he touched it with the spur and cantered off, turning round in the saddle to wave his hat to me.

My eyes followed him with admiration, for he was a graceful rider, and his horse was a magnificent animal, moreover I felt grateful to the man, for he had undoubtedly saved me from serious injuries, if not death.

I walked slowly home, thinking over the whole affair, and feeling very light-hearted. A bit of romance had come into my hitherto quiet life, and I was pleased. In future, I should have someone to talk to, and to walk with. I had an idea that Mr Randolph and I would often meet, but I had not the least thought of harm. On reaching the house, I found Miss Dean looking, as usual, sweet and placid, making shirts for ragged fugitives. Kissing me affectionately, she said:

'You are looking very blooming, Dorothy. What has made your cheeks so rosy this evening?'

I laughed, telling her that I had been frightened by a bull, but I did not inform her of the danger I had been in, nor did I mention Mr Randolph. I thought it best to keep silence about him, for Miss Dean was very strict in her ideas, and she would never have allowed me to meet him.

I took off my hat, and we went in to tea, which was also our dinner, and was a plentiful meal, consisting of fried trout, grilled wild turkey, corn bread, buckwheat cakes and honey. The evening was spent in the usual way and we read and sewed till it was time to go to bed.

Next day, at the appointed hour and place, I met Mr Randolph. He was evidently glad to see me, and taking both my hands, he held them, gazing with a look of admiration in my face. A woman always knows when she is admired. After exchanging greetings, he politely offered me his arm, which I took, and we strolled along the road until we came to a secluded dell with mossy banks shaded by trees. In this nook we sat down side by side on the grass, and then he questioned me about myself. I told him I was an orphan, and that I had no relations of any sort. I also informed him how I had become companion to Miss Dean, but of course I did not hint at our reasons for coming to live in Virginia.

His manner to me was perfectly respectful, and I remained chatting with him for upwards of an hour. Then I went home, after promising to meet him again in three days' time.

I did meet him, and from that time we became very friendly, seeing each other two or three times a week. I did not love him in the least, but I liked being in his company, as he was so utterly different from any man I had ever known. He amused me with his stories of adventures – he had travelled all over the world – and interested me by his descriptions of European countries which I was always longing to visit.

I had soon found out that he was cynical, having a very low opinion of women, and from the way he sometimes talked, I had an idea that his disposition was cruel.

However, he seemed to exercise a sort of fascination over me, so I invariably met him whenever he chose to ask me.

So far he had treated me politely, but in a condescending sort of way, and I was quick-witted enough to perceive that he considered me very much his inferior – and so perhaps I was. He was a rich planter, one of the aristocracy of the south, and a member of one of the 'F.F.V's,' as they called themselves, meaning 'First Families of Virginia,' while I was only the daughter of a poor clerk of no particular family, earning my living as companion to a Quaker lady.

As time passed, I got to like him a little better, and consequently was more familiar with him, while he became warmer in his manner towards me, but as yet he had not attempted to take the least liberty. He was waiting for a favourable opportunity. He lent me books of poetry, which were a great source of delight to me, and he used often to read aloud to me passages from Byron, Shelley, or Keats.

One afternoon, we were sitting side by side in our favourite nook, and he was reading poetry to me. I do not know who was the author, but I remember that the poem was about love. He had a musical voice, and he read with passionate

31

feeling, every now and then looking into my eyes. I became deeply moved by the sweet but rather warm verse; my cheeks flushed, my heart began to beat rapidly, and my bosom heaved, while a sensuous feeling, such as I had never experienced, took possession of me. I closed my eyes and sat in a soft, waking dream.

He ceased reading, and everything was perfectly still except for the far-off song of a mocking bird. Presently I felt his arm steal round my waist, then he drew me on his lap, and pressed his lips to mine in a long kiss. It was the first time I had ever been kissed by a man, and I felt a thrill pass through me from head to foot, but I did not attempt to get away – the kiss seemed to have mesmerized me. Pressing me to his breast, he covered my face with kisses, calling me all sorts of endearing names and telling me that he loved me. But still I lay quietly in his arms, feeling unable to move.

My quietness emboldened him; so after a moment or two, he put his hand up under my petticoats and felt my bottom through the slit of my drawers. Then my senses returned. The touch of the man's hand on such a part of my body acted like a galvanic shock; my sensuous feeling was instantly changed to a feeling of outraged modesty; I realized my danger, and began to struggle violently in his arms, at the same time calling out to him to let me go. But he paid no attention to what I said, and I was unable to free myself from his powerful grasp.

Laying me down upon my back, he pulled up my clothes, and tearing open my drawers, tried to separate my thighs which I instinctively kept pressed together.

I resisted with all my power, shrieking, and buffeting him in the face with both my hands, but he soon prevented me doing that, by seizing my wrists and holding my arms down at my sides. Then pressing his chest upon my bosom, he crushed me under his weight, and thrusting his knees between my legs, he forced my thighs apart in spite of all my efforts to prevent him; then I felt his stiff member touching my belly in different places as he tried to penetrate me. But he could not; for though I was filled with horror, and burning with shame, I did not lose my head, and I was sure that he could not effect his purpose as long as I kept moving my loins. So I did not exhaust myself by violent struggling, but merely twisted myself about, and every time I felt his 'thing' touch the right spot, I jerked my hips to one side, and by so doing prevented him getting into me.

Again and again, he tried to sheath the weapon, but could not manage to do it. I was strong, healthy, and in good condition, so I fought hard in defence of my virginity, at the sime time uttering a succession of loud shrieks.

It was a terrible fight! All my muscles were aching with the strain; every nerve in my body was strung to the utmost tension; the weight of his body was squeezing the breath out of me; my bosom heaved as though it would have burst; my eyes were starting out of my head, and I was filled with a horrible feeling of loathing.

But I continued to resist stubbornly, until at last, fearing I suppose, that my screams would be heard, he ceased his efforts to rape me, and uttering a bitter curse, let me go. Then rising to his feet, he buttoned up his trousers.

I sprang to my feet, panting for breath and trembling all over; tears were streaming down my cheeks, and I was hoarse from screaming. My clothes were torn, and my hair had come down and was flowing in disorder, partly hiding my scarlet face. Overwhelmed with shame, I was about to run away, when he seized me by the arm, and glaring at me with a cruel look in his eyes, hissed out in a savage tone:

'You little fool! Why did you resist me?'

'Let me go you, horrid wretch!' I exclaimed fiercely. 'How dare you look me in the face after what you've done to me? Oh! you beast! But I will have you prosecuted. I will go to the police and have you put in gaol.'

He smiled an evil smile, and darted a baleful glance at me:

'Oh, no, my little girl; you won't go to the police when you have heard what I am going to tell you,' he said, pinching my arm. 'Now you needn't struggle, I've done with you for the present, and I'll let you go in a moment, but you must first listen to what I have to say. I know what Miss Dean and you are doing here. You are keeping an "underground station." I suspected you both from the first, so I watched the house at night on several occasions, and I soon found out the game that was being carried on. For certain reasons, which I dare say you can guess, I did not give information to the police, but you and Miss Dean are in my power, and if I choose now to let the authorities know what you have been doing, you will find yourselves, in a very short time, at hard labour in the State's prison.'

I was startled and frightened, for I saw at once that we were entirely at the man's mercy, but I was so thoroughly upset by the outrage I had suffered, that I could not find a word to say. I could only weep.

Changing his tone, he went on:

'But I don't want to inform against you. I wish to be your friend. I am fond of you, and when you let me kiss you so quietly just now, I thought you were willing to let me go further. I am sorry I treated you so roughly, and I apologize. But I want you. Leave Miss Dean, and come and live with me. You shall have everything a woman can desire; I will settle a thousand dollars a year on you for life, and promise not to lay information against Miss Dean, or to interfere with her in any way.'

As things turned out, it would have been far better for me had I then accepted his offer. But at that moment I was full of rage and shame; moreover, being a perfectly pure girl, I was utterly revolted by the cool way he offered to buy my virtue; and though I dreaded the prison, I said to myself that I would rather go there than yield myself up to this man.

'No! No!' I exclaimed. 'I will not leave Miss Dean. You may tell the police, if you are such a brute. I will go to gaol, but I will not go and live with you. I hate the very sight of you! Oh! go away and leave me, you wretch!'

Again the cruel look came to his face, and he pushed me roughly, saying in a tone of suppressed anger:

'Very well, Miss Dorothy Morton, I will go away now, but we shall meet again some day, and I think you will be sorry for having refused my offer.'

34

Then after bowing to me with mock politeness, he turned on his heel and walked rapidly away, leaving me weeping and dishevelled.

Chapter Four

The results of my resistance – The inutility of goodness – An unwelcome visit, which leads to the humiliation of our persons and the ravishment of my virgin state.

As soon as he was out of sight, I twisted up my hair, and arranged the disorder of my attire as much as was possible; then I hurried home, and fortunately got up to my room without being seen by either Miss Dean or Martha.

Locking the door, I undressed, as my clothes were in a dreadful state; my frock, a white one, was torn at the gathers nearly all the way round, and the back was stained green, the strings of my petticoats were broken, my chemise was torn, and my drawers were hanging in ribbons about my legs. My thighs were covered with black marks made by the pressure of the man's fingers, and I was sore and bruised all over.

After I had put on clean things, I threw myself on the bed, buried my face in the pillow, and cried. But my tears were now angry ones, as the keenness of my shame had somewhat worn off.

I was enraged at my foolishness in having trusted myself

alone with Randolph, for whom I had a feeling of distrust ever since he had expressed to me his low opinion of the virtue of women. I also felt degraded in my own estimation, that he should have taken for granted that I was the sort of a girl who would give herself up to a man for the asking. I am sure I had never granted him the least encouragement.

Then I remembered that he had said I should be sorry for not accepting his offer. I had made an enemy of him, so most probably he would give information to the police about us.

It was not pleasant to think of. I felt I ought to let Miss Dean know that we have been found out, but had I done so, I should have been obliged to enter into all the details of my affair with Randolph. And I could not bear to tell her of the outrage I had been subjected to.

Altogether, through my imprudence, we were in a dreadful fix, and there was nothing to be done but wait miserably for the end, which would be the gaol.

Already in my mind I pictured Miss Dean and myself clad in coarse prison garments, and with our hair cropped short, toiling at some hard labour.

Presently, Martha knocked at the door to tell me that tea was ready; so I had to pull myself together and go down to the parlour. I could not eat much, and Miss Dean noticed at once my want of appetite. She also saw that my face was pale and my eyes red, and asked me what was the matter.

I told her I had a bad headache, which was the truth. On hearing that, the kind-hearted woman made me lie on the sofa, while she bathed my forehead with *eau de Cologne*. Then she recommended me to go to bed, so that I might have a long night's rest and sleep off the headache.

But I did not sleep well, as my rest was broken by a succession of horrid dreams, in which I fancied I was struggling in the arms of a man with an enormous member, who always succeeded in overcoming my resistance and taking my maidenhead. In the morning while dressing, I wondered where we should be in twenty-four hours time, for I fully expected that Miss Dean and I would be arrested before the night came.

The day wore slowly away; I was uneasy and restless, and could not settle down to my usual routine of work, but I was constantly peeping out of the window, watching for the arrival of the police.

They did not come. But at nine o'clock, a runaway made his appearance in a starving condition; and in attending to the poor creature's wants, I forgot for the time, my own precarious position.

Several days went by quietly, and I began to think that Randolph after all was not going to be so mean as to inform on us.

But all the same I was very anxious to get out of the state of Virginia, so I said to Miss Dean that I thought we had now done our share of the work, and ought to go back to Philadelphia. Miss Dean however, would not hear of such a thing. She said we were doing good work and that we must go on with it, for some time longer at any rate.

Another fortnight passed, during which period three fugitives arrived, two men and a woman, all of whom we sent on to the next station, without exciting any suspicion as far as I knew, and as nothing had occurred to alarm me, my spirits rose, and I became quite myself again.

I had never seen Randolph since the day he assaulted me, but I often thought of the shameful affair, the recollection of it always sending the blood in a hot flood to my cheeks.

I had hatred for the man and hoped I should never set eyes on him again.

But alas! I was fated to see him before long, under the most painful circumstances. One afternoon, about five o'clock, we were sitting in the veranda at the front of the house. Miss Dean, looking very sweet and pretty in a dove-coloured dress, was as usual usefully employed in making shirts for the runaways, while I was engaged in trimming a hat for myself. Martha was in the kitchen washing up plates and dishes, as we had just finished tea. I was in good spirits, and as I worked I sang to myself in a low voice a plantation song I had learnt from the negroes, called: 'Carry me Back to Ole Virginny.'

It was strange that I should have been singing that

particular song, for I was very anxious to get away from 'Ole Virginny,' and had I been out of the State I certainly would not have asked anyone to carry me back to it.

Presently the stillness of the evening was broken by the clatter of horses' hoofs, mingled with the sound of loud voices in the distance, and on looking down the lane I saw a number of men, some of them mounted, some on foot, coming towards the house.

Miss Dean and I gazed at them as they came along, and we wondered where they were all going; people very rarely entered our secluded lane.

To our surprize, the party stopped at the house, the men on horseback dismounting and hitching their horses to the fence, then the whole crowd came into the veranda and gathered round us as we sat, in silent astonishment, on our chairs.

I noticed however, that there was a hard stern look on the face of every man, while some of them scowled at us with angry glances. There were fifteen men, all of whom were quite unknown to me, even by sight.

Most of them were bearded, rough-looking fellows, dressed in coarse cotton shirts of various colours, with their trousers tucked into boots reaching to the knees and wearing slouched hats on their heads. But there were some men better dressed, and evidently of a higher class.

My heart began to flutter, and a vague foreboding of evil came over me, for though I had not the least suspicion of what the men's intentions were, I guessed from their looks that they had not come to pay us a friendly visit.

One of the intruders, a man about forty years of age, who was addressed by the others as 'Jake Stevens,' and who appeared to be the leader of the band, stepped forward, and laying his hand on Miss Dean's shoulder, at the same time looking at me, said sternly:

'Stand up you two, I've got sumthin' to say to you.'

We both rose to our feet, and Miss Dean asked in a quiet tone:

'Why have you and your companions invaded my house in

39

this rough manner?'

The man laughed scornfully, saying:

'Well, I should say you orter pretty well guess what's brought us here. You ain't so innocent as you look, by a long chalk.' Then with an oath, he went on: 'It has come to the knowledge of the white folks in these parts, that you are keeping an "underground station" and since you have been ere you have got away a great many slaves. Now I jest tell you that we Southerners don't allow no derned Northern abolitionists to run off our slaves. When we ketches abolitionists we makes it hot for them, and now that we've ketched you and your assistant, we are going to bring you before Judge Lynch's court. The boys who have come here with me are the gentlemen of the jury. Isn't that the right talk boys?' he said to the men round him.

'Yes, yes, Jake. That's the talk. You've put it the right way,' shouted several voices.

I sank down horribly frightened on my chair. I had heard dreadful stories of the cruelties perpetrated under the name of 'Lynch.' Miss Dean again spoke calmly:

'If you have found out that we have broken the law of the State, why have you not informed the police? You have no right to take the law into your own hands.'

There was an angry movement among the men, and a hubbub of voices rose.

'We've got the right to do as we please. Lynch Law is good enough for the likes of you. Shut your mouth. Don't waste any more time talking to her, Jake. Let's get to business,' was shouted.

'All right, boys,' said Stevens, 'we'll go into the garden right away and settle what shall be done with the prisoners. We know they are guilty, so we've only got to sentence them, and then we'll proceed to carry out the sentence of the court.'

Miss Dean and I were left in the veranda, while the men, all trooping out into the garden, gathered in a cluster and began to talk; but they were too far off for us to hear what was being said.

I sat huddled up in my chair, with a dreadful sinking at my

heart.

'Oh, Miss Dean,' I wailed, 'what will they do to us?'

'I do not know, dear,' she replied, coming over to me and taking my hand. 'I am not very much concerned about myself, but oh! my poor girl, I am so sorry for you. I should never have allowed you to come here.'

Too miserable to say another word, I sat pale and silent. The men continued talking together, and there seemed to be differences of opinion amongst them, but I could not catch a word that was said. The suspense to me was dreadful, my mouth was parched and I turned alternately hot and cold.

But Miss Dean who still held my hand, occasionally pressing it, was quite calm. At last, the men seemed to have agreed, and they all returned to the veranda.

Then Stevens, assuming a sort of judicial manner, addressed us, saying:

'The sentence of the court upon you two is, that you are each to receive a whipping with a hickory switch on the bare bottom; then you are both to be made to ride a rail for two hours, and further, you are warned to leave the state of Virginny within forty-eight hours. If at the end of that time, you are found in the State, Judge Lynch will have something more to say to you.'

When I heard the shameful and cruel sentence which the lynchers had passed upon us, my blood ran cold and I trembled all over; there was a singing in my ears, and a mist came before my eyes. I rose from my seat, my legs shaking under me so much that I had to hold the back of the chair to support myself.

'Oh, you surely don't mean to whip us!' I exclaimed in piteous accents, stretching out my arms appealingly to the men. 'Oh! don't put us to such awful shame and pain. Have pity on us! Oh! do have pity on us.'

But there was not the least sign of pity on any of the faces surrounding us. All were stern, or frowning, or stolid. And one man called out:

'Sarves you right, you darned little abolitionist. You ought both to be stripped naked, and tarred and feathered after the

41

whipping and then perched on the rail. You would look a queer brace of birds.'

At this coarse joke, there was a burst of laughter from the other men, and I again sank down on my chair, wringing my hands in despair, while the tears streamed down my white cheeks.

Miss Dean, however, faced the men boldly. She had turned very pale, but her eyes were bright and she showed no signs of fear.

Addressing the leader, she said without a tremor in her voice:

'I have often been told that the Southerners were chivalrous in their treatment of women, but I find that I have been misinformed. Chivalrous men do not whip women.'

'I don't know nothing about chivalrous,' said Stevens gruffly, 'but when women acts like men, and sets to running an "underground station" they must take the consekences.'

The men in various terms, garnished with oaths, expressed their approval of what their leader had said.

Miss Dean calmly continued:

'I wish you all to know that I am the only person in this house responsible for what has been done. The young lady is not to blame in any way. She is my paid companion and has acted entirely under my orders. You must let her go free.'

'Oh no! we won't,' exclaimed several voices at once. 'She must have her share of the switch.'

'Let me do the talking,' said Stevens. 'We know very well that you are the boss of this yer show, but the girl has been helpin' you to run it, so she's got to be whipped, but she wont git such a smart touchin' up as you will. Isn't that right, boys?' he asked.

'Yes, yes! That's all right,' some of them answered. 'Let the gal off a bit easier than the woman.'

Just then one of the men called out:

'Whar's the hired woman? She ought to have her bottom switched, and get a ride on the rail as well as the others.'

'Certainly she ought,' said Stevens. 'A couple of you go and bring her here. I guess she's hiding somewhere in the house.'

Two of the men went into the house, and while they were away the others talked and laughed with each other, making ribald remarks that caused me to blush and shiver.

But Miss Dean did not appear to hear what was being said, she stood quite still; her hands loosely clasped in front of her, and with a far-off look in her great soft brown eyes.

In about five minutes' time, the two men returned, and one of them said with an oath:

'We can't find the bitch anywhere in the house though we have looked well. She must have run off into the woods.'

'It's a pity she's got away,' said Stevens, 'but anyhow we've got the two leading ladies of the show, and I guess we'll make them both feel sorry that they ever took a hand in the game.'

'You bet we will, Jake,' shouted the men. 'We'll make them sorry they ever came to Virginny. Let's get to work at once.'

'Very well,' said Stevens. 'Bill, you run to the barn and fetch the ladder you'll find there. Pete and Sam, you go and cut a couple of good, long, springy hick'ry switches and trim them ready for me to use.' Then he added with a laugh: 'I daresay these yere Northern ladies have often eaten hick'ry nuts, but I reckon they never thought they would feel a hick'ry switch on their bare bottoms.'

The men all joined in the laugh, while I shuddered, and my heart swelled with bitterness at our utter helplessness.

The ladder and the switches were brought, then all the men went into the garden,.

The ladder was then fixed in a sloping position against the rail of the veranda on the outside, and Stevens took up his position near it, holding one of the switches in his hand; while the other men stood round in a ring, so that they might all have a good look at what was going to be done.

'Bring out the prisoners,' said Stevens.

Some of the men took hold of us by the arms and led us out of the veranda to receive the cruel and indecent punishment.

I was trembling and crying; but Miss Dean was calm and silent. Stevens said to her:

'As you are the boss, you shall be whipped first. Tie her up,

43

boys.'

She was seized by two men, and laid upon the ladder; her arms being stretched to their full extent above her head; her wrists tied with thick cords to the rungs of the ladder, and her ankles also securely fastened in the same way.

She had not made the least resistance nor had she uttered a word while being tied up, but now she turned her head, and looking over her shoulder at Stevens, said:

'Can you not whip me without removing my clothes?'

'No, certainly not,' he replied. 'You was sentenced to be whipped on the bare bottom. Turn up her clothes, boys.'

Her skirt, petticoats and chemise were rolled high above her waist, and tucked under her body so that they could not fall down. She had not on the ordinary drawers with a slit behind, such as are usually worn by women, but she was wearing long pantalettes, buttoning up all round, fitting rather closely to her legs, and reaching down to her ankles, round which the little frills at the end of the garment were drawn in with narrow ribbons.

'Why darn me, if she ain't got on white trousers!' ejaculated Stevens in a tone of astonishment. 'I never seed such things on a woman before.'

The other men also seemed surprised, and very much amused at the sight of the trousers, and various remarks were made about them by some of the spectators. I suppose the women of their class in that part of the country never wore drawers of any sort.

'Take down her trousers,' said Stevens.

Again Miss Dean looked round:

'Please leave me my pantalettes. They won't protect me much. Do not expose my nakedness to all these men,' she pleaded earnestly.

But no attention was paid to her entreaty. One of the men roughly put his hands in front of her belly, and after some fumbling, unbuttoned the pantalettes and pulled them down to her ankles, leaving her person naked from the waist to the tops of the black silk stockings she was wearing.

When her last garment had been removed, her pale cheeks

44

blushed scarlet, even the nape of her neck and her ears became red; a shudder shook her body from head to foot, she bent her head down and closed her eyes.

I was being held by two men close to the ladder, so I could not help seeing everything.

Miss Dean, as I have said before, was a tall, slim, slightly-built woman. Her hips were very narrow and her bottom very small, but it was round, well-shaped and fairly plump; her thighs and legs were also well-formed though slender; her skin was of a delicate ivory tint, smooth, and fine in texture.

The men pressed closer to the ladder, and I could see their eyes glisten as they fixed them with lecherous looks on Miss Dean's half-naked body.

And Stevens after gazing for a moment or two at her straight figure, exclaimed with a laugh:

'Je-ru-sa-lem! what a little bottom she's got. It ain't no bigger than a man's. By gosh, boys! perhaps she is a man?'

This was meant for a joke. It amused them and they all laughed, one of the men calling out:

'Well, Jake, you can easily find out whether she's a woman or not.'

'Why so I can, now that you have put it in my head,' drawled Stevens, grinning and affecting to be surprised at the suggestion.

Then he thrust his hand between her thighs.

She flinched convulsively, uttering a startled cry, then looking round at the man with an expression of intense horror on her face, and with her eyes flashing, exclaimed:

'How dare you touch me like that? Take your hand away! Oh, whip me and let me go!'

She writhed and twisted, but the man kept his hand in the cleft of her thighs, saying with a coarse laugh:

'She's a woman sure enough, boys. I've got my hand on her slit.' Then he said to her:

'My hand won't hurt you. But if I and these other gentlemen were not sorter decent chaps who only intend to carry out the sentence of Judge Lynch, you would soon find something different to a hand between your legs. Now I'll flog you right away, and I guess you'll soon be begging me to stop whipping you.'

He withdrew his hand, and Miss Dean ceased struggling, her head drooped forward; she again closed her eyes, and lay silently awaiting the shameful punishment.

Stevens raised the switch and flicked it about, so as to make it hiss in the air, then he brought it down with considerable force across the upper part of her bottom; the tough hickory spray making a sharp crack as it struck the firm flesh which quivered involuntarily under the stinging stroke.

She winced, drawing her breath through her teeth with a hissing sound, and a long red weal instantly rose on her delicate skin. Swinging the switch high, he went on whipping, laying each stroke below the preceding one, so that her skin was striped in regular lines. Each stroke smacked loudly on her flesh, and raised a fresh, red weal which stretched across both sides of her quivering bottom.

She began to writhe, and clenched her teeth so tightly that I could see the outlines of her jaws through her cheeks, but no sound came from her lips.

The man laid on the strokes with severity, and I wondered how she could bear the pain in silence. I felt inclined to scream, and I shuddered every time I heard the horrid sound made by the switch as it fell on her flesh.

He continued to whip her ruthlessly and slowly, pausing between each stroke, while the weals increased in number and her skin grew redder, until at last there was not a trace of white to be seen on the whole surface of her bottom. Her flesh twitched, she winced more sharply, writhed more, and jerked her loins from side to side as the hissing strokes fell. Then, raising her head and looking over her shoulder, she fixed her eyes, which had become dilated and wild-looking, on the switch every time it rose in the air; her lips were quivering, her pretty face was distorted with pain, big tears were streaming down her scarlet cheeks and she began to moan. Still he plied the hickory, drops of blood began to show all over the surface of the skin, her contortions became more violent, and she uttered a groan every time the switch

46

raised a fresh weal on her bleeding bottom.

But the brave woman never once screamed, nor did she make an appeal for mercy. Her fortitude amazed me.

At last he stopped whipping, and threw down the switch which had become quite frayed at the end. Then bending down, he closely examined the marks of his handiwork on the sufferer's bottom.

I also gazed at it, shuddering. The whole surface, from the loins to the thighs, was a dark red colour; covered with livid weals crossing and recrossing each other in all directions, and plentifully spotted with blood. It was dreadfully sore-looking, and its extreme redness contrasted with the ivory-like whiteness of the untouched skin of the thighs.

She had been most severely whipped. I think she must have received forty or fifty strokes.

'There, boys,' said Stevens looking round at the spectators, 'I guess that will do for her. I touched her up pretty smartly, as you can see from the state of her bottom. She won't be able to sit down comfortable for two or three days, and I don't think the marks of the whipping will ever be quite rubbed off her skin.'

He then pulled down her clothes and unfastened her wrists and ankles. She stood up, twisting her loins in pain, with her pantalettes hanging about her feet; her face was now pale and drawn with suffering, her bosom was heaving, her tears were flowing, and she was sobbing.

She seemed oblivious of everything except her pain. But after a few moments she recovered herself a little, and taking her handkerchief from her pocket, wiped the tears from her eyes; then she pulled up her pantalettes, and with some difficulty, as she was trembling very much, buttoned them round her waist, her cheeks again reddening when she noticed the grinning faces and leering looks of the men standing round her.

Two of them took her by the arms and led her into the veranda, where they left her. She laid herself down at full length upon a couch and hid her face in the cushion, weeping.

Chapter Five

I am myself stripped naked and receive a most terrible whipping –
The coarse observations of the men – My shame and terror,
showing from experience that chastisement by the opposite sex
awakens sensations sometimes far from pleasurable – Jake
Stevens's fearful crime – How Peachie was raped.

I have told you all these things precisely as they happened,
and I have used the exact words and phrases that were spoken
by the band of Lynchers who tortured us that day. I daresay
you wonder at my remembering all the little details. But such
an experience can never be forgotten. All the incidents that
occurred during that dreadful period were indelibly printed
on my memory, so that I have still a vivid recollection of
them.

But to resume. You can imagine my feelings as I listened to
the coarse language of the men, language such as I had never
heard before, and watched the proceedings, at once so cruel
and so utterly revolting to feminine delicacy. I was torn with
various emotions. I was horrified at what I had heard and
seen. I was filled with pity for Miss Dean, and consumed with

impotent rage against the men in whose power we were. I dreaded the coming exposure of my person, and I was awfully afraid of the whipping before me.

I never could bear pain with any fortitude. In fact I must confess that I am morally and physically a great coward.

Stevens picked up the unused switch, and straightened it by drawing it through the fingers of his left hand.

'Now, boys,' he said, 'put the gal on the ladder and tie her up; but let me do the stripping.'

The awful moment had come, and I became quite frantic at the thought of the shame and pain I was about to undergo, and an insane idea that I might escape, came into my head.

The men were holding me loosely, so I easily slipped from their grasp and made a dash for the garden gate.

Several of the men gave chase, and though I exerted myself to the utmost, I was soon caught and dragged to the ladder, shrieking, struggling, and begging them not to whip me.

But my entreaties only evoked laughter. I was lifted up, placed in position with outstretched arms, and securely fastened by the wrists and ankles.

Stevens began to strip me, and seemed to take as long a time over the work as possible, slowly rolling my garments one by one till he came to my drawers; then he paused. I was wearing the usual feminine drawers that are open behind.

'Look, boys,' he observed, 'this gal has got on trousers too, but they are different to the ones the woman wore. These are loose, and are real dandy ones, all pretty frills and lace, and ribbons, and you see there is a big slit at the back. I suppose that's made so as her sweetheart can get at her without taking down her trousers.'

The men all laughed loudly, while I, on hearing the shameful words, shrank as if I had received a blow.

He untied the strings of my drawers and pulled them down to my knees, and then I could feel the breeze fanning my naked bottom and thighs. A sensation of unutterable shame overwhelmed me. To be exposed in such a way before fifteen men!

And such men! Oh! it was horrible! I knew that they were

all gloating over my nakedness and I seemed actually to feel their lascivious glances on my flesh.

I was hot with shame, yet I shivered as if with cold. But worse was to come. Stevens put his hand on my bottom, stroking it all over and squeezing the flesh with his fingers, making me thrill and quiver with disgust. In fact, my feelings of shame and horror at the moment were far greater than they had been when Randolph assaulted me.

'Ah!' said Stevens, chuckling and continuing to feel me with his rough hand, 'this gal has got something like a bottom. My! ain't it jest plump, and firm, and broad. There's plenty of room here for the switch, and her skin is as soft and smooth as velvet, and you can see how white it is. I've never before had my hand on such a scrumptious bottom. It's worth feeling and no mistake.' I writhed and moaned. He went on: 'I should like you all to have a feel of it, but as leader of this yer party, I can't allow you to touch the gal, for fear some of you might want to do more than feel her; and that would lead to difficulties among us. Now, as to the punishment of the gal, I propose to give her a dozen strokes, but not draw blood. Remember she is only an assistant in the business.'

The men were divided in opinion. Some said that I ought to be whipped just the same as the 'missis'; but the majority was in favour of my receiving only twelve strokes. And so it was settled. Even in my fear and shame, I felt a sensation of relief at hearing that I was not going to be whipped so severely as Miss Dean had been. One of the men called out:

'Mind you lay the dozen right smart, Jake. Make the young bitch wriggle her bottom.'

'You bet I'll lay them on smart, and you'll see how she'll move. I know how to handle a hick'ry switch, and I'll rule a dozen lines across her bottom that'll make it look like the American flag, striped red and white. And when I've done with her I guess she'll be pretty sore behind, but you'll see that I won't draw a drop of blood. Yes, gentlemen, I tell you again that I know how to whip, I was an overseer in Georgia for five years.'

All the time the man was holding forth, I lay shame-stricken at my nakedness, and shivering in awful suspense, the flesh of my bottom creeping, and the scalding tears trickling down my red cheeks. The man raised the switch and flourished it over me; while I held my breath and contracted the muscles of my bottom in dread of the coming stroke.

It fell with a loud swishing noise. Oh! it was awful! The pain was even worse than I had anticipated. It took my breath away for a moment and made me gasp, while I uttered a loud shriek, writhing and twisting my loins in agony.

He went on whipping me very slowly, so that I felt the full sting of each stroke before the next one fell; and every stroke felt as if a red-hot iron was being drawn across my bottom.

I winced and squirmed every time the horrid switch fell sharply on my quivering flesh. I shrieked and screamed, and I swung my hips from side to side, arching my loins at one moment, and then flattening myself down on the ladder, while between my shrieks, I begged and prayed the man to stop whipping me.

I had forgotton all about my nakedness, the only sensation I had at the moment was one of intense pain, and when the twelve strokes had been inflicted I was in a half fainting state.

I was left lying with upturned petticoats, on the ladder, while the men all gathered round me and looked at me.

As I was a strong healthy girl, the faintness soon passed off, as also did the first intense smart of the whipping, but my whole bottom was sore, and the weals throbbed painfully.

The feeling of shame again came over me as I began to notice the way the men were looking at my naked body, and I tearfully begged them to pull down my clothes.

No one did so however, and Stevens pointing to me said:

'There, boys, look at her bottom. You see how regularly the white skin is striped with long red weals; but there is not a drop of blood. That's what I call a prettily whipped bottom. But the gal ain't got a bit of grit in her. Any nigger wench would have taken double the number of strokes without making half the noise. Now the other woman is a plucky one; she took the whippin' well.' He then pulled up my drawers

51

and tied the strings round my waist, saying with a laugh. 'This is the first time I've ever fixed up a woman's trousers, and it's the first time I've ever whipped women who wore pants.'

Pulling down my clothes, he loosed me from the ladder, and led me crying, sore and miserable, back to the veranda where Miss Dean was still lying on her stomach on the couch, with her hands over her face.

The conduct of these wretches towards two women of whom one was young and pretty, and desirable anyway, may appear strange. How was it that their brutal, lustful natures were not inflamed by the intoxicating sight of my dazzling nudity?

The agonizing anticipation of torture did not cause me to prefer the ignominy which was bound to result from the defeat of my virtue, but in the inmost depths of my soul, I hoped nevertheless that the sight of my youthful charms, sharpening the concupiscent instincts of these brutes, might cause them to quarrel among themselves.

Although still innocent, in spite of the lesson the infamous assaults of Randolph had taught me, I knew that the exposure of my frame was capable of awakening the vile desires of these low and bestial men; so I hoped that they might have disputed about the possession of my body, and allowed me to escape under cover of a free fight.

Alas! I knew not then that they were Randolph's own creatures, and generously paid by him to carry out his barbarous orders.

In their hearts, for once, cupidity spoke louder than lewdness.

Besides, bushwackers did not always behave in this way unless the greed for gold dictated their motives, and this very Stevens had eluded the efforts of justice to overtake him when he had been guilty of the crime of murder preceded by rape, perpetrated under particularly atrocious circumstances.

The story of this monstrous offence was told me later, by an old quadroon, one of the slaves of Randolph's father, and she had had it recounted to her in the fullest possible way.

I venture to give the woman's tale here, apologizing for the digression.

'In spite of the slaves being overworked, and extra labour exacted from all the women, Randolph senior could not manage to satisfy the demands of the cotton-dealers; so that it became urgent for him that his human flock should increase in number.

'The planter consequently bought at Richmond market three blacks, among whom was an octoroon about thirty years of age, named Maria de Granier, as in some parts of the South, slaves born on a plantation had their master's title following their proper names.

'This woman, who had formerly been very pretty, was in a most lamentable condition at the moment of being put up for sale. She had been buried in a sliding mass of earth, while working with a spade, and was taken out half dead, and infirm for the rest of her life, incapable in future of being used for the rigorously severe labour which she had been forced to undertake.

'Maria de Granier, as damaged goods, fetched a very low price. But what tempted Randolph senior to buy her was that in spite of her terrible accident she was soon about to become a mother.

'He doubtless hoped that the young invalid woman could manage light jobs, and the child in her womb would increase the number of his slaves, and render him slight service some day or the other.

'Although this calculation was abominable, it was none the less true. The octoroon, in the family way by a white man, gave birth to a charming little girl, whom she called Peachie. The child grew up and attained the age of fourteen, carefully tended by the women of the plantation, who ofttimes risked a flogging in order to hide her childish faults; while Peachie was adored by the poor blacks who stoically put up with a whipping when the overseer caught them helping the child in its work.

'Nevertheless, Peachie had become a delicious young

creature with refined and regular features, white teeth, and large black eyes. The incomparable beauty of her form was already revealed beneath her ignominious rags of slavery, and her naked arms, with their soft and dazzling skin, could be seen scarcely tinged with the sepia hue betraying the hybrid.

'At that epoch, George Randolph, who had just reached his eighteenth year, was inflamed with a violent passion for Peachie, a case of lust at first sight. He persecuted her with his assiduous attentions, and was only waiting for some favourable opportunity to doom the child to the fate awaiting nearly all young slave-girls.

'But Peachie, who by a kind of foresight of the threatening danger, perceived the true nature of George's feelings, avoided every chance of meeting, and therefore only accepted the presents and caresses of the youth in the presence of the blacks, before whom the young fellow did not dare to make an attempt upon her, despite the impunity he enjoyed.

'But finally, one day, when Peachie, all by herself, was carrying a bale of cotton to a shed which was used as a warehouse, and stood on the outskirts of a forest, George, during the absence of the overseer, sent away by him under some specious pretext, threw himself on the child, covered her with scalding kisses, and under the influence of a violent erotic spasm, ordered her to lie down and pull up her clothes.

'Peachie, cleverly disengaging herself from his grasp, refused to obey his vile commands and fled into the forest, where Randolph, raging furiously, pursued her for some time.

'The lass clambered over fences, dashed through canebrakes, and prickly bushes, running along paths unknown to her; so much so, that exhausted, panting for breath, she let herself fall near a bypath, and half dead with fatigue, fell fast asleep.

'Night came on, and soon the dead leaves and brushwood encumbering the narrow path creaked beneath the heavy boots of a band of men. This noise, suddenly breaking out amidst the calm of the tangled wood, woke the little girl up. Then she remembered and was sore afraid. But reassured by the thought that the footsteps resulted from the approach of some blacks who were scouring the forest to find her, she stood up and called out. At the same moment she felt the cool caress of the night breezes stirring the leaves on the trees and fanning her naked, amber flesh.

'In her mad flight her clothes had come undone; and falling one by one, had left her without a rag to cover her exquisite nudity. So now she was ashamed, and it seemed to her girlish brain that unwholesome curiosity lurked in the dread shadows.

'The childish voice had been uplifted. Men's gruff notes had replied. But did these answering shouts come from her dusky mates?

'No, it was Stevens, escorted by the two companions wearing leather pants, and carrying repeating rifles.

'"By the sheriff's guts!" exclaimed Jake, catching sight of the damsel, "here's a coon gal noways skeared at the notion of catching cold." He added, as he approached her: "Gee whillikins! she desarves to be invited to come and stay over and have a real good time in the fairy palace belonging to Jake Stevens. Our boss, old Nick, has most sartinly heard as how we're devilishly sharp set for fornicating fun, and that's why he's mailed up this tit-bit, all charges paid, from his hot old town where there ain't no snowballs."

'Peachie quickly grasped the frightful meaning of these words. She made a movement as if to retreat.

'Stevens quickly covered her with his gun, exclaiming:

'"Hands up – and legs up too – beaut'! My sight's kinder short by daylight, but I kin see in the dark like a wild cat, I guess, and kin put a bit o'lead through the joker, moon or no moon. So jist hev your best company manners, and put on yer go-to-meeting bonnet, if you kin spy it lying around. Leastways, get a hustle on, and come along of us!"

'Being now surrounded by the three men, the maiden felt that any resistance was impossible. Red with shame, and terrified in anguish, she clasped her hands and implored them:

'"Be good to me, gentlemen! Have pity on me! I'se only a

poor coon gal! See, I's but a slave, and not fifteen yet!"

'The three men's eyes sparkled.

'"Not fifteen!!" exclaimed Stevens, whose authority seemed to regulate the acts and words of his mates. "By Christ, if this ain't manna in the wilderness, may I never taste old Rye again in the whole course of my nat'ral life! She is a windfall of ripe fruit, just spoiling to be sarved up for dessert, with the bloom on, boys, and which aren't never been bitten by no teeth at all. By Jacob's naval, you shall have a go at this here treat, a goddarned sight better nor any pumpkin! This beats corned-beef hash by a long chalk, and there'll be enough to go round for you, my sons, when Jake Stevens has had first pick o' the dish, and don't you forget it!"

'All hope faded out of her mind, but courage came back to the girl, and she cried out:

'"Well then, kill me if you like, but I'll not go with you!"

'Peachie, as she spoke, crossed her trembling hands across her breast, trying to hide her small, hard, budding bubbies; and squatted down in the cold grass, already wet with night dew.

'Peachie struggled in vain in the rough hands of the bushwackers; supplicating, and imploring once more to no purpose. The men paralyzed her movements by means of a lasso wound round her, and they carried her off through the wood, where, as her prayers and cries for mercy had no effect on her captors, she resolved in her despair to utter piercing shrieks, hoping thus to be heard from afar.

'She knew perfectly well what kind of punishment awaited her at the plantation as a reward for her rash escapade, but although she as yet had never been under the cowhide, she however preferred such torture, which she knew to be cruel, to the fate reserved for her by the bandits.

'They were far from being at their ease, although they made all possible haste to get away from the track of the search-party, that they guessed was now out on the hunt for Peachie; and the rough wretches were annoyed at the girl's cries, which might perhaps guide the blacks in their direction. So they made up their minds to gag her, and

Stevens, fishing out of his leathern wallet a cotton rag, rolled it up in the shape of a ball, and thrust it deeply into his victim's mouth.

'In this way the abductors arrived at Jake Stevens's log-hut. It was a cabin built up of rough boarding, old wooden cases, and trunks of fallen trees; the roof formed of intertwined branches, and all its fissures were blocked up with heavy lumps of earth. The hut looked like some sinister, criminal retreat, hidden in the deepest, thickest undergrowth, shaded in the midst of high trees, growing between huge rocks. Jake Stevens and his two cronies were the only beings who knew of the existence of this lair. It was here that they came and hid the booty resulting from their highway robberies, effected as far away as possible from their hiding-place.

'Stevens, who carried the child in his arms, put her softly down upon a rough kind of bed, and took away the stifling gag. One of the men then drew a flint and steel from his jacket of buffalo-hide, and lit a hemp-stalk, while his mate got the lamp ready.

'A dull glare lit up the cabin, and some eatables, drawn out of their wallets, were placed on a large plank, a few inches off the ground.

'"I reckon our saloon aren't no great shakes," said Stevens, whose lustful glance, since the lamp had been lit, seemed as if searing Peachie's body, "but yer kin say what yer like, it's kinder commodious, and home-like. Jim," he added, with a lecherous wink, "I guess we'll have to do without terrapin and canvas-backs just this once, but you had better put some ginger spice and seasoning on our bit o' old horse, just to make us spunky. Joey, old son," said he, turning to the other, "fill up the pannikins with the old pisen."

'When the meal was ready, Stevens said to the girl:

'"If the spirit moveth, my kiddy, and missy feels a bit o'appetite, sure there'll be a mouthful for you, my bronze beaut'."

'Peachie did not reply, but stifled sobs stuck in her throat. She had picked up an old leather waistcoat and tried to cover her nakedness with it. Stevens noticed her efforts.

'"Drop yer draperies, my angel!" he exclaimed. "No masks here, missy. All's fair and aboveboard in this air shanty, and silks and satins, my gal, 'ud cut no figure alongside of your natty little limbs."

'He rose to his feet, tore the ragged garment from her, preventing her from accomplishing the design she had of covering her bosom and the mark of her sex, and came back to the table chuckling hideously.

'All this time they were eating, the man called Jim never took his eyes off Peachie's marvellous body. His gaze seemed to be revelling in the slightest details of the charms which were sure to be in his possession before he was a few minutes older, and if now and again, his looks wandered towards his chief, they were brimming with jealousy and envy. Morcover, grief became the child's style of beauty and it seemed as if the lowly hut was warmed by her body and scented by the intoxicating odour of her dying virginity.

'Joe gulped down mug upon mug of fiery spirit. At the close of the repast, with his brain muddled by the thick vapours of intoxication, he went and stretched himself on a bed of dried leaves and remained half-asleep, without, however, losing sight of the smallest incident in the scene which was about to take place.

'The talk of Stevens and Jim was commonplace, when it was not coarse and smutty. Both were under the influence of the same preoccupations. Each guessed what was passing in the other's mind.

'But Stevens, absolutely master of his mates, knew how to make Jim cower beneath the yoke of discipline which it would have been dangerous to resist, and it often happened after one of their thieving raids that Stevens kept all the loot for himself, leaving his two companions naught but the glory of the expedition to "cut up" between them.

'"Say, cully, maybe you're sorter sick; suffrin' from swelled head, like? Own up. Be a man, and tell us how you got so all-fired sassy as to think you might be a-goin' to *begin?*" said Stevens, breaking silence.

'"Maybe too, matey, as you thinks you're God-Almighty? Waal, I 'spect you'll find out diff'rent on Judgement Day. P'raps afore – who can savey?"

'Such was Jim's tranquil reply as he ostentatiously patted the handle of a formidable bowie knife, comfortably nestling in the sleeve of his dirty red flannel shirt.

'"The coon bitch is as much mine as yours, I reckon, and for once in a way – say, for the fust time in your darned existence, it might happen that you'd have to share and share alike with your pard. See? So let's draw lots as to whom shall open de ball, and walk for de angel, maidenhead cake wid little brownie ober dere."

'"I calkilate I've won afore we start," replied Stevens, who, rising and dropping on one knee, popped a heavy revolver under Jim's nose. "I've got a full hand! The jackpot's mine! Throw that razzer away, or I'll put daylight through yer!"

'Jim hurriedly drew the formidable blade out of his sleeve, and dashed it from him across the rude apology for a table. Stevens stepped quietly backwards, still keeping the muzzle of his sixshooter in a steady line with Jim's face, and picking up the weapon, slipped it into his hip pocket.

'"Now," said he, "the marriage ceremony is about to take place with every formality known in the land where the blamed drunken hog, Joe, first saw whuskey, and he stands on the Catholic platform. So you, Jim, 'ull be my best man and give the bride away as well; and if Joe wasn't as drunk as Noah, he'd say mass and tip us the nuptial blessin'. One hour 'ull fix me, and arter that, I hands you the box o' toys, and climbs down from the position of husband, gettin' divorced in your favour, Jim, sonny! A married man hornified by his little wifie sixty minutes after the knot's been tied! Guess that licks creation, and you've got to be invited to be a summer boarder at Jake Stevens's country residence to see a sight like that!"

'Heavy laughter convulsed the speaker, lighting up his wild-beast features, and every fresh guffaw of Stevens sent a thrill of horror through the lithe and supple frame of the poor girl.

'He approached the shuddering child, who now began to
sob, and without speaking, his face fearfully congested as
though about to have an attack of apoplexy, covered her with
hot, disgusting kisses, licking her face like a dog, and
thrusting his tongue into her unwilling mouth, sucking her
ears, and tasting the interior of her nostrils. His breath came
in gasps, and his horny hands rummaged and pinched every
charm, inflicting bruises wherever the eager fingers
wandered. The small hard bubbies were scratched and
pressed, the nipples bitten; the firm buttocks, of light bronze
hue, were kneaded, slapped and nipped, and his crooked
digits dared to invade the secret orifice behind. Peachie felt
her blood course hotly through her veins, and mount to her
affrighted brain; her heart seemed as if breaking, as she
endured the vile and painful caresses – if they can so be called
– of the brute; she felt the repugnant breath of the monster on
her lips, as he slobbered and frothed his tobacco-laden saliva
in her pretty, pure mouth; and between the repeated
onslaughts, which made her think her last hour had come,
she experienced a most horrible sensation, for it seemed to
her that some enormous animal clutched her, and pumped
her breasts with tepid viscous tentacles.

'Jim's lust was fearfully inflamed at the vile sight; his virile
organ swelling to bursting, so he gave it full liberty, and the
long tool sprung out of its place of hiding and stood up arched
towards his navel, slowly jerking itself spasmodically, as the
excited ruffian felt the pent-up sperm striving to escape.
With flaming eyes, and foaming mouth, Jim waited for the
finish, eager for the moment when his turn should come at
last.

'Stevens did not hurry; and he was probably endeavouring
not only to prolong his own pleasure but also to annoy his
partner by delaying his.

'Peachie was too frightened to try and struggle; she lay
with closed eyes and pallid cheeks. Perhaps she had fainted?

'Little recked Stevens. He parted the girl's unresisting
thighs, and gazed for a moment ecstatically at the little lass's

tiny slit. He roughly pulled it open with his fingers, and caught a glimpse of the pink lining. It looked like the interior of some delicate sea-shell; nothing could be fresher, and more unsullied. Stevens pulled out a tremendous virile organ; the skin having long since sprung back, disclosing a violet-red head, looking like an egg-plant, had it not been for the white matter that partially covered it. He pressed the point to the miniature gap, and throwing himself with all his weight on the wretched little girl, her head and breast disappeared from view. Nothing could be seen but his burly back and the pushing movements of his arse as he crushed into the body of his victim. He was soon engulfed and Peachie gave a fearful shriek, as with a last despairing effort she managed to push him up and free her face from the weight of his body.

'At this moment, an oath of delight proved that Stevens had spent in her, and she fell back, her lineaments distorted by pain to such an extent that all her beauty left her, and the erstwhile pretty features were twisted into the semblance of a Japanese mask.

'Jake stood up, his tool suffused with blood, and a stream of gory fluid slowly issued from the now swollen and tumefied parts of the outraged virgin.

'Nothing daunted by this shocking spectacle, Jim rushed forward, prick in hand, when the rough door of the cabin was broken down with a loud crash, and a band of niggers, who had tracked Peachie by the clothes torn from her during her flight, invaded the hut.

'Lust left the bandits at the thought of danger, and Stevens rushed for his rifle, overturning the lamp with a blow of his left hand as he did so. Joe's bed flared up like tinder, and the coons retreated for one short instant, long enough to enable Jake to fight his way through them, and disappear in the darkness without; leaving the frightened blacks busy trying to put out the flames, amid the heartrending shrieks of Joe, who danced about the hut, a living torch. Jim seized the plank that formed the table, and with his clothes aflame clubbed his way through the blacks, who made but a feeble resistance before the infuriated figure of a man, who, with hair and beard on fire, and his private parts exposed, rushed at them with a long piece of wood, grasped in both hands.

'Joe had fallen a blackened mass of burnt flesh, emitting a sickening odour, but Peachie had escaped the flames and still lay without movement; her thighs outstretched, and a bloody patch between them. The overseer approached her, and as she never stirred, he took his cowhide out of his belt and lashed the childish body with the long leather thong. But she remained as still as the bronze statuette she resembled; the poor raped maiden was dead – the terrible thrust of Stevens's formidable organ had killed her!

'Joe, blinded in one eye and maimed for life, alone had to answer to justice for his crime, but as he had only played a minor part in this drama of lust and blood, and had suffered terrible injuries from which he never wholly recovered, he was acquitted. Some little time afterwards, the news came that Jim had been shot at Richmond – on sight – by someone he had tricked; while Stevens got off scot free. No one ever knew by dint of what lucky circumstances he escaped without being prosecuted, or how he was taken back into Randolph's good graces.'

After Stevens had conducted me to the side of Miss Dean, he went off to the other men, a few of whom I saw were engaged in work of some sort near the fence. But I was so thankful at having got out of their hands and sight that I did not particularly notice what they were doing.

I thought they would soon go away and that all our troubles were over. I had quite forgotten that Stevens had said we would have to ride a rail for two hours after being whipped.

Miss Dean looked mournfully at me, her sweet face very pale and her soft eyes full of tears, but the tears were not for herself; they were for me. She beckoned to me, and when I went to her, she folded me in her arms, pressing me to her bosom:

'Oh! my poor, poor girl;' she murmured in tones full of compassion, 'how I have felt for you! Your shrieks pierced my heart. Oh! the cruel, cruel man to whip you so severely.'

She seemed to have quite forgotten the shame and pain of

her own whipping in her pity for me.

'He did not whip me nearly so severely as he did you,' I said. 'He only gave me a dozen strokes and no blood has come. But I could not help screaming. I am not so brave as you are.'

Then we kissed and cried, and sympathized with each other, comparing notes as to our feelings while on the ladder exposed to the eyes of the men.

After a moment or two, I put my hand under my petticoats and touched my smarting bottom, feeling the weals which had been raised on the flesh by the switch. They were exquisitely tender, and I could hardly bear to touch them.

'Oh! dear me!' I wailed, 'How dreadfully sore I am. But you must be much sorer?'

'I certainly am very, very sore,' said Miss Dean, wiping her eyes. 'I can neither sit down nor lie on my back. My bottom is still bleeding I think, and my pantalettes are sticking to my flesh. But oh, oh! the awful exposure, and the shameful touch of the man's hand was worse than the whipping,' she exclaimed, wringing her hands, while the tears again began to trickle down her cheeks.

I pressed her hand in mute sympathy, and she went on:

'Our sufferings are not over yet, Dorothy. Don't you remember the man said we would have to ride the rail for two hours?'

I now did call to mind what Stevens had said about our riding a rail, but I was not much frightened at having to do so. Of course I knew that it would be very uncomfortable, if not painful to have to sit with a sore and smarting bottom on a rail for two hours. That was all I thought about the matter at the moment.

Ah! I little knew what a terrible torture riding a rail would prove to be.

I don't know whether Miss Dean had any notion of what it actually was, but anyway she did not say a word more on the subject, and we stood – both of us being too sore to sit down in comfort – with our arms round each other, weeping silently and waiting miserably for the men to come for us.

We had not long to wait. In a couple of minutes, four of the band came, and taking us by the arms, led us out of the veranda to the fence, beside which the other men were standing some of them holding pieces of rope in their hands.

The fence was about five feet high, and of the ordinary pattern, made of split rails, the upper edge of each being wedge-shaped and sharp. Stevens, with a cruel smile on his face, said:

'Now you are going to receive the rest of your punishment – a two hour ride on the rail. I guess your bottoms must be very hot jest now, but they'll have plenty of time to cool while you are having your ride, and to prevent you from falling off your horses, we'll tie you on them. Get them ready, boys.'

I thought that we should be merely tied in a sitting posture on the fence with our clothes down. But I was soon undeceived! We were each seized by two men who held our arms, while a third man, in each case, raised our petticoats and pulled our drawers entirely off our legs. Then our garments were held high above our waists so that the whole lower parts of our persons, both behind and before, were exposed to the lustful eyes of the horrid men.

And as they had already seen our bottoms, they all crowded in front of us, gloating over the secret 'spots' of our respective bodies, while we, crimson with a greater shame than ever, struggled and wept, and entreated the wretches to cover our nakedness.

But they only laughed, and two or three of them put their hands on the 'spots' – 'pussies,' they called them – the touch of their fingers making us start and shrink with a horrible feeling of disgust.

Stevens, however, stopped them, by saying:

'No, no, boys, you must not touch the prisoners, but you may look at them as much as you like.'

And the men did look, making remarks, speculating as to whether we were virgins or not, pointing out the difference in the shape of our figures, and observing the colour of the hair on our respective 'spots' while we blushed, and cried with shame.

You have seen my 'spot' and know what it is like; there is nothing strange about it. But Miss Dean's 'spot' was somewhat remarkable. I had never seen it before and I could not help looking at it with astonishment. It was covered with a thick forest of glossy, dark brown hair, which extended some distance up her belly and descended between her thighs in curly locks nearly two inches long, the fissure being completely hidden and not a trace of the lips to be seen.

One man, after a prolonged stare, exclaimed:

'By Gosh! I've never seen such a fleece between a woman's legs in my life. Darn me if she wouldn't have to be sheared before a man could get to her.'

The men roared with laughter at the remark, while Miss Dean groaned, and writhed in the bitterness of her shame.

After looking at our naked bodies for fully five minutes, the men went on with their work.

A long piece of rope was passed several times round our bodies, so that our arms and wrists were closely lashed to our sides. We were then lifted bodily up, and to my intense horror, seated astride one of the topmost rails of the fence, facing each other and about six feet apart.

The rail passed between our naked thighs, and our bare bottoms rested on the sharp edge of it. On each side of the fence and close to it, the men had driven stakes into the ground, and to these stakes our ankles were securely tied.

When the men had fixed us in this painful position, they allowed our clothes to fall about our legs. Our nakedness was covered, but our torture had begun.

Stevens looked at us with a grin on his face, saying:

'There now; you are properly mounted on your horses. We've done with you and we're all going away, but at the end of two hours one of us will come back and loose you. And I reckon you'll both be mighty stiff after your ride.'

Then the band of lynchers took their departure, laughing, and shouting coarse jokes which made us, even in our pain, grow hot with shame. The clatter of the horses' hoofs and the loud laughter of the men gradually died away in the distance; then all was perfectly still.

Chapter Six

On the rack – Moral torture is allied to the physical – I make the great decision of my life and consent to become Randolph's mistress – His revolting cynicism.

It was a beautiful, calm, bright evening, the sun was just setting, so the house, the garden, and our two unfortunate selves were all bathed in a flood of amber light.

At first, I had a faint hope that Martha would come back – now that the men had gone – and release us, but she never came, and there was not the slightest chance of any one else coming to the house at that hour.

There was no escape possible, so we would be obliged to undergo the whole of our dreadful punishment.

From the first moment of our being placed astride the rail we had been suffering pain, and it was increasing every minute. We did not speak to one another, as our sufferings were too great, so we sat in silence, with the tears, which we could not wipe off, trickling down our pale cheeks, while every now and then a shuddering sob, or groan of anguish would break from our parched lips.

As our legs were rather widely stretched apart, the rail was in the cleft of our thighs, and the weight of our bodies forced the sharp edge deeply into the division between the cheeks of our bottoms, and consequently the most delicate part of our persons was hurt by the pressure of the rail.

Just imagine our position, and think what it meant to individuals of the female sex!

Miss Dean, throughout the whole time we were on the rail, bore her sufferings far more quietly than I did.

The minutes passed slowly, the pain growing more and more excruciating, and in addition, my bottom was still smarting and the weals on it were still throbbing. I felt as if the wedge-shaped rail was slowly splitting me; sharp lancinating pains darted through my loins and up my back, and as my ankles were tightly fastened to the stakes I could not alter my position in the slightest degree.

If my arms had not been bound to my sides, I might have got a little temporary ease by resting my hands on the rail, and thus taking some of the weight off my bottom.

But the men, in their devilish ingenuity, had taken care that we should not have a moment's respite from our tortures. Even if we had fainted, we should not have fallen from the fence. The upper part of our bodies would have dropped either forward or backward, but our legs, tied to the stakes, would have remained straddled over the rail, and its sharp edge would have still remained between the cheeks of our bottoms.

By this time every nerve in my body was thrilling with agony, and a cold dew of perspiration had broken out on my forehead. I groaned and writhed and twisted myself about, but the more I did so, the more the sharp rail was forced against the tender space between the cleft of my thighs.

I began to scream, and I think I cursed.

Miss Dean was crying, and her face showed the anguish she was feeling, but she made no outcry.

A few minutes more of agony slowly passed, then I saw a man enter the lane and come towards the house. He was not one of the lynchers, so my heart bounded with joy. We should be released in a few moments!

I redoubled my cries, begging him to come quickly to our assistance. He did not however hurry himself in the least, but walked on deliberately and when he had got a little nearer I saw that it was Randolph.

A few days previously I had hoped never to set eyes on him again; but now I was intensely delighted to see him.

'Oh! Mr Randolph,' I gasped out in a choking voice, with the tears streaming down my cheeks, 'take me down! Oh! take me down quickly!'

He came close up to the fence and stood looking at us with a smile on his face.

'Oh! dear Mr Randolph, take me down! do be quick and take me down!' I again wailed.

But, to my horror, he did not move.

'Well, Miss Ruth Dean, and Miss Dorothy Morton;' he said mockingly, 'this is what slave-running has brought you to. And it is to me that you owe your present position. I let the white people know of your doings, and you have been rightly and smartly punished. I told you, Dolly, that we should meet again, and we have. I knew the men were to pay you a visit this evening, so I came with them, and although you did not see me, I saw both of you getting your bottoms whipped. And I must say, Dolly, that you squealed just like a pig being killed.'

He paused to laugh, and a sickening feeling of despair came over me. The cruel man, not content with having set the lynchers on us, had come to mock us in our agony.

He continued:

'I am afraid your bottoms, especially yours, Miss Dean, must be very tender after the smart switching, and I am sure you must both be extremely uncomfortable on your present seats. The edges are sharp, and I have no doubt they are pressing sorely on a certain delicate spot between your thighs.'

Miss Dean's face was working with pain, and her eyes were full of tears, but when she heard Randolph's cruel and indecent words, her pale cheeks grew red.

Looking at me, she said in a weak quavering voice:

'Dorothy, do you know this man?'

He answered for me:

'Oh yes, she does. Miss Morton and I were once great friends, but we had a little tiff one day and she told me to go away. Is not that the case, Dolly?'

I hated the man, but at that moment the dreadful pain I was suffering overpowered every other feeling.

'Yes! Yes! that is the case,' I exclaimed fretfully. 'But don't stand talking, take us down at once.'

He smiled, but did not make a movement to release us.

'Oh! Oh!' I shrieked with pain, and enraged at his utter callousness. 'How can you stand there and watch two poor women suffering agony? Oh! why don't you release us? Have you no mercy or pity?'

'I am not a merciful man, and as a rule, I have no pity for abolitionists when they get into trouble for interfering with our slaves,' he replied coolly. 'But I don't mind making an exception in your case, Dolly. I will take you down, if you promise to come and live with me.'

On hearing what he said, Miss Dean again fixed her eyes on me, saying earnestly:

'Oh! Dorothy! don't listen to the man; he is a cruel scoundrel to try and take advantage of your sufferings. But be brave, dear. Don't give way. I am suffering as much, if not more than you are, but I would not accept release on such disgraceful terms as he offers.'

Randolph laughed scornfully.

'I have not the least intention of offering the terms to you, Miss Dean,' he said. 'As far as I am concerned, you may sit on the rail till the two hours are over. The view I had of your naked charms did not tempt me in the slightest degree. You have no figure. You are quite straight up and down. Your bottom is too narrow, your thighs are too small, and your legs are too thin. I like a woman to have a broad bottom, plump thighs, and good legs such as Dorothy has got.'

'Oh! you hateful man,' exclaimed Miss Dean, angrily; as after all she was a woman, and no woman likes to hear her charms, whatever they may be, spoken of in disparaging terms.

'Now then, Dolly, you have heard what I said. Do you intend to come home with me to-night?'

The coarse way he put the question shocked me, so I tried to pluck up a little spirit, and I partly succeeded.

'No, no, I won't go home with you,' I said, but not in a very determined way.

'Very well then, stay where you are. You have an hour and a half more to sit on your perch, and by that time you'll be in a terrible state between the legs, and half dead with pain. Rather a dreadful prospect, isn't it?'

Alas! it was. I moaned and shuddered at the thought of the long period of agony before me, and again I piteously entreated him to take me down.

He made no answer, but coolly lit a cigar and began to smoke. Then leaning his back against the middle of the rail at the ends of which we were straddled, he looked first at one and then at the other, with perfect unconcern, while we writhed, wept, and groaned in anguish, as the sharp edge of the rail pressed harder and harder against the tender flesh between the cheeks of our bottoms.

For a few minutes more I bore the pain which was growing more and more intense: then I gave way utterly. I could no longer endure the anguish. I said to myself:

'What does anything matter, as long as I escape from this terrible torture. I can't bear it for another hour and a half. I should go raving mad, or die. Oh! take me down! Take me down at once, and I promise to go home with you,' I cried.

No doubt it was weak of me, but I was in a half-fainting state, and as I have before told you, I am physically and morally a coward.

When Miss Dean heard me promise to go with Randolph, she said:

'Don't, oh! don't go with him, Dorothy. Don't wreck your life. Try and bear your sufferings. They will soon be over. If I were you, I would die rather than yield my body to that man.'

'Have you quite made up your mind, Dolly?' said Randolph laying his hand on the knot of the rope binding my arms.

'Yes, yes,' I cried impatiently. 'Oh! do be quick and release me.'

'Oh, Dorothy, my poor girl, I pity you,' said Miss Dean in a sorrowful tone. 'You do not know what is before you.'

Randolph soon untied the ropes that fastened my arms and ankles; then putting his arms round my waist, he lifted me off the rail, carried me into the verandah, and laid me, limp and faint, on the couch. I was stiff and sore, and aching from head to foot, but I was not suffering much pain. Oh! the intense relief it was to find myself no longer astride the sharp rail.

He got me a glass of water which I drank thirstily, as my mouth was parched, and I was quite feverish from the torture I had undergone.

When I had recovered a little, I thought of Miss Dean, and I asked Randolph to release her.

He was however very bitter against her, and at first refused to let her go, but I begged hard for her, and at last he said that he would release her before we went away.

'Now, Dolly,' he said, 'I'll go for the buggy. I left it just round the corner of the lane. I shan't be gone long, so you lie quietly here till I come back.' Then he added, in a meaning way: 'You had better not attempt to leave the house, for the men are still somewhere in the neighbourhood and if they see you they will put you on the rail again.' So saying, he went away.

But the thought of escape never entered my head. At that moment, I was weak and frightened; all my senses were in a half-torpid state, and I had not fully realized my position. So I lay languidly on the couch, thinking how delightful it was to be free from pain.

Presently, Randolph drove up with the buggy to the garden gate, and after hitching the horse, he came to me:

'Now then, Dolly, come along,' he said. 'Never mind your things. My women can supply you with everything necessary for the night, and I will send for your trunks to-morrow morning. Can you walk to the buggy, or shall I carry you?'

I replied that I could walk, but on attempting to do so, I

found myself too shaky and so stiff that I could hardly put one foot before another.

Noticing how feeble I was, he lifted me up in his arms, and carrying me to the buggy, put me in and wrapped a rug round my knees. Then going to Miss Dean, he untied the ropes binding her, but he did not take the trouble to help her down; so the poor thing had to get off the rail without assistance.

She was weak, pale, and suffering, so she had to lean against the fence for support; but her thoughts were still for me.

'Don't go with that man, Dorothy,' she again said in a most earnest way. 'Never mind your promise. It was extracted from you by torture, so you are not bound to keep it. Stay with me.'

I did not want to go with Randolph, and I would have been only too glad to stay with her, but my cowardice prevented me. I was afraid of again falling into the hands of the lynchers. So I only cried, saying feebly:

'Oh! I must go with him, I am in his power.'

'Yes, yes, you are;' he observed, 'and if you were to attempt to break your promise you would very soon find yourself astride the rail again.' Then addressing Miss Dean, he said: 'Remember what the men told you. If you are not out of the State before forty-eight hours are over, you will receive another visit from Judge Lynch.'

He then got into the buggy beside me, and as he did so, I shrank away as far as possible, hating him, and despising myself.

He touched the horse with the whip, and we drove off, leaving Miss Dean standing with drooping head by the fence.

After we had gone a short distance I looked back, and I saw the lonely figure still in the same position. She did not move, and I kept my eyes fixed upon her until the buggy turned the corner of the lane; then I sank back on the seat, and covering my face with my hands, wept bitterly. I had parted with the only friend I had in the world.

Chapter Seven

At Randolph's house – I make Dinah's acquaintance – Her sympathy for me, and her contempt for unsophisticated 'whites.' – My attempts to escape are frustrated.

Randolph did not say a word to me, but just let me cry away, which was the best thing he could have done at the moment.

The buggy, drawn by a fast trotter, rolled rapidly along the road, and as Randolph's plantation was only three miles distant, we soon reached the closed avenue leading to the house. The gates were thrown open by two negroes, and we entered the avenue which was about a quarter of a mile long, shaded throughout its length with tall trees. In a few minutes we arrived at the house, a very large and handsome building, consisting of a central part with a cupola on top, and wings on either side; in front there was a broad terrace sloping down to a lawn, flanked with well-kept beds of beautiful flowers.

Several negroes were on the terrace, waiting to receive their master, and when he pulled up the horse at the door, the men came forward and took charge of the animal.

The wide door of the house was opened; then Randolph, lifting me out of the buggy, carried me through a spacious hall into a handsomely furnished room, and placed me on a couch.

'There, Dolly,' he said, smiling down at me, 'You are safe from the lynchers now.'

He then rang the bell, which was immediately answered by a good-looking quadroon woman, about thirty-five years of age. She was very tall, stout, and broad-shouldered; neatly dressed in a well-fitting print frock, with white apron, collar and cuffs; she had very black, glossy, wavy hair, and on her head she wore a smart cap.

The woman looked hard at me, but there was not the least expression of surprise on her face.

'Dinah,' said her master, 'this lady has met with an accident. Carry her up to the pink room, and attend to her. See that she has everything she wants, and take great care of her. Do you understand?'

'Yes, massa,' she replied.

Turning to me, he said:

'I am going to dinner now, but Dinah will look after you, and I think you had better let her put you to bed. You are quite feverish. You shall not be disturbed to-night,' he added, meaningly.

I understood the significance of the last words, but I made no remark, and a blush dyed my cheeks. I was still dazed and stupid. The rapid succession of painful and startling events had been too much for me.

Dinah came to the sofa, and lifting me in her strong arms, as if I had been a baby, carried me out of the room, up a broad flight of stairs, to a most luxuriously furnished bedroom, and laid me gently on the bed. Then closing the door, she came back to the bedside and looked at me with a kind, motherly expression on her pleasant face.

'I know who yo' is, missy,' she said. 'Yo' is one of de good Northern ladies who keeps the unnergroun' station. All de cullud folks in dese parts has heard ob yo'. But it was none of dem dat set de lynchers on you'. I know de lynchers has been

74

after yo' to-day, honey. What did dey do to yo'? Did dey ride yo' on a rail? Dey offen does dat to ablishinists. Don't mind tellin' me all about it, little missy. I'se fond of yo' for what yo've done for de runaways.'

The woman's sympathy was most grateful to me, so I told her all that had been done to Miss Dean and myself.

'Oh! you poor young lady! I'se so very sorry for yo',' she exclaimed, in tones full of pity. 'Yo' mus' be drefful sore. But I will bathe yo' an' make yo' as comfortable as I can, an' den yo' mus' go to bed.'

It was rather dark, so she lit the lamps and drew the curtains. She then left the room, returning in a few minutes with a can of hot water.

'Now, honey,' she said tenderly, 'I'll fix yo' up.'

She undressed me to my chemise, then asking me to lie on my face, she rolled up the garment, and after separating my legs a little, examined my body.

'I see dat dose horrid men gave yo' twelve strokes with de switch;' she observed, 'de weals is quite plain on your poor bottom, missy, an' yo' is all bruised an' marked between de thighs where de rail hurt yo'.'

She then sponged my bottom with cold water, and gently rubbed the weals with some soft stuff, saying:

'Dis is 'possum fat, missy, it will take de smart out ob de weals. We always uses 'possum fat to take away de sting of a whipping.' The stuff certainly did seem to make my bottom feel easier. 'What a bootiful figure you've got, and such pretty legs, and such a lubly white skin. I'se never seen such a white one in my life.'

When she had 'fixed' my bottom, she turned me over on to my back, and fomented with warm water the 'spot' and the parts adjacent, uttering all the time expressions of pity for me, and abusing the lynchers whom she called a pack of 'mean white trash.'

It is a curious fact that the slaves in the South used to have a contempt for the white people who did not own a negro. I may also say here that Dinah never knew that it was her master who had set the lynchers on us.

75

As the parts were very tender and also a good deal swollen, the fomentation gave me great relief, and when Dinah had finished bathing the sore 'spot,' she went to a drawer, which to my surprise, I saw was filled with all sorts of feminine undergarments.

Taking out a lace-trimmed night-dress she brought it to me, then removing my chemise, put the night-gown on me, and made me get into bed.

She then went away, but soon returned with a tray, on which were dishes and plates, and also a small bottle of champagne.

She placed a little table by the bedside, and spreading a cloth, laid out the good things she had brought; saying:

'Now honey, here is a nice wee dinner. Yo' must try and eat a bit, and drink some of dis wine. It will do yo' good.'

As I had been a teetotaller all my life I did not want the wine, so I asked Dinah to get me a cup of tea.

She soon did so, then propped myself up in the bed, taking care to press as little as possible on my bottom, and as I was feeling very faint, I began to eat, and was able to make a very fair meal, forgetting, for the moment, the past, and not thinking of the future. While I was having my supper, Dinah talked to me freely, but always with perfect respect. The fact of my having been indecently whipped by a band of men had not lowered me the least in her estimation. To her, I was still a white lady from the North, while she was only a slave.

She informed me with an air of pride, that she was the housekeeper, and had twenty female servants under her. Then she gave me some particulars about herself. She had been born on the plantation, and had never been more than twenty miles from it in all her life. She had once had a husband, but was now a widow without a child. She further informed me, in a most matter-of-course way, that she had often been whipped.

When she had cleared away the dinner things, she brushed my hair – it was the first time I had ever had such a thing done for me since I had become a woman – then she put a bell on the table beside the bed, and, after turning down the lamp,

76

she bade me good night, and left the room.

When I woke next morning, the hands of the handsome Dresden china clock on the mantelpiece pointed to half-past eight. Sitting up in bed, I looked about me with the puzzled feeling one always experiences on first waking in a strange place.

Then my brain cleared, and I vividly remembered all the dreadful incidents of the previous day. The horrible exposure of my most secret parts before a number of rough men, the ignominious and painful whipping, and the agonizing ride on the rail! I shuddered. Next I thought of Randolph, and of the promise I had given him. He might come to me at any moment! I felt my cheeks flush, and in a sudden, unthinking impulse, I jumped out of bed, and ran to the door to lock it. But there was no key. Then it struck me that locking the door – even if I had been able to do so – would not save me. I was in the man's power, and would have to submit to him sooner or later. So I crept back to bed again, lying trembling, and wondering whether he would do the horrid deed some time during the day, or wait till the night.

However, as it turned out, I did not meet my fate that day or night.

At nine o'clock, Dinah came in with a cup of tea for me, bringing with her a letter from Randolph, saying that he had been unexpectedly called to Richmond on urgent business which would probably detain him four or five days. He also said that he had made arrangements for my trunks to be brought to Woodlands; and he had given orders to all the servants that they were to look upon me as their mistress, and he finished the note by telling me that Dinah knew where everything was, and that she would take good care of me. Feeling very thankful for my temporary respite, I drank the tea and lay down again.

Presently, a smart young quadroon chambermaid brought in a large tin bath which she filled with water; then after laying out towels and all the other articles necessary for my toilet, she left the room. I had my bath, and while drying myself, looked at my bottom in the pier-glass, finding that the weals had gone down considerably, but they still showed in long red stripes on my skin, and were still tender to the touch. I was also still very sore between the legs, where the rail had bruised the flesh. In fact, it was a week before all the marks and bruises on my body had entirely disappeared. The tears rose to my eyes, and my heart swelled with rage and bitterness as I gazed at the traces of the shameful punishment that had been inflicted on me.

Dinah came back, helped me to dress, and also arranged my hair. Then she showed me down to a snug, well furnished room, where I sat down – my bottom was rather tender – to breakfast, waited on by two pretty quadroon girls, who gazed at me curiously with their big, soft, black eyes, but treated me with the utmost deference.

Just as I had finished breakfast, Dinah came to inform me that my trunks had arrived; she told me also she had heard that Miss Dean and Martha were going to start that evening for Richmond on their way North.

Oh! how I wished I was going with them. Then the idea of escape flashed across my mind, and I determined to try and get away from Woodlands. If I could get to Miss Dean, she would be delighted to see me, and to know I returned to her as pure as when I left her. She would take me back with her to Philadelphia. Filled with new hope, I went up to my room, finding that Dinah had unpacked all my things and put them away in the drawers.

I was glad to be able to change my clothes, so I dressed myself in clean garments from head to foot; and then putting on my hat I went downstairs to the hall, finding Dinah standing near the open door. I told her I was going out for a walk.

'Oh! missy,' she said, 'I know what yo' is thinkin' of. Yo' wants to get away to Miss Dean. But oh, honey, yo' can't. De massa has gib strict orders to de men at de gate not to let yo' out, an' all de place is watched. Yo' can't get away nohow.'

My hopes of escape were dashed to the ground. I felt utterly miserable, and throwing myself on a seat I wept bitterly; while Dinah hovered about me, looking sympathetic, but saying nothing.

I saw at once that if I could not reach Miss Dean before she started, all chance for me was gone, for even if I managed to get away from Woodlands, I had no money, nor had I any place to go to; moreover, I had been warned by the lynchers to leave Virginia in forty-eight hours. If they caught me wandering about – which they would be sure to do – they would either whip me or ride me on a rail again, perhaps both.

The prospect was too awful to contemplate, so with a heavy heart I gave up all thought of leaving Woodlands. I would have to remain and submit to my fate when the time came.

After a few minutes I grew calmer, then Dinah, with the intention of diverting my thoughts, asked me if I would come and see the house.

I answered in the affirmative, and she showed me all over the place from the attics to the kitchen.

It was a very large mansion, beautifully furnished throughout: it had long corridors, and two flights of stairs, one at the front of the house and one at the back, and there were twenty bedrooms, each one decorated in a different style. There were several sitting-rooms and boudoirs, a spacious dining-room and an immense drawing-room; there was also a billiard table, and a large library, well filled with books of all sorts.

I had never before been in such a grand house, nor had I seen such splendid furniture – the pictures though, in some of the rooms, made me blush.

There were twenty female servants, slaves of course, living in the house. All were dressed alike in well-fitting pink print frocks, with white aprons, caps, collars and cuffs. They all wore neat well-polished shoes and white cotton stockings, and everyone of them looked trim and clean. In fact they were obliged to be always tidy and properly dressed, any slovenliness being punished. The cooks and kitchen servants were black, or mulatto women, but all the parlourmaids and housemaids were young quadroons, or octoroons, from eighteen to twenty-five years of age.

All of them were pretty, while two or three of the octoroons were really quite handsome and so light in colour that they might easily have passed as white girls anywhere except in the South. People there can at once detect the least trace of black blood in a man or woman.

Some of them had full, voluptuous-looking figures, and as none wore stays, the rounded contours of their bosoms were plainly outlined under their thin bodices. There were several children of both sexes about the place, but no male servants lived in the house.

When Dinah had shown me everything that was to be seen in the establishment, she left me, and I went out in the grounds. They were extensive and beautifully kept. There were flower gardens, fruit and kitchen gardens, shrubberies, and hot-houses, the whole place being surrounded by high iron railings, the only means of exit being the gate at the entrance to the avenue.

I wandered about listlessly, but I noticed that the men who were at work about the grounds kept a watch on my movements. I walked down to the gate, and just to see if I was really a prisoner I tried to open it, but two men instantly came out of the lodge, and one of them said civilly:

'Yo' can't go out missy. De gate is locked, by de massa's order.'

I then returned to the house, and went up to my grand bedroom, all pink and white and gold, with two large windows looking on to the gardens at the back. It was partly furnished as a sitting-room, with a comfortable sofa and easy chairs, a round table, and a large, well-fitted writing cabinet.

Drawing an easy chair to one of the windows, I sat down and had a long think. I thought what a cruel man Randolph was to have betrayed us to the lynchers and then to have taken advantage of my agony to extract the promise from me.

Oh! why had I not sufficient fortitude to bear the pain? If I had refused to accept release on the shameful terms he had offered me, I should in a few hours have been on my way to Richmond with Miss Dean.

I thought of her, and contrasted her position with mine.

She was all right, except for the whipping, and in a couple of days she would be safe at home in Philadelphia, still in possession of her virgin treasure, while I would be at Woodlands, a prisoner in the hands of a man who had shown himself to be utterly unscrupulous.

And what was to become of me afterwards?

'Oh, dear! oh, dear!' I said to myself. 'How I wish I had never persuaded Miss Dean to let me come to Virginia with her!'

The morning passed, and at one o'clock Dinah came to tell me that lunch was ready. I went downstairs and managed to eat something, then I betook myself to the library where I remained for the rest of the afternoon trying to divert my thoughts by reading a novel.

At seven o'clock, I sat down to a dainty, well-cooked little dinner – a better dinner than I had ever seen, as Miss Dean always lived very plainly. The two quadroon parlourmaids, whose names were Lucy and Kate, waited on me, while Dinah, as 'Butler,' overlooked them.

Dinah had the key of everything, and was entirely trusted by her master. She offered me champagne, claret, and bottled ale, but I refused them all. However I made a fair meal, as I was a healthy girl, and my appetite asserted itself in spite of the depressing nature of the position I was in at that moment. When dinner was over, I went into one of the smaller sitting-rooms, where the lamps had been lighted, the curtains drawn, and everything made snug for me. But the evening seemed very long, and I felt very lonely. I should have liked Dinah's company even, as her quaint talk would have amused me a little, but I did not think it would be quite correct for me to send for her, while she, I suppose, did not think it right to intrude upon me, so I did not see her until I went up to my room, when she came to brush my hair and help me to undress.

Chapter Eight

News arrives that the 'massa' is returning – My virginity to be sacrificed – Fears and dread – I am given a scented bath – Tortured in the tyrant's bed – The pain and horror of the 'wedding-night' – The 'lust of his eyes' – The terror of his tearing, iron-made tool.

Four days passed in the quiet way narrated in the preceding chapter. On the fifth morning of my captivity, when Dinah came in with my usual cup of tea, she informed me that she had received a letter from her master – she could read, but not write – telling her he would be home at seven o'clock to dinner, and that she was to take care it was a good one.

I sat up in bed, looking blankly at Dinah, and feeling a sinking sensation at my heart, for though I had known the fatal moment would come, I was startled at hearing that it was so close at hand.

I got up, had my bath, and dressed myself mechanically, then went downstairs; but I could not eat any breakfast, though I thirstily drank two cups of coffee. All day long, I was restless and uncomfortable, roaming about the great house with a sort of feeling that I was in a dream, and would soon wake. Sometimes I would sit down on a chair, with my mind quite blank, then, in another moment, the thought of what was going to be done to me would strike my brain with a sudden shock that sent the blood to my cheeks.

I dreaded the ordeal before me, morally as well as physically. Even a newly-wedded bride on the day of her marriage feels a little shame and fear at the thought of what her husband will do to her at night.

The afternoon wore slowly away, and at five o'clock I was sitting listlessly in my room, when Dinah came in, followed by one of the chambermaids carrying the bath. Placing it in the middle of the room she filled it with warm water, then she went away, but Dinah remained.

As I had taken my bath in the morning, I could not understand why the girl had again filled it, and with hot water too. I was not in the habit of bathing in hot water.

'I don't want a bath, Dinah,' I said.

'No, missy, I knows yo' don't, yo' is bootiful clean. But I'se had orders in de letters from de massa, to give yo' a scented bath. I must obey his orders whatever dey is, or he will whip me. Now den, honey, yo'll let me give you de bath.'

I flushed with a strong feeling of indignation. I also felt deeply humiliated. The victim was to be bathed and perfumed before the sacrifice!

However, Dinah could not help it, she had to obey orders, so I told her that she might bathe me.

She was evidently relieved, and at once began to prepare the 'scented bath.'

First, she poured some fluid from a phial into the water; she next threw in a quantity of white powder which had a delicate perfume of roses; then she stirred the water till the powder was completely dissolved. I found out afterwards that the fluid and the powder were Turkish preparations used by the ladies of the harem to impart a softness and gloss to their skins.

When everything was ready, she undressed me, then

making me stand up in the bath, she sponged me all over with the warm perfumed water, at the same time praising the symmetry and plumpness of my figure and the whiteness of my skin.

When she had finished bathing me, she dried me with soft warm towels, then rubbed me with her hands from head to foot, and with her fingers gently kneaded my titties and arms, also my bottom, thighs, and legs, until my flesh seemed to become firmer, and my skin smoother and more velvety than usual.

She then began to dress me, putting on my nicest things, and I had some pretty undergarments. She first put on me a lace-trimmed chemise with blue ribbons on the shoulders, then my finest drawers with deep lace frilling and bows of pink ribbon at the knees. Next she drew on my legs a pair of white silk stockings, fastening them above my knees with dark blue satin garters with silver buckles – these garters were produced from her pocket; I did not possess such fine ones.

Then she cased my feet in my neatest shoes, put on my nicest petticoats, and laced me tightly in my stays, and finally helped me on with my prettiest white frock. Then she brushed my hair, and arranged it most elaborately. She was delighted with my appearance and after turning me round two or three times, exclaimed:

'Oh, missy! yo' is a bootiful young lady for true. De massa will be pleased when he sees yo'.'

Dinah knew that she had bathed, perfumed, and dressed me for the sacrifice, but she did not understand what a dreadful thing it would be to me. She was not a virtuous woman herself, and her ideas, like those of most slave women, were very loose on the subject of feminine virtue.

Besides, I think she considered I was rather a lucky young lady to have attracted the notice of 'De Massa,' who in her eyes was a very exalted personage indeed. Now that I was dressed, she suggested that I had better go down to the drawing-room so as to be in readiness to receive the master on his return.

Accordingly I went down to the great room, which had been brilliantly lighted, and seated myself on a sofa.

I had become dully resigned to my fate, but my heart was heavy as I waited in the gorgeous apartment for the man who was going to rob me of my virginity.

If I had had the slightest liking for him, I should not have felt the thing so much. But I did not like him. I hated him. Presently I heard the sound of wheels on the terrace, and then I heard the hall door being opened and shut. He had arrived! My heart began to flutter, though not with the pleasurable anticipation of a young girl waiting for her lover.

But he did not make his appearance, so I supposed he had gone straight to his own room to change his travelling garments. Such was the case. In a short time he came into the drawing-room, dressed in evening clothes.

I rose from my seat, and he came to me, took both my hands in his, and kissed me hotly on the lips, making me shrink and tremble. Then, holding me at arms length, he looked at me from head to foot in a critical way, as if he were appraising my charms, while I stood with flaming cheeks and downcast eyes.

'You are looking very charming, Dolly,' he said. 'The frock you are wearing becomes you, but in future you must always put on a low-necked dress for dinner.'

He already considered me his property!

'I have not got one,' I murmured, without looking up.

'Well, you shall soon have more than one,' he observed, laughing and patting me on the cheek. 'Now tell me: have you been comfortable during my absence; has Dinah taken good care of you, and have the servants been attentive?'

I did not answer the first part of his question, for though my body had been comfortable after it had recovered from the first severe effects of the punishment, my mind had been extremely uncomfortable the whole time. I replied:

'Dinah has taken very good care of me, and the servants have been attentive.'

'So much the better for them. If they had not, I would have made all their bottoms smart, from Dinah downwards,' he observed, coolly.

His words jarred upon me. I thought he need not have said anything about the women's bottoms.

He asked two or three other questions, which I answered, and then one of the parlourmaids announced dinner, so we went into the big dining-room.

The table had been beautifully decorated with flowers and fruit; the glass, linen, and other appointments were of the finest description, and the great sideboard of old, polished mahogany glittered with massive silver plate which had been in Randolph's family for generations. It was the first time I had seen the precious metal. The dinner was of many courses, with all sorts of dishes that I had never heard of, and it was accompanied by wines whose names were also new to me.

Randolph talked away gaily, eating heartily, and drinking a bottle of champagne; but I, being nervous and depressed, hardly ate anything. I could only answer in monosyllables, and I blushed whenever I happened to catch his eye. I was constantly thinking of the dreadful thing he was going to do to me that night.

In order I suppose to cheer me up, he filled my glass with champagne and insisted on my drinking it, but the wine only went to my head and made me giddy without exhilarating me in the least. So when he saw the effect the liquor had on me, he did not give me any more.

When dinner was over and he had smoked a cigar, we went back to the drawing-room. Seating himself comfortably in an easy chair, he continued to talk, not taking any notice of my silence, or making any remark about my downcast looks.

He was in high spirits, induced I suppose, by the thought that he would soon be in possession of my virgin body.

He told me he had heard that Miss Dean had got safely home to Philadelphia, and he added with a laugh:

'I don't think the prim Quakeress will ever again take to running an "underground station." She got a real smart whipping and she will always carry the marks of it on her bottom. But you won't be marked in the least, Dolly, as your skin was not cut.'

I shuddered, and my bottom seemed to tingle as I thought of the whipping.

At ten o'clock he rose from his seat and said jocularly:

'Now, Dolly, as this is our wedding night, we'll go to bed early. Come upstairs.'

I blushed furiously and began to cry. After all, I could not resign myself quietly to my unhappy fate. I thought I had become resigned, but now that the moment had arrived, all my feelings of modesty rose in revolt against the sacrifice of my maidenhead. I made a despairing appeal to him for mercy:

'Oh! Mr Randolph,' I exclaimed, 'will you not spare me?'

His countenance grew dark, he frowned, and a hard look came into his eyes.

'Don't be a fool, Dolly;' he answered harshly, 'you gave me your promise, and I thought the whole affair was settled. Come along.'

'Oh, do not hold me to my promise!' I wailed. 'You know that when I made it I was half-mad with pain. Oh! do let me go away from your house.'

'Now listen to me,' he said, in cold, incisive tones. 'I am not going to stand any nonsense. You are completely in my power, and I don't intend to spare you, as you call it. If you do not come upstairs and submit quietly, I'll have you carried up by four of the women, and I will make them hold you down upon the bed, so that I shall be able to do what I like to you at my ease. Now, will you come quietly, or must you be carried up and held?'

My appeal for mercy had failed, and I was thoroughly frightened by his threats. To be held down by four women while the deed was being done would only add to my shame, the very idea of such a thing made me thrill with horror. Resistance would be useless. So there was nothing left for me but to submit.

'I will go quietly,' I sobbed out in a low voice, with the tears trickling down my cheeks. Oh! how wretched I felt as I said those words.

'That's right,' he said.

Then taking me by the hand he led me up to my own room.

The shaded lamps had all been lit, so the apartment was filled with a bright soft light, and I at once noticed that a large bath towel had been spread over the silken coverlet of the bed, and a nightshirt of his had been placed on one of the pillows.

He closed the door, then turning to me, said:

'I am glad you have come to your senses. I hate struggling with a woman, but I would have had my way in the end. Now continue to be sensible, and let me do whatever I like to you, without making any more remonstrances. First of all, I am going to undress you with my own hands. I like undressing a pretty girl.'

He did the work in a way that showed it was by no means the first time he had stripped a woman.

Making me stand in front of the pier-glass, he unfastened my dress, and taking it off, threw it on a chair, then he deftly unlaced my stays and removed them, thus exposing the upper part of my bosom which I endeavoured to hide by crossing my arms over it.

Next he loosed the strings of my petticoats, letting them fall to the floor and making me step out of them, then kneeling down, he took off my shoes, after which he slipped his hands up my legs, unbuckled my garters, and pulled off my stockings. Then putting both his hands under my chemise, he untied my drawers and drew them off my legs. As his hands strayed over my body and limbs while he was thus slowly stripping me, I shivered, but offered no resistance. It would have been of no avail. He had determined to do the deed in his own way, so there would have been no use in my resisting. Nothing now remained but my chemise, and that he soon pulled off over my head, leaving me standing nude before him, and I saw my whole figure reflected in the pier-glass. I could not help uttering a little cry of shame, and I instinctively covered the 'spot' with both my hands, while my face, neck, and the upper part of my bosom became scarlet. I shut my eyes, but the tears forced their way between my closed eyelids and trickled down my cheeks.

Of course it was very horrid to be obliged to stand naked before a man, and I had a strong sense of shame, but I did not feel so horribly ashamed as at the time when my person was exposed to the lascivious eyes of the lynchers, and my ears shocked by their obscene remarks.

He turned me round and round, looking at me on every side, and holding my hands so that I could not screen any part of my body, but he did not feel me. When he had sufficiently gratified the lust of his eyes, he lifted me up in his arms, carried me to the bed, and laid me down upon it on my back. Covering the 'spot' with one hand, and with the other hiding my scarlet face, I lay trembling, while he quietly undressed himself and put on his nightshirt.

I hoped he would extinguish the lights, but he did not. Getting up on the bed beside me, he removed my hand from my face, then clasping my naked body in his arms, he kissed my lips, eyes, and cheeks, saying:

'Now my dear little girl, I've got you at last!'

It was the first time he had made use of a tender word to me that night. While stripping me, he had not spoken a word but had treated me as if I had been merely a lay figure. After kissing me, he proceeded to gratify his sense of feeling. Laying both his hands on my bosom, he played with my titties, squeezing them, tickling them, and moulding the flesh with his fingers, then bending his head, he took one of my nipples in his mouth and nibbled it with his teeth.

Uttering a startled cry, I shrank away from him, plucking my nipple out of his mouth.

'Keep still, whatever I do,' he said sharply.

Then taking my other nipple between his lips, he sucked it, and rolled his tongue over it as if it had been a bit of candy.

I forced myself to lie still, and after a moment or two he let go my nipple. He next stroked my belly and ran his hands several times over each of my thighs; then separating my legs a little, he touched the 'spot,' twining his fingers in the hair and pulling it rather hard, then he inserted the tip of his forefinger between the lips, making me squirm, and quiver from head to foot – but not with pleasure – and extracting from me a stifled shriek.

'Oh! oh! don't do that!' I exclaimed. 'Oh! do take your hand away!'

'Don't be silly,' he said. 'You'll feel something else there in a minute or two.'

With a strong effort I controlled myself and lay quiet again. Turning me over on to my face, he looked at my bottom, saying: 'The marks of the whipping are not quite gone; there are still a few faint pink lines on your skin.'

Then he played with my bottom in all sorts of ways, stroking it, pinching it all over, gently spanking it, and squeezing the flesh with both his hands; finishing up by separating the cheeks and rubbing his hand up and down the division from the upper part to the cleft of my thighs.

The whole of these proceedings had been intensely repugnant to me, making me feel quite sick; moreover they were totally unexpected. When he laid me down on the bed, I thought he would at once have embraced me. I had not the slightest idea that I should first have to go through so much preliminary handling.

I afterwards discovered that Randolph was a man who always liked to spin out his pleasure as long as possible.

He now turned me on to my side and again took me in his arms, kissing my face, throat, and bosom, and inhaling the sweet odour emanating from my flesh. He was evidently pleased with the charms of his victim.

'You are a pretty little woman,' he said. 'Your figure is very good, and you are plump without being fat. Your skin is beautifully white and smooth, your flesh is firm, and you are as fresh as a rose, and as fragrant as one. I am fond of the delicate perfume of roses on a woman when I have her naked in my arms, and that is why I told Dinah to give you the bath with the Turkish powder in it.'

After toying with me a moment or two longer, he laid me on my back, saying:

'Now, Dolly, I am going to do the job. To use plain words, I am going to poke you. You will feel a little pain, but you must bear it. Every woman suffers more or less, the first time she is poked by a man; but afterwards she feels no pain at all, but only pleasure when in the arms of her lover.'

The fatal moment had come!

Closing my eyes, and covering my face with my hands, I waited for the stroke, feeling greatly frightened, very much ashamed, and intensely sorrowful.

Taking hold of my knees, he stretched my legs widely apart, then getting between them, he laid himself down upon me with his breast on my bosom, at the same time removing my hands from my face and pressing his mouth on my lips. Then with his fingers he opened the way, and immediately after, I felt the tip of his member inserted between the lips of my 'spot.' I shuddered and uttered a low cry. My martyrdom had commenced!

Clasping his arms round me with his hands under my bottom, and holding me tightly, he began to move his loins up and down, and I felt the column beginning to penetrate me, stretching the parts and causing great pain.

As I was utterly ignorant of the size of the erect male organ, and as I was in a state of great fright, the weapon seemed to me to be of enormous dimensions – it really was not very big – and I thought it could not possibly be got into the sheath.

'Oh! oh! you are hurting me dreadfully,' I shrieked, beating my hands on the bed and shrinking away from him as much as I could. 'Oh! Oh-h! I can't bear it! Oh-h-h! Take it away! Oh-h! Stop! Stop! Oh-h-h!'

He worked away steadily, gradually forcing the implement deeper. I felt as if a wedge was being driven into me, and that I was being split. I winced under his thrusts, quivering all over, kicking up my legs and squealing with pain.

The weapon, however, was driven deeper and deeper, until its further progress was checked by something inside the sheath.

My ravisher – for such in reality he was – had reached the membrane that barred the passage: my maidenhead! Increasing the vigour of his strokes, he battered at the opposing membrane. The pain grew sharper, the tears rolled down my cheeks, I writhed, and I squealed, but at the same time I instinctively arched my loins to aid his in his efforts to break through the barrier.

He paused for a moment to take breath, then gripping me tighter he again began the assault vigorously.

Oh, how it did hurt me! I was small in comparison to him, and the parts now seemed to be stretched to bursting. Stiffening myself and clenching my teeth, I lay groaning, as the horrid thing was being driven with increased force against the obstruction. He quickened his strokes, the membrane began to yield, then suddenly it gave way and his member went right into me up to the roots, and at the same instant I felt a sharp, tearing pain which made me utter a shrill cry.

He went on working, while I, quite involuntarily, moved my bottom up and down, keeping time with his thrusts, though I had not the faintest sensation of pleasure – quite the reverse.

His movements became quicker and quicker, I writhed with pain but still kept heaving up my bottom to meet him. He gave me two or three more furious pushes, then the gush of fluid came, and at the same moment a curious spasm seized me, and I could not help wriggling my bottom, and squirming from side to side as I felt the stuff spurting in hot jets up to my very vitals.

However, the warm thick fluid, as it flowed over the lacerated edges of the ruptured membrane, seemed slightly to assuage the pain, and when all was over, I lay in his arms panting, my naked bosom heaving, my face wet with tears, and my whole body jerking spasmodically. There was a buzzing in my ears, a mist before my eyes, and I thought I was going to faint.

After a moment or two he got off me, and giving me a kiss, said:

'There, Dolly, it's all over now. It won't hurt you so much next time.'

When I had recovered myself a little, I became aware that I was wet between the legs, and that something was trickling down my thighs. So sitting up on the bed, I looked at the

92

'spot,' and saw that blood was oozing from it, I also noticed that the towel under me was stained with the proof of my virginity. I was dreadfully frightened, as I had no idea that there would be an effusion of blood, and my terrified imagination made me think that I had actually been split open.

'Oh! Oh! I am bleeding. What shall I do!' I exclaimed, wringing my hands and beginning to cry again.

He took me in his arms, and petted and soothed me, saying:

'That's nothing, Dolly. You needn't be alarmed. Every woman bleeds a little the first time she is poked.'

Then getting off the bed, he brought a basin of water and a sponge, and making me again lie on my back with outstretched legs, sponged the 'spot' and my thighs until he had removed all outward traces of his bloody deed. He then told me to put on my nightgown and get between the sheets.

I did so, glad to be able at last to cover my nakedness.

After he had washed himself, he put out all the lamps, except a small one, then he got into bed beside me, but did not touch me. He seemed to be tired, and after giving me a kiss, he turned over on to his side with his back towards me, and in a short time I knew by his quiet breathing that he had gone to sleep. I heaved a sigh of relief, heartily glad that all was over – for a time at any rate. The 'spot' was sore, and the parts felt stretched; I had a curious sensation as if his stiff member was still sticking in me, and I kept as far away from him as I could in the broad bed.

At first I could not go to sleep. I was far too miserable, and I lay crying bitterly for the loss of my virginity.

'Oh what an unfortunate girl I am! What shall I do? What shall I do?' I kept on saying to myself despairingly.

After a time, however, my tears ceased to flow, though I continued to sob, then a dull apathetic feeling came over me, I grew drowsy, and at last I sobbed myself to sleep.

Strange to say, I slept soundly, and when I woke it was broad daylight. Sitting up in bed, I looked at my ravisher who was still sleeping calmly and I wondered how he could rest so quietly after having ruined a poor defenceless girl.

I had a headache, and also a heartache, and on looking at myself in the glass on the toilet table near the bed, I saw that my face was pale, and that there were some dark patches under my eyes. I felt very wretched and forlorn, but my brain was quite clear, so I was able to review my unhappy position with a certain amount of calmness.

And it was an unhappy position without doubt. I was a ruined girl. I had no money, and I had lost my only friend, for I felt that I could never, under any circumstances, go back to Miss Dean. What then was to become of me?

I thought over everything and at last came to the conclusion that I should have to remain at Woodlands, for a time at any rate; after all, it was the only thing I could do, so I determined to try and make the best of my position as it was at the moment and to trust to chance for the future.

As I have already told you, I disliked Randolph, but as I was going to stay at Woodlands, I made up my mind to conceal my true feelings, and let him think that I was quite willing to live with him. It would be to my interest to do so.

Presently he woke, and after yawning and stretching himself, he kissed me, saying with a smile:

'Well, Dolly, how do you feel this morning? A little sore between the legs, I suppose.'

I blushed, but acting up to my resolution to make the best of things, I forced myself to smile answering lightly:

'Yes, I am rather tender, but I suppose the soreness will soon pass off.'

He kissed me again, saying:

'I'm glad to see you are taking the affair sensibly, not whining or complaining. The thing's done and can't be undone. I'll make you very comfortable at Woodlands, and it will be your own fault if you are not happy. I am an easy man to get on with, when I have my own way,' he added with a laugh.

He then played with my titties, and felt my bottom till he was ready, then placing me in position, he rolled my nightdress up to my chin and got into me for the second time.

94

As there was now no obstacle in the way, a very few movements of his loins were sufficient to drive the weapon up to the hilt in the sheath, and then he poked me with full force.

I suffered a good deal while the great thing was being worked up and down in the sore, raw folds of my 'spot,' the pain making me grind my teeth and utter little cries, but again I was forced by nature to heave my bottom up and down to his strokes, and again when the spasm seized me, I wriggled and squirmed till I had received every drop of his offering.

I did not by any means like my second poke, but it had not been so intensely repugnant to me as the first.

Randolph sat up and looked at me as I lay on my back, breathing hard, with flushed cheeks, and moist eyes.

'It did not hurt you so very much that time, did it Dolly?' he observed.

'No'o, not-so-very-much,' I replied in a shaky voice, and feeling rather inclined to cry, for the 'spot' was smarting dreadfully.

'Oh, you'll soon get used to it, and then you'll like it,' he remarked, laughing at my woebegone face.

I thought to myself that I might get used to it, but I did not think I should ever get to like it.

Just then there was a knock at the door, and Susan, one of the chambermaids came in with tea and toast. She came to the bedside and placed the tray on a little table, her eyes resting for a moment on us as we lay side by side.

The girl's face was perfectly expressionless, but I felt ashamed that she should see me in bed with her master; my cheeks grew hot, and I did not know which way to look.

She got my bath ready and tidied the room, picking up my clothes which were all scattered about the floor, where Randolph had thrown them when he stripped me overnight.

Then she left the room, and we drank our tea, which was most refreshing to me, as I was faint and thirsty.

Randolph then got up, and taking his garments, went away to his own apartments leaving me alone to dress.

While having my bath, I examined the 'spot' finding that

the inner lips were red and swollen, so I bathed them well with cold water. After completing my toilet I went downstairs, and going out to the garden, betook myself to a secluded spot where I sat down on a long cane chair under a magnolia tree.

It was a beautiful morning, the sun, though not high, was shining brightly in a cloudless sky of pale blue, the birds were twittering, a soft breeze was blowing, drops of dew were still sparkling on the gossamer festooning the bushes, and the air was filled with the sweet scent of flowers.

I felt very languid, so putting my feet upon the chair, I leant back, inhaling the fresh morning air and feeling a great sensation of relief at being alone.

After the trying time I had gone through, the calm and quiet of everything had a soothing effect upon me, and my heart seemed to grow a little less heavy.

In about half an hour's time I returned to the house, and went into the breakfast room. Randolph soon made his appearance and we sat down to the morning meal.

My appetite was not so good as usual, I felt ill at ease in the presence of the man who had taken my maidenhead, and whenever I caught his eye I could not help blushing. He, however, was quite at his ease, chatting away gaily throughout the meal; when it was over, he ordered his horse to be brought, and then went off to the plantation to make a round of inspection after his absence.

Shortly after he had gone, Dinah came into the room, and handing me a basket of keys, asked me respectfully to give her my orders for the day. I noticed that she no longer called me 'missy,' but addressed me as 'missis.'

As I did not want to be bothered with the housekeeping of such a large establishment, I told Dinah to keep the keys, and to carry on the management as before.

She appeared glad to hear that she was not going to be deprived of her authority, and taking the basket of keys went away smiling. Randolph did not come back to lunch, so I had it by myself in the big dining-room, waited on by Lucy and Kate.

When I had finished, I went to the library where I spent the afternoon, reclining on a couch reading.

I did not feel inclined to take walking exercise that day. Randolph came home later, so I did not see him till we met at dinner at seven o'clock. My appetite was returning, so I managed to partake of some of the tasty dishes, and I also drank a glass of champagne, which I liked, as it exhilarated me slightly without affecting my head.

The evening passed, and we went away upstairs to my room at eleven o'clock.

Randolph allowed me to undress myself, and while I was doing so he sat on a chair watching me. We were soon in bed, and a few moments afterwards I found myself groaning and wincing, as the dart was being forced for the third time into my still tender flesh.

And before I got up in the morning, I had twice again wriggled my bottom and squirmed in Randolph's arms.

Chapter Nine

I learn some cunning tricks of the 'ars amandi;' loving, without loving – Randolph's amorousness – I become a 'past-mistress' in the joyful craft of arse-wriggling, but find withal no mental joy therein.

Some time passed. I had settled down to my life at Woodlands, adapting myself to my surroundings at the time, and endeavouring not to think of the future.

A dressmaker from Richmond had paid several visits to the house, and I was well supplied with pretty frocks of all sorts, for morning and evening wear, as well as a quantity of fine, richly-laced undergarments, silk stockings of all colours, and numerous pairs of shoes. I had also a riding costume with breeches and boots, a horse was always at my disposal, and I was learning to ride. Randolph had also given me a lot of jewellery, he always made me dress for dinner in a low-necked frock, and one of the octoroons, a girl named Rosa, had been specially appointed to act as my maid.

Randolph was a clever man, and well read, but he was a thorough libertine who considered women merely toys to be used for the gratification of his sensual desires.

Before my arrival at Woodlands, all the pretty quadroon and octoroon slave girls had been his concubines. Not that he had been in the habit of sleeping with any one of them, but whenever he wanted a girl, he would give her orders to be in his room at a certain hour of the day, or night, as the case might be, and then after he had amused himself with her for an hour or two, he would send her away.

But though he used the girls as playthings whenever he felt inclined, he had not the slightest soft feeling towards them. They were his slaves, nothing more; and whenever a girl misbehaved or offended him in any way, he would either send her to one of the overseers to be whipped, or he would inflict the punishment with his own hands.

He did not love me in the least, but he admired me, often telling me that I was a pretty girl and that I had a good figure: he was fond of seeing me naked, and posing me in various positions before the large pier-glass in my room, in order that he might be able to see both the back and front of my body at the same time. He soon made me acquainted with the meaning of all the naughty words in the vocabulary of 'Love' – words that I had never heard before – and in course of time he taught me practically, all the different positions in which it is possible for a man carnally to possess and enjoy a woman, either by day, or night; in bed, or out of bed.

I was invariably submissive to all his whims; he was a masterful man, and his strong will dominated my weak one; moreover I was always rather afraid of him. In my innocence I had thought that there was only one way of administering the stroke, and, at first, I was greatly astonished at the number and variety of the positions in which he rogered me. He would 'have' me lying on my back, or on my side; also standing, kneeling, sitting, or on all fours. He would 'do it' to me from behind, while I leant over the side of the bed, or the back of a chair, or the edge of a table, and he would sometimes lie on his back and make me straddle over him on my knees with my back turned towards his face, so that he could see my bottom; then I had to fix the weapon in the sheath, and do all the work by raising myself up and down on my knees.

Sometimes he rode me when I was stark naked, or when I was half dressed, or in my chemise, stockings and shoes, or perhaps with nothing on but my drawers, and frequently after dinner he would 'have' me in full evening dress with tightly-laced stays.

On these occasions he would sit on a chair while I would stand in front of him with my back turned; and putting his hands up my clothes, he would feel me until he was properly excited. He would then unbutton his trousers, letting out his member in full erection, with the red tip uncovered ready for action. I had then to pull open the slit of my drawers myself, hold my petticoats above my waist; and lower myself down upon the dart until it was into me as far as it could go, and my bottom rested on his thighs.

In that position he would possess me. He used to say that a woman should never be 'had' twice in succession the same way, and he told me that if a man always poked a woman in the same position, he would get tired of her sooner than if he varied the embraces.

After my shame had worn off, and I had got used to being stroked in this way, I discovered that there was a strain of voluptuousness in my disposition, and although I never liked Randolph, I was not averse to his embraces, so I always let him do what he liked to me by day or night, without murmuring; and he often told me: 'I was a very good mount.' Randolph was a man who always called 'a spade a spade'.

I don't think that after my arrival in the house he had much to do with the slave girls; anyhow he always slept with me, and it was rarely that a night passed without his poking me once at least.

I should have been better pleased had he let me more alone at night, for I was a sound sleeper, and I hated being woke up to be pulled about in all sorts of ways, and then poked in some uncomfortable position. I had gradually got accustomed to him, and called him by his first name, George, and though he was often very ill-tempered, and sometimes spoke extremely

100

harshly to me, he never laid his hand upon me in anger during the whole time I lived with him.

Randolph was one of the richest planters in Virginia, and his family was one of the oldest, but I soon found out that he was not, so to speak, in 'society.' His character as a libertine was well-known throughout the State, consequently no ladies ever came to the house. But he often gave dinner parties, at which I always took my place at the table opposite him.

On these occasions, all the young women in the house, chambermaids as well as parlourmaids, were very smartly dressed in well-fitting black frocks, with white caps and aprons, and it often happened that three, four or even more of the gentlemen, who had come from a distance, would remain in the house all night.

These parties wound up regularly with high card play, during which a good deal of liquor was drunk, and the house became a regular 'Liberty Hall,' as Randolph allowed his guests to do whatever they liked. I always went to bed as soon as the gambling began.

If a guest took a fancy to any particular girl he had seen about the place, all he had to do was to inform Randolph, who would at once send for the damsel. The gentleman would then take her up to a bedroom and poke her, returning afterwards to the card-room. And every guest who stayed in the house for the night could take a woman to bed with him if he felt inclined to do so. However, I was never treated but with respect by the men – to my face at any rate – for Randolph having chosen to put me at the head of his table, always insisted on his friends behaving as if I had really been the lady of the house, and as he was known to be a dead shot with a pistol, and always ready to use it, not one of the gentlemen who visited Woodlands ever attempted to take a liberty with me, nor did one ever speak to me in an improper manner.

Chapter Ten

*The slaves get to know me – Voluptuous effects of flagellation –
My maid, Rosa, is whipped for impertinence – Description of her
bottom and legs – Randolph's opinions on the right of raping
coloured women – Randolph puts me on the sofa and does the
'usual thing.'*

The weeks slipped away. My health continued good, my
spirits had revived and I was not unhappy. I had plenty of
books to read, I rode nearly every day, sometimes alone,
sometimes with Randolph, and he also often took me for a
long drive in the buggy.

We occasionally spent a few days in Richmond, staying at
the best hotel, and going every night to the theatre, or some
other place of amusement. Before that time, I had never been
in a theatre, so I enjoyed the performances immensely, and
wished very much that I could go on the stage. I told
Randolph so one day, but he only laughed, telling me that I
was 'a little goose,' and that I had not enough 'go' in me to
make an actress.

At Woodlands I often amused myself by roaming about the

plantation, which was a very extensive one, with upwards of two hundred field hands, male and female, all of whom were engaged in cultivating the cotton. Randolph fed his slaves well and did not overwork them, but otherwise he was a hard master; and his four overseers had orders never to pass over a fault, or allow the least shirking of work, consequently the strap, switch, and paddle were constantly being used on the plantation, both to men and women.

The slaves' quarters were divided into three blocks of 'cabins' – as they were called – one block was for the married couples, another for the single men, and the third for the unmarried women and girls. But as soon as work was over for the day, all the slaves of both sexes met together round a fire, where they spent most of the night, dancing, singing, and playing the banjo, and as a matter of course there was a great deal of poking. However, no notice was taken of what they did with themselves at night, so long as they were present next morning, when the roll was called by the overseers, before the gangs were marched off to work.

The slaves soon got to know me well, and as I took an interest in them, and was often able to do them little kindnesses, they all became fond of me. I liked the poor good-natured creatures who were always lighthearted, except when they happened to be smarting from a whipping.

Although I had often seen the marks of the lash on the bodies of the runaways who had passed through our station, I had hitherto never seen a slave whipped. Dinah, in her capacity as housekeeper, maintained strict discipline, so she often brought one of the women or girls before Randolph for neglecting her work or some other offence, and he sometimes himself gave the offender a whipping on her bottom with the switch. I had occasionally heard the squeaks of a culprit, but I had always avoided being present at the punishment.

Whipping a girl seemed to have an exciting effect on Randolph, for, after switching one, he used invariably to come to me, wherever I happened to be, and poke me with great vigour.

I thought it strange at the time, but I have since found out that men's passions are inflamed by whipping the bottom of a female till she cries and writhes with pain, and if they can't do it themselves, they like seeing it done. This is a curious, but undoubted fact, and it shows what cruel creatures you men are.

I have already mentioned that an octoroon girl named Rosa had been appointed to act as my maid. This girl had formerly been Randolph's favourite, but since my arrival at Woodlands he had had nothing to do with her.

When Rosa found that she was entirely neglected, and obliged to serve as my maid, she had been filled with resentment. In fact the girl was bitterly jealous; she had shown her vexation from the first, by constant sullenness, and at times she was very impertinent to me. But I had borne with her ill-temper, and had always been kind to her, trying to make her like me, as I pitied her and all the other slave girls. However, nothing that I could do had any effect in softening the girl; she continued to be sulky and disrespectful, though I had managed to make all the other women and girls fond of me.

I knew that if I reported her to Randolph he would have her punished, but as I did not wish to get her into trouble I did not say a word. Rosa was twenty years of age, a tall, handsome girl, and as she was an octoroon, she was not darker than an ordinary brunette; her complexion being a clear olive, with a tinge of pink showing on her cheeks. She had a well-rounded figure, with a full bust and broad hips; her feet were small, and her hands were smooth, as she had never done any hard work. She had a profusion of long wavy, dark brown hair; her eyes were also brown, large, and soft; she had white, regular teeth, and full, red, moist lips. Her voice was low and musical, but she was perfectly uneducated, not being able to either read or write, and she spoke in the usual 'nigger' way.

One morning, when she was assisting me to dress she appeared to be in a worse temper than usual, and while brushing my hair, she pulled it so roughly that I several times had to tell her to be more careful. I spoke gently, but my remonstrances only seemed to irritate her. Tossing her head, and giving my hair a nasty pull, she said in a most saucy way:

'I oughtened to be brushing yo' hair at all. Becos, you is white, yo' tinks yo' is a very fine lady; but yo' is not a bit better dan me. Yo' isn't married to de massa, yet yo' sleeps wid him ebery night.'

I flushed with anger, and rising from my seat, ordered the girl to leave the room. She did so, laughing.

The tears came into my eyes, my heart swelled, and I felt a deep sense of degradation. It was hard that owing to a series of misfortunes, I should have come to be spoken to in such a coarse way by a slave girl. But, alas! what she had said was the truth. I really was no better than her.

After a moment or two, I put up my hair, finished dressing, and went down to breakfast. I had not intended to say anything to Randolph, but he noticed that I was put out, and asked me what was the matter.

'Oh, nothing much,' I replied; 'Rosa has been a little impertinent to me.'

Not being satisfied with my answer, he insisted on knowing what the girl had said to me.

So I told him what had occurred, adding that she had always been more or less impertinent to me, and I suggested that if he spoke to her, she would probably be more respectful in future.

'I will speak to her presently,' he said. Then he went on quietly with his breakfast.

I thought no more about the affair, and when the meal was over we left the room, and went into an adjoining apartment, where I amused myself reading the newspaper, while Randolph smoked his cigar. When he had finished, he rang the bell, which was answered by one of the parlourmaids, named Jane.

'Go and tell Dinah and Rosa I want them here, and come back yourself,' he said to the girl.

She went away, returning in about five minutes accompanied by the two other women. Randolph rose from his seat with a stern expression on his face, and turning to

Rosa, who was looking rather frightened, said angrily:

'You young hussy! I have been hearing about your conduct. How dare you speak to your mistress in the way you have done? Did you think I would let you insult a white lady? You are getting too saucy, but I will take the sauce out of you. I am going to whip you.'

Rosa turned as pale as her olive complexion would allow, a frightened expression came into her eyes, and she burst into tears.

'Oh! massa!' she exclaimed. 'Don't whip me! Oh! please don't whip me! I'se very sorry I was sassy to de missis. Oh! do let me off an' I will be a good gal and never be sassy again.' Then turning to me, she said imploringly: 'Oh! missis, forgib me, an' ask de massa not to whip me dis time.'

I did not wish the girl to be whipped, so I asked Randolph to let her go away, saying that I was sure she was sorry for what she had said, and I did not think she would offend again.

But her master was very angry with her, and would not consent to let her off, although I begged him hard to do so.

Turning to Dinah, he said curtly:

'Take her up.'

I had no idea what was meant by the words, but Dinah knew what to do. She had often 'taken up' naughty slave girls on her broad, strong back. Going up to Rosa, she seized her by the wrists, and turning round, drew the girl's arms over her shoulders; then bending well forward, she raised the culprit's feet off the floor, so that her body was brought into a curved position.

Not wishing to see the punishment inflicted, I walked towards the door, but Randolph peremptorily ordered me to remain in the room.

'Turn up her clothes, Jane, and mind you hold them well out of the way,' he said.

Jane went to the right side of the delinquent, and rolling up her skirt, petticoats, and chemise, held them high above her waist.

The girl's underlinen was perfectly clean, but she wore no

drawers – none of the slave women possessed drawers.

She had a fine, big, well-shaped bottom, and owing to the curved position in which she was being held, the large, plump, round cheeks swelled out in high relief at a most convenient angle for receiving the switch. Her olive-tinted skin was perfectly smooth, her thighs were large and well-rounded, her legs were shapely and her ankles were trim. She was wearing tightly fitting white stockings, gartered with bows of blue ribbon and she had on neat shoes. Randolph went to a cabinet from which he took out a hickory switch – he kept a switch in nearly every room – then placing himself at the left side of the culprit, said:

'Now, I'll teach you to respect your mistress. I have not whipped you for some time, but I'm going to make your bottom smart now.'

Rosa had not struggled or uttered a word while she was being 'taken up' and prepared for the switch, but now she turned her head, looking at Randolph, with a dog-like expression of appeal in her great, brown eyes, and said beseechingly, while the tears ran down her cheeks:

'Oh massa, don't whip poor Rosa hard.'

He began to flog her, laying on the strokes smartly, and as calmly as if he were merely beating a dog. The girl winced, drawing in the cheeks of her bottom with a jerk each time the switch fell; long, red, weals rose on her skin, her plump flesh quivered, and she kicked up her feet, squealing shrilly and exclaiming in gasps:

'Oh, massa! – Oh, massa! – Don't, oh! whip – me – so – hard! Oh! massa! Oh! – good massa please – don't whip – me – so – hard! Oh! Oh! Stop massa! Oh! please – please – stop. My bottom – is – so – sore! – Oh! Oh!'

The switch continued to stripe her writhing bottom, extracting loud cries from her, making her struggle and plunge violently, but Dinah, slightly separating her legs and bending well forward, easily held the shrieking girl in position. Randolph whipped away steadily; Jane held up the girl's petticoats and Dinah gripped her wrists tightly, while Rosa, squealing and twisting herself about, drew up her legs one after the other, then kicked them out in all directions, and in her contortions opened her thighs so that I could see the curly dark brown hair shading the 'spot' and every now and then I caught a glimpse of the pink orifice. Her skin was rather fine, and she appeared to feel the pain acutely, begging piteously for mercy, but Randolph, utterly regardless of her cries and entreaties, went on whipping her till the whole surface of her bottom from the loins to the thighs was covered with red weals.

Then throwing down the switch he said:

'Let her go.'

Jane let the sufferer's petticoats fall, and Dinah released her wrists. She then stood on her feet, twisting her hips and wailing with pain, while she wiped the fast-flowing tears from her eyes with her apron.

'There, Rosa,' said Randolph; 'I have let you off rather easily this time, but if I ever again hear that you have been saucy to your mistress, I will whip you until the blood runs down your thighs. Now you can all go back to your work.'

Rosa, still wailing, slunk out of the room with her hand pressed to her smarting bottom; the other two women followed, and Randolph and I were left alone.

He put away the switch, then turning to me, said:

'I don't think she'll give you any more trouble, but if she does let me know.'

'Oh, George!' I said. 'How could you bring yourself to whip the girl so severely? She is a pretty creature and I know you have often "had" her.'

He laughed.

'Yes. I have often "had" her and will "have" her again if ever I feel inclined to do so, and I will also whip her whenever she requires punishment. She is only a nigger, though she is so light in colour. You are a Northern girl, so you don't understand how we Southerners look upon our slave women. When they take our fancy we amuse ourselves with them, but we feel no compunction in whipping them whenever they misbehave. Their bodies belong to us, so we can use them in any way we please. Personally I have no more regard for my slaves than for my dogs and horses.'

Though I had got to know Randolph pretty well by that time, I felt rather shocked by his unfeeling sentiments; however, I made no remark. He was standing in front of me, and I noticed that there was a protuberance in a certain part of his trousers. I guessed what was coming!

He went:

'You know, Dolly, that whipping a girl always excites me, so I am going to "have" you.'

Then laying me on the couch, he pulled up my petticoats, took down my drawers, and entered me with more than usual vigour. Whipping Rosa's bottom had certainly acted on him as a powerful aphrodisiac.

When all was over, and I had fastened up my drawers, we went to our respective rooms, and made ourselves tidy. Then he ordered the buggy, and we went for a long drive in the country, lunching at a farm house, and not returning home until it was time to dress for dinner.

When I got to my room I found Rosa there, as usual, waiting to assist me in making my toilet. She was looking very subdued, and her manner was humble and submissive. She had received a severe whipping, and her bottom must have been very sore. I felt for her, knowing as I did, how dreadfully the switch could sting.

'I am sorry for you Rosa,' I said. 'Did the whipping hurt you very much?'

'Oh! yes, missis,' she answered, giving a little shudder at the remembrance, 'it did hurt me most drefful. De massa never gib me such a hard whippin' before. Dinah has rubbed my bottom wid possum fat, an' dat has taken de sting out of de weals some, but I'se very sore, an' I can't sit down easy.'

She helped me to dress, seeming very anxious to please me in every way, and always speaking most respectfully. From that day she was a changed girl, so far as regarded her behaviour to me, and I never had occasion to find fault with her during the rest of my stay at Woodlands.

Chapter Eleven

A Rabelaisian banquet of nude damsels – A shocking orgie – Ten naked waitresses and their bashfulness – Hot viands and bottom-spanking escapades – Original racing in the corridors, and the inevitable sequel.

Three months passed, during which period I went through some varied experiences, and saw some curious sights, but if I were to relate everything that occurred, my story would be too long.

However, I will describe one or two of the incidents, just to give you an idea of the sort of man Randolph was.

I have already mentioned the dinner-parties he frequently gave to his male friends, and I have told you that these gatherings were always of a very free and easy sort.

At one of these dinners the proceedings were of a more licentious character than usual. Randolph had invited ten guests, which was the usual number – the parties, including our two selves, never exceeding twelve.

He was very particular on these occasions that all the girls should be nicely dressed, so Dinah used to parade them for my inspection just before the guests arrived. I merely had to see that the girls should be nicely attired outwardly, but Dinah before bringing them to me, had to see that each girl was clean in person, and that she had on fresh underlinen.

On the day of which I am speaking, after my own toilet had been made, I went down to the hall and inspected the girls, finding them all looking clean and smart.

Then I went into the drawing-room where Randolph was lounging on a chair turning over the leaves of a large illustrated book of Rabelais, which he was very fond of reading.

I told him I had seen the girls, and that they were all looking very nice in their black frocks. To my astonishment, he burst out laughing, and said:

'Oh, they won't wear frocks this evening. I have got such a splendid idea from a picture in this old book. I wonder it never struck me before.'

'What is it?' I asked.

'I have just been reading the chapter which tells how Pantagruel and his companions were entertained at a banquet by the Papimanes, and were waited on by a bevy of nude damsels. The dinner to-night shall be a reproduction of the scene described. There are ten men coming, and each man shall be waited on by a naked girl. It will be great fun, and also quite a novel entertainment for my guests.'

Although I was accustomed to his vagaries, this new freak horrified me. I should have to sit at the table with ten men, while the same number of women displayed their naked bodies.

The idea was most repugnant and I blushed, a thing I had not done for many a day.

'Oh George!' I exclaimed, 'don't do such a thing. It is too shameful.'

'Yes, I will,' he said, laughing heartily. 'Why Dolly, you are actually blushing! I thought you had got over all your squeamishness by this time.'

'Oh, but this is a particularly horrid idea,' I observed. 'And if you are determined to carry it out, don't make me come to table. Just fancy what a dreadful position it would be for me to have to sit among a lot of men, surrounded by naked women. I should not know which way to turn my eyes!'

He again laughed, but there was in his pupils a stern gleam which I had got to know, meaning that he had determined to have his way.

'It does not matter which way you look,' he said. 'You are looking very pretty and that's sufficient. You will have to take your place at table as usual, and you must appear to be quite unconscious that the women are naked. None of my guests will insult you by word or glance.'

I still remonstrated, but he sternly told me to shut up, or it would be the worse for me. I held my tongue, for I was afraid of him, knowing him to be a man who would stick at nothing, and it struck me that if I made any more objections he might take it into his head to whip *me*.

Sending for Dinah, he told her what he intended to do, and gave her orders to have ten of the young women stripped naked in readiness. He named the ones he wanted, selecting those who had the best figures. Seven of them were quadroons, the other three were octoroons, one of them being Rosa. Dinah received the order, and also some further instructions he gave her, with a perfectly unmoved countenance.

'All right, sah,' she said. 'De gals shall be ready.'

She then left the room.

It was nearly seven o'clock, and the guests began to arrive. Some came on horseback, others in buggies, and in a short time the whole party had assembled. All the gentlemen were more or less known to me, and everyone on entering the room shook hands with me in a most polite manner. They were of all ages: the youngest being about twenty-five years of age, while the oldest was upwards of fifty. Most of them were bachelors, but I knew that some of them were married men.

Presently Dinah, looking very smart in her black frock and white cap, made her appearance with a tray of cocktails, and while the guests were imbibing them, Randolph said with a smile on his face:

112

'I suppose, gentlemen, that most of you have read Rabelais. Those who have perused the book will remember the description of the banquet given to Pantagruel in the island of Papimany. I intend our dinner to-night to be, as nearly as possible, a counterpart of that celebrated banquet. I think I can give you as good fare and as good wine as Homenas gave Pantagruel and his companions. I also think that the "she-butlers" will please you. They may not be so fair-skinned as were the damsels of Papimany, but in all other respects you will find that the "waitresses" will answer the description of the ones mentioned in the book. They are "tight lasses," good-conditioned; comely, waggish, and fit for business.'

The men who had perused Rabelais and knew what was coming, laughed and clapped their hands, but the men who had not read the book looked puzzled. However, knowing Randolph's little ways, they guessed that something funny was going to happen. In a short time, dinner was announced, and then the oldest of the guests, a gentleman named Harrington, who I knew had grown-up daughters, offered me his arm and led me into the brilliantly lighted dining-room. The other men followed, and we took our places at the table, which was beautifully decorated with flowers, and glittering with plate and glass.

Randolph took his place at one end of the table; I faced him at the other end, and five of the guests sat on each side.

When everyone was comfortably settled, Randolph touched a small handbell beside him, and then the door at the far end of the room was opened. Dinah came in, followed by the ten naked young women with their long black, or dark brown hair flowing loose on their shoulders; each girl, without hesitation, taking up her position behind one of the guests. Dinah had told each waitress where she was to go. They all, without exception, showed signs of bashfulness, for although every one of them had passed through the hands of gentlemen on various occasions, singly in a bedroom, they had never been exposed stark naked before the eyes of a number of people. Some of the girls blushed, the colour

113

showing plainly on their olive cheeks; others cast down their eyes and fidgeted as they stood, while all of them placed their hands over the 'spot' between their legs.

I felt horribly uncomfortable, hot thrills passed over me, and my cheeks grew scarlet. The men smiled, casting amused glances at one another, then they looked with gleaming eyes at the naked girls. Some were slim, and some plump, some tall; some of medium size, and some short; but all of them were pretty and had shapely figures, with firm, round titties and good bottoms, while the brilliant light, shining on their naked bodies, made their smooth, olive-tinted, and in some cases, nearly white skins, glisten. The hair covering the 'spots' was, in all cases, black or dark brown, and one of the quadroons, a plump little girl, nineteen years of age, named Fanny, who had been whipped a couple of days before, still bore on her bottom the pink stripes left by the switch. Rosa was the prettiest of all the girls; she had also the best figure, and she was the lightest in colour; consequently she attracted the most admiration. The dinner was soon in full progress; the girls, directed by Dinah, bustled about bringing in the dishes, changing the plates, and filling the glasses with champagne. Some of them, not being accustomed to waiting at table, were rather awkward, but whenever a girl make a mistake she received from Randolph the next time she came within reach of his arm, a sounding slap on the bottom which made her jump and squeal, and clap her hand to the place.

But no one took the least notice of these little occurrences, the gentlemen continuing to talk and laugh as unconcernedly as if they were quite accustomed to being waited on by naked women, and also to seeing them smacked whenever they made a mistake. But it was a most trying time for me. I sat with my eyes fixed on my plate, and with a very red face, making a pretence of eating, and hardly listening to the conversation of Mr Harrington, the old gentleman who had taken me into dinner, and who was sitting on my right. He chattered away to me, but I noticed that he kept leering lecherously at Rosa's full bosom and broad bottom, as she tripped gracefully here and there. She had evidently taken his

114

fancy more than any of the other girls, and I felt sure that later on, my pretty maid would be poked by the old satyr. The dinner was a long one, but at last it was over, and the gentlemen settled down to smoke their cigars and sip their coffee, while the conversation turned upon slaves, and the price of cotton.

No improper remarks of any sort were made by the men, but their eyes were frequently turned with lustful looks on the naked girls standing in various attitudes about the room.

When the cigars had been smoked, we all went into the drawing-room, the girls being told to follow. I tried to slip away, but Randolph ordered me to remain. He told his guests to sit down on a row of chairs at the end of the room, and when they had done so, he posed the naked girls in groups in various positions with their arms round each other, some standing, some kneeling, and some lying on their sides at full length, so that their figures could be seen both back and front. These *poses plastiques* greatly pleased the spectators, and they gloated over each lascivious tableau, applauding vigorously; while the girls, utterly astonished at what they were being made to do, gazed timidly at the men with their big, ox-like eyes. At last, Randolph exhausted his ingenuity in inventing fresh tableaux, and I thought he would at least let the girls put on their clothes. But he did not. He had not yet done with their naked bodies.

'Now gentlemen,' he said, 'if you will go into the corridor I will let you see young mares' races. Some of them are rather fat, but I dare say I shall be able to make them show their best paces.'

The men, laughing boisterously, trooped out of the room and stationed themselves at intervals on each side of the long, broad corridor. The races were to be run in heats, the course being from one end of the corridor to the other and back, twice over. Before starting the girls, Randolph got a long heavy whip, and cracking it in the air, warned them that they had better run as fast as they could. Then as soon as the first lot was off, he took up his position at one side of the corridor half-way down, and as the runners dashed past him in the

115

several heats, he flicked the bottom of any girl who appeared not to be exerting herself, the touch of the whip extracting a shrill cry from the victim, and making her increase her speed, while a red mark instantly showed on her skin where the end of the lash had fallen.

The men grew excited, they laughed, cheered and betted on the girls as they raced up and down the corridor, their long hair flowing loose behind them, their titties undulating and their bottoms swaying.

The final heat was won by a tall, slender octoroon girl, twenty-one years of age, named Jenny.

After the runners had a rest, there was what Randolph called a 'Jockey race.' The five strongest girls had to take on their backs the other five girls, who held on by putting their arms round the necks, and their legs round the loins, of their respective 'mounts.'

This time the course was once up and down the corridor, and heavy bets were laid by the men on the women they fancied.

The signal to start was given, and the race began, the gentlemen whooping and shouting as they watched the extraordinary sight. Five naked women staggering along the corridor as fast as they could, each woman carrying on her back another naked female!

The muscles of the thighs and bottoms of the carriers quivered under the strain, while the legs of the riders, being stretched apart by the position in which they clung to their steeds, the cheeks of their bottoms were slightly separated, so that the spectators could see the hair in the cleft of the thighs. And nearly every one of the bottoms was marked either with the prints of Randolph's fingers, or with the red dot made by the flick of the whip. Two of the girls had both finger-marks and whip-marks, and when all was over only three girls out of the ten had spotless posteriors.

The men's eyes gleamed, their faces were flushed, and I could see that they were all in a state of great sensual excitement. After a close struggle, the race was won by a sturdy young quadroon woman, twenty-five years of age, named Eliza, who had carried the youngest of all the girls, a slightly-built, shapely octoroon named Helen, who was only eighteen years old.

Then we went back to the drawing-room, the girls being allowed to sit down, and Randolph told Dinah to give each of them a glass of wine and water. They were all very thirsty, some of them had tears in their eyes, and one or two were rubbing their bottoms, while the girls who had been carriers were panting for breath; their bosoms heaving tumultuously, and their naked bodies moist with perspiration. As soon as they had recovered their breath, the ten were made to stand in a row with their hands by their sides. Then Randolph said:

'Now, gentlemen, will you each choose a girl, either for a short time, or for the whole night? You can please yourselves.'

The men laughing and joking, began to make their selections, and in cases where two or three wanted the same girl, the matter was settled by tossing up a coin.

Rosa was the favourite, five of the men, including Mr Harrington, wanting to have her, but finally the old gentleman, as the senior member of the party, was allowed to take her. The selections being made, each man, followed submissively by the naked girl he had chosen, left the apartment and went upstairs to a bedroom.

Randolph and I were left alone.

He had been very much pleased with his evening's amusement.

'Oh Dolly,' he said laughing, 'what fun it has been! I've never had such a game before. I'll do it again some day or other and when I do, every woman in the house shall strip for the races.'

I did not feel at all mirthfully inclined. I had been wretched and uncomfortable throughout the whole proceedings, moreover the sight of so many bare bottoms, naked bosoms, and uncovered 'spots,' had given me a feeling of disgust. A woman is not excited by seeing the nakedness of other women. At any rate I never am.

'I think it was all very horrid and shameful,' I observed.

117

'I don't care what you think,' he replied. 'It pleased me, and amused my guests, and that's all I care about. But it has been very exciting work, I am feeling very randy, and my tool is aching from its prolonged erection, so I must take the stiffness out of it at once. I will "have" you sitting down, so as not to crumple your pretty frock.'

So saying, he seated himself on a chair and let loose his member, which stood straight up with its red tip uncovered.

'Come along now, Dolly, you know what to do;' he said impatiently.

I did know what to do. Turning my back to him, I raised my petticoats above my waist, and pulled open the slit of my drawers as widely as possible, exposing the whole of my bottom; then straddling over his thighs, with a leg on each side of him, I lowered myself down upon his upstanding member, which he guided between my thighs into its place, and the weight of my body forced the weapon up to the hilt in the sheath.

He clasped me round the waist under my clothes, while I, raising myself up and down on my toes, did all the work until the spasm seized me, and I felt the hot torrent inundating my inside. Then I lay back panting against his breast. As soon as I had received all he had to give me at the moment, I got off his lap, pulled my drawers into their place, and shook my petticoats straight, as some of the men might be coming back at any moment. As it was, we got done only just in time, for we had hardly sat down before one of the gentlemen made his appearance, and he was followed at intervals by others, until at last all had re-assembled except three, who had elected to stay all night with their girls. The other lasses, after being poked, had been allowed to go away to their own part of the house. Dinah brought in a tray of liquors and the men refreshed themselves. Then they all sat down to play cards, and I slipped out of the room and went to bed, glad to get away from the men, although not one of them had said an improper word to me during the evening.

It was very late, or to speak more correctly, it was early in the morning, when Randolph came to bed. I was fast asleep, but he soon woke me up by pinching my bottom, and then in a moment or two he was working away at me. As I was very tired and sleepy, I did not respond to his movements in the least, so when he had finished, he said crossly:

'Damn it, Dolly, you lay just like a log of wood. You did not even move your bottom at the finish. What's the matter with you?'

I said that there was nothing the matter with me only that I was sleepy. He growled out something uncomplimentary, then turning his back to me, went to sleep, and I speedily did the same.

Chapter Twelve

Mr Harrington's copulative capabilities – Randolph goes to Charleston on shipping business – I am left in charge with instructions to whip and spare not – I witness more whipping scenes – How the overseers lashed delinquent women – How differently women bear punishment – Description of the bottom in the Quadroon and Mulatto female.

We got up late next morning, and after he had gone to his dressing-room, Rosa came to help me as usual. While she was brushing my hair, I asked her how she had got on with Mr Harrington during the hour she had spent with him the previous night.

She looked at me with a comical expression on her pretty face.

'Oh, missis,' she replied, giggling; 'I tell yo' all 'bout it. De ole genterman was no good at all. He couldn't do nuffin to me. He try, an' he try, an' he try. He feel me all over, he play with me with his finger, an' dat did make me squirm, an' he make me rub him, but it was all no use, his ting would not get stiff enough to go into de place. Den he lay me on my face, an'

120

say I got very fine bottom, an' he asked me if de massa often whip it. I tole him dat de massa sometimes whip it. He laugh, den he gave me a little spankin', an' afterwards he gib me two dollars, an' say dat I was a pretty wench, an' dat he would buy me if de massa would sell me.' I smiled, and Rosa went on: 'But, oh, missis, ask de massa not to sell me to de genterman. I'se fond ob yo' now, an' I don't want to leave de ole plantation. I was born on it.'

I told her that I was sure her master would not sell such a pretty girl as she was to anyone. She seemed pleased at what I said, and went away with a smile on her face.

I went down to the breakfast-room, where I found Randolph, and in a short time the three gentlemen who had stayed in the house all night came into the room.

They greeted me politely, without the least sign of embarrassment, but I felt rather uncomfortable when I met their eyes. The cook had sent up an excellent breakfast, to which we all did justice. The three girls who waited looked fresh and clean, for though they had taken part in the races, and had been poked, they were not the three who had been kept at work all night.

When breakfast was over, and cigars had been smoked, the buggies were brought round to the terrace; the gentlemen bade me good-bye, and smilingly thanked their host for the pleasant night's entertainment he had given them. Then they drove away to their respective homes; Randolph went off to look round the plantation, while I betook myself to the library and amused myself with a novel.

A few days after the 'races,' Randolph found that he would have to go to Charleston on some business connected with the shipping of his cotton. So Dinah was told to pack her master's portmanteau with things for an absence of ten days. On the morning he left Woodlands, he spoke to me about the slaves, telling me that I was on no account to interfere with the overseers in their management of the field-hands, but he gave me full authority over all the women and children in the house. And he said that if any of them misbehaved, I could, with Dinah's assistance, whip the offender myself, or send her to the overseers to receive the whipping. In the latter case, I was to send a note to the man specifying the instrument of punishment that was to be used, whether strap, switch, or paddle, and also stating the number of strokes the culprit was to receive.

I told him I would look after the women, but I said to myself that I would neither whip them with my own hands, nor send one to be whipped, under any circumstances. The idea of grown-up women being whipped was intensely repugnant to me, and is still, but I think that children of both sexes require an occasional spanking. Randolph went away, and I was glad to be temporarily my own mistress. It was pleasant to be able to come and go as I pleased, and not to be at the beck and call of a master; for such Randolph was to all intents and purposes, and as I have before told you, I was always more or less afraid of him.

The days passed quietly. Dinah was most attentive to me, and I had no trouble with any of the women. I read a good deal, and nearly every afternoon I took a long canter in the country on the quiet old horse Randolph had given me. I had learnt to ride pretty well, but I was always rather nervous when I was on horseback. I also often walked about the plantation, watching the field-hands at work under the supervision of the overseers, each of whom carried a whip. It was the cotton-picking season, the picking being done entirely by women. Every one had to pick a certain quantity each day, and at the hour when work ceased, each picker carried her basket of cotton to the weighing-shed, where one of the overseers was in waiting to check the day's work.

Each woman's basket was weighed to find out if it contained the right quantity, and if it did not turn the scale, the woman who brought the basket was whipped there and then, receiving twelve strokes. No excuse was ever taken, and the punishment was always inflicted with the strap, which gave great pain, but did not cut or injure the skin. I once heard an overseer say that he could whip a nigger wench's bottom with the strap for half-an-hour without drawing a drop of blood, and her skin at the end of the time would be as smooth as a peeled onion. There were seventy female field-hands employed in the cotton-picking, and nearly every evening one or two, and sometimes three or four of the women, would be punished for not bringing in proper weight. I will give you a description of what I once saw, and you must remember that it was almost a daily occurrence, not only on Randolph's plantation, but on most, if not all, of the other plantations in the South.

I have often heard people – not Southerners – defend slavery and say that it was a fine institution, but those people had never seen what slavery really was. To this day the thought of slavery makes me indignant. But to proceed.

One evening, I was returning from a stroll, and happened to be passing near the weighing-shed, just at the hour when work ceased for the day, and the women were bringing their baskets of cotton to be weighed. I stopped to watch the scene, and, as there was a hedge between the shed and the path where I was standing, no one saw me, though I could see through the leafy screen. I knew the rules of the plantation, and as I looked at the women, I hoped for their own sakes that they had all picked their proper weight of cotton. They were of all ages, from eighteen up to forty. Some were married, but most of them were single, and of various shades, the majority being black, but there were many mulattoes and also several quadroons. All of them were strong, healthy-looking women, dressed in cotton gowns of divers colours; their heads, as a rule, being covered with brightly-coloured handkerchiefs, but some of the younger and lighter-skinned women wore linen sun-bonnets or wide-brimmed straw hats, while every one had on shoes and stockings. They came along the path carrying their baskets on their heads, chatting and laughing as if they had not a care in the world, but I noticed that a few of them were looking rather grave, and I thought to myself that they had probably been idling, and were not quite sure that they had picked the full weight. The overseer, with a note book in his hand, and attended by four field-hands, stood in front of the shed, near a large pair of scales. The women came up one by one, each handing her basket to be weighed by the men. If the weight was correct, the overseer ticked off the woman's name in his book, and she went away to her cabin, free to do what she liked till next morning, but if a woman's basket proved to be of short weight, the overseer put a mark against her name and told her to remain. The weighing was quickly done, so in a short time all the women had gone, except six poor things whose baskets had been found to be light. They knew what they were going to get, and stood in a row, all of them looking doleful, while three of them were also whimpering.

If I had possessed any authority on the plantation, I would have saved the women from the lash, but I had none. If I had showed myself to the overseer at that moment and asked him to let the culprits off the regulated punishment, he would have laughed at me. I knew all the delinquents, three of them being black women; two, mulattoes; and one was a quadroon.

The overseer did not make a single remark to them, nor did they attempt to excuse themselves – they knew that no excuse would have saved them. Turning to the woman whose name was first on the list, he said sharply: 'Lie down.' The woman, without hesitation, extended herself upon the ground. Two of the men then knelt down and held her arms stretched out at full length, while the other two men, also kneeling, grasped her legs by the ankles. She was a big, very stout coal-black woman, forty years of age, married; and having two strapping daughters, both of whom were pickers in the same gang as herself. The two girls, who were both over twenty years of age, and quite black, had brought in their proper weight, and had walked away a little distance from the shed, but when they saw their mother had been kept back, they stopped, and standing side by side, looked on in silence while she was being whipped. I dare say it was not the first time they had seen such a sight. Members of families, of both sexes, were often whipped in each other's presence on Southern plantations. The overseer turned up the woman's scanty garments, which consisted only of a skirt, a stuff petticoat, and a coarse chemise, laying bare her great posteriors. Her bottom was enormous, and so fat that it was dimpled all over. Her thighs were colossal, and her legs immense; her black skin however, was quite smooth, and it shone like polished ebony. It was the first time I had ever seen a black woman's bottom fully exposed, and the sight of it rather astonished me.

The overseer took out of his pocket a strap about two feet and a half long, three inches broad, and an eighth of an inch thick, and then standing over the prostrated woman, he gave her twelve sharp strokes, the leather making a loud crack, like the report of a pistol, each time it fell on the culprit's great big bottom.

The tears rolled down her cheeks, and her fat buttocks quivered involuntarily, but otherwise she did not move a muscle, nor did she utter the least sound during the whipping, and when it was over, she got up and went to her daughters, who put their arms round her, and then the three walked away. I noticed that the broad stripes made by the strap showed a livid colour on her black skin.

The next on the list was the quadroon: a slim, rather pretty girl, not more than eighteen. She was in a great fright, tears running down her cheek, and she did not place herself in position when ordered.

'Put her down,' said the overseer.

She was seized by the men, and in a moment more was lying flat on the ground, with her petticoats up to her shoulders. Her bottom was small, with pear-shaped cheeks, and at the upper part of her thighs there was a small space through which peeped the crisp black hair shading the 'spot.'

She received her dozen, and although the overseer did not whip her as hard as he had the black woman, the girl twisted her loins, and squealed loudly from the first stroke to the last, and when all was over, her olive-skinned little bottom had become a dusky red colour. When she rose to her feet, she danced about for a moment with the smarting pain, and then she walked stiffly away, wailing loudly, with both hands pressed to her bottom.

The third culprit was a sturdy mulatto woman, thirty-five

years of age. She submissively laid herself down when ordered to do so, and the overseer soon stripped her. She had a big, round, plump bottom; its skin was smooth, and of a yellowish tint, not at all pretty. The strap cracked on her yellow bum, striping it with twelve red bands, and making her wince, wriggle, and cry aloud, but she never once screamed.

The other delinquents, two black women aged respectively twenty-seven and thirty, and a mulatto girl aged twenty, were then disposed of by the overseer in the same way. The black women bore their punishment with a certain amount of fortitude, but the mulatto girl writhed and squealed, making almost as much outcry as the quadroon.

I will here state that from what I saw of whipping during my residence in the South, I came to the conclusion that the light-coloured slave-women had finer skins than the darker women, consequently the former felt more pain while being whipped than the latter. Moreover, the whipping of females by men, besides being cruel and most indecent, was also in my opinion, extremely unfair as a punishment. For instance: if an octoroon woman and a full-blooded black woman, both of the same age and physique, were to undergo exactly the same punishment, the octoroon would suffer far more than the black.

When the overseer had finished whipping the last culprit, and she had gone whimpering away, he told his assistants to go to their quarters, then rolling up the strap, he put it in his pocket, and strolled leisurely away in the direction of the overseer's house. The four men lived together, and I have no doubt they had carnal intercourse with all the best looking field-girls. But the man had been perfectly unmoved throughout the whole affair, not appearing to be the least excited at seeing the naked bottoms of the women writhing and twisting with seemingly lascivious movements under his strokes, and he had whipped the poor creatures with as little compunction as if they had been dogs. However, as it was his almost daily work, he was quite accustomed to it, and I don't suppose that the cruelty of the thing ever struck him. Slavery had a demoralizing effect upon most of the white people in the South; and they hardly looked upon slaves as human beings. I often heard white men use the expression 'a nigger is no better than a hog.' But I am again digressing.

Chapter Thirteen

Randolph is detained – Dinah wants a woman whipped – Her opinion on the disciplinary power of chastisement – Cruelty to a cat – My first experience of spanking others – The negro child's codpiece – Early puberty of the black female – Dinah's delight.

By this time everyone had disappeared, and I was left alone in the fast-gathering dusk. My ears still seemed to be ringing with the sharp cracking sound of the strap striking the flesh of the women, and I kept fancying I heard the cries of pain. I felt pity for them, but my feelings of commiseration were not so keen as they had been a few months previously. I had grown accustomed to seeing women whipped, although I had never before seen six turned up one after the other. Moreover, since my own shameful whipping and the events that had followed, my nature had become hardened.

I walked back to the house without meeting anyone, and went up to my room, where I found Rosa waiting for me. I changed my dress and bathed my face, and after having my hair brushed, I went down to dinner, which I ate with my usual good appetite, although now and then I could not help thinking of the scenes I had witnessed. After dinner, I amused myself with a book until bedtime. Next morning, I received a letter from Randolph, telling me that business matters would oblige him to go on to New Orleans, and he did not know exactly how long he might be detained. The news did not trouble me. I did not care for him, so I did not miss him, and I liked to be sure of having the days to myself without being poked. A nice quiet embrace in bed at night was all very well, but I disliked being poked by day with all my clothes on, and that was what Randolph often did to me. He was a man of strong sensual passions, and the least thing inflamed them: a paragraph in a newspaper, a picture in a book, or a passage in one; an unexpected glimpse of my ankles, or some other trifle would set him off, and then in a twinkling, I would find myself turned up in some ridiculous position.

After breakfast, I went to the library to answer his letter, and just as I had finished writing, Dinah, looking annoyed, came into the room, with a long story of how Emma, one of the mulatto kitchen-girls, had lately been neglecting her work. Said Dinah:

'I scold her, an' I scold her, but she don't mind me one little bit, an' dis very mawnin' de ornery nigger wench was sassy to me, who am de housekeeper of Woodlands;' added Dinah, her ample bosom swelling with wrath. Quadroons always call anyone darker than themselves, niggers. She continued: 'Now missis, yo' jus' send for her, I'll take de gal "up," an' den yo' gib her a good whippin' wid de switch.'

'No, Dinah, I cannot do that,' said I.

'Well den, missis, send her to be oberseer.'

'No, I won't do that either.'

Dinah looked very much surprised. She could not understand why I would neither whip the girl nor send her to the overseer.

'Oh, but, missis,' she said, 'if dis yer gal isn't whipped for her sassiness to me, all de odder nigger wenches will get sassy to me, an' I shan't be able to keep dem in order.'

I could hardly keep my countenance on hearing the

contemptuous way Dinah spoke about nigger wenches. Although she was a slave herself, and liable at any moment to be whipped if she committed an offence, she had a great idea of her own importance as housekeeper of Woodlands. I said:

'Wait until Mr Randolph comes home, then report Emma to him, and he will very likely punish her.'

Dinah was not satisfied with my suggestion, so she remarked that if I did not like to whip the girl with the switch, or to send her to the overseer, I might at least give her a spanking with a slipper.

But as I would not consent to do even that, she went away fuming and muttering something about my being too easy with 'sassy nigger wenches.'

A week passed uneventfully, and then a little event happened which annoyed me very much, and caused me to do a thing I had never done before in my life.

I was fond of reading out of doors in fine weather, and one bright afternoon, taking a book, I set off to a secluded part of the grounds where there was a little lake or pond full of beautiful water-lilies, and surrounded by flowering shrubs of various sorts. On the bank of the pond was a creeper-covered summer-house, furnished with a couple of long, softly-cushioned chairs, and a small round table, the floor being covered with Chinese matting. It was a comfortable little place, and a favourite resort of mine.

On approaching the pond, I saw at the edge of it two children, busily engaged in throwing stones at something struggling in the water. I knew the children, as they lived in the house; they were brother and sister, their mother being a fine mulatto woman named Margaret, who was one of the kitchen maids, and as both the boy and the girl were quadroons, their father, whoever he was, must have been a white man. The boy was eleven years old, and the girl thirteen. They had no business to be at the pond at all, and I expected to see them run away when they caught sight of me, but they were so absorbed in what they were doing that they did not notice my approach.

When I had got close to the pond, I saw that the object they

130

were stoning was a kitten, which as soon as it had managed to struggle to the shore, they threw back into the water, to be again a target for their stones.

I am very fond of all animals, especially cats, and any cruelty to a dumb creature always makes my blood boil. So feeling very angry, I rushed down to the edge of the water, and picking up the half-drowned kitten when it had again managed to reach the shore, I placed it on the bank, hoping that the poor thing would recover. But the creature had been injured by the stones; it was at its last gasp, and in a few seconds was dead.

I was now more angry than ever, and going to the two children, who had not attempted to run away – not that flight would have saved them – I took each of them by the hand, and led them into the summer-house intending to give them both a good spanking.

They were slaves and belonged to the house, therefore they were under my authority. As I have said before, I think that all children need corporal punishment at times, and in my opinion the two children who had stoned the kitten to death richly deserved a whipping for their gross cruelty. The girl especially, as she was old enough to have known better, and it was she who had led her little brother into mischief. I scolded the young wretches heartily, winding up by telling them that I was going to give them both a good spanking.

They did not appear to be very much frightened, but stood staring at me with their large brown eyes, without saying a word. I suppose both had been often spanked before, and I knew that three weeks before, the girl had been well beaten by Dinah, by order of Randolph, for pilfering. They were both very light-coloured; the boy was a sturdy little fellow dressed in a white cotton shirt and trousers; and the girl was pretty, with long, curly, dark brown hair flowing loose over her shoulders. She was dressed in a pink print frock, reaching a little below her knees, and showing her legs clad in clean white cotton stockings. Sitting down upon a chair, I took off my slippers, then told the boy to come to me, and he at once obeyed my order. I had never spanked a child, but I remembered the position in which my father used to place me for punishment, so seizing the boy, I laid him across my knees. I then unbuttoned his trousers, pulled them down to his knees, and tucked up his shirt, laying bare his posteriors.

I gazed at the chubby little bottom laying upturned on my lap, and passed my hand two or three times over the smooth, olive-tinted skin. Then a desire came over me to feel what the member of a boy of his age was like, so slipping my hand under his belly, I took hold of his little 'thing,' which felt like a thick, warm worm. Having satisfied my curiosity, I proceeded to business. Holding him down with my left arm over his loins, I applied the slipper smartly to his plump little bottom, each smack leaving a red mark on his skin, and extracting a howl from him. He kicked up his heels and wriggled about, squealing lustily and trying to roll off my lap: but holding him tightly, I spanked away steadily till the whole surface of his bottom was red. Then I stopped, and placed him kneeling on the floor with his trousers down and his bottom turned towards me, telling him not to move until I gave him permission to do so. He did not attempt to stir, but remained where I had put him, crying loudly, with his fists in his eyes, while his little red buttocks shook with the sobs that were bursting from him.

While I had been spanking the boy, his sister had looked on with a perfectly unmoved countenance, and when I told her to come to me, she did so without hesitation. Taking hold of her, I placed her in position, saying to myself that I would make her show some signs of feeling before I had done with her. I whisked up her short and scanty garments, at once baring her bottom, as she wore no drawers: everything she had on was perfectly clean. Although the girl was only a little over thirteen years of age, she was remarkably well developed. Before taking her up, I had noticed that her bosom was already showing a slight swell under her thin bodice, and now on looking at her bottom, I was quite astonished at its size. It was well-shaped too, the plump, firm cheeks standing out in rounded curves, and her thighs also were fairly well rounded. She had good legs for so young a girl; her skin was soft and smooth, and of a pretty olive tint. Putting my hand under her, I touched her 'spot,' and finding that there was a good deal of downy hair on it, I felt pretty sure that the girl had come to puberty. Quadroons, and in fact all females with negro blood in their veins, become marriageable at an early age. I began to spank her, laying on the slipper with considerable force, making her wince and writhe, but she bore several smacks in silence, and then bursting into tears, began to squeal and kick, at the same time putting both her hands behind her to shield her bottom from the hot slaps. Catching hold of her wrists, I held them tightly with my left hand and went on spanking her, as she wriggled, twisted, bounced, and bawled: her olive skin growing redder and redder every moment, while the summer-house echoed with her shrill squeals, and the smacking noise made by the slipper as it struck her bottom, the flesh of which was as firm and elastic as possible. But I felt no pity for the cruel little girl; so, quite regardless of her cries and her entreaties for mercy, I gave her the soundest spanking she ever had in her life; and when the punishment was over, her bottom was a dark red colour from the loins to the thighs.

I made her kneel beside her brother, and hold her petticoats above her waist; and then I put on my slippers and leant back in the chair, taking breath after my exertions, which had been considerable, for I had found it no easy task to keep the struggling, kicking girl on my lap while I was whipping her. While resting, I looked at the red marks of my handiwork on the children's bottoms. The boy had ceased crying, but he still sobbed at intervals, while the girl, who must have been smarting dreadfully, wailed aloud. After a short time, I told them that they might go, and they at once stood up, with the tears trickling down their cheeks; the girl letting her petticoats fall, and the boy buttoning up his trousers. Then they slunk out of the summer-house, and went off home.

Feeling quite a glow of satisfaction at having punished the naughty children, I made myself comfortable, with my legs up on the chair, and began to read the novel I had brought with me.

I read quietly for about an hour, then went back to the house. That evening after dinner, when I was sitting in the small, cosy drawing-room, Dinah came in to ask what I wished done in connection with some household affairs. When I had given her my directions, she did not go away, but stood fidgetting about and looking at me as if she wanted to say something.

'What do you want, Dinah?' I asked.

'I don't want nuthin', missis,' she replied. 'But I want to tell yo' how glad I is dat yo' spanked dose drefful chillen dis afternoon. De kittin de little beasts killed belonged to me.'

'How did you come to know that I had spanked them?' I inquired.

'Oh, dey came home cryin' and rubbin' deir bottoms, an' dey tole us dat de missis had gib dem a spankin' in de summer-house for trowin' stones at de kittin.'

I smiled, and asked Dinah if she knew who was the father of the children. She knew everything connected with Woodlands, and informed me that the father was a white man, who, at one time, had been an overseer on the plantation. I then asked her several more questions, and as she was always ready to chatter to me on the least encouragement, I heard some very curious stories about the doings of slave-women and girls. She also gave me many particulars, that I had not heard before, about herself and the Randolph family. Dinah was very fond of hearing herself speak, and she used a great many more words then were necessary, so I will only give you a summary of what she told me.

She was exactly the same age as Randolph, both having been born on the same day, thirty-five years back. Her mother had been Randolph's nurse, and the two children had been brought up together, and had played with each other in their young days. But when George grew to boyhood, he became the young master, and she had to submit to all his caprices. He was the only child, and his parents spoilt him, allowing him to do what he liked. He was very precocious,

134

and before he was fifteen years of age he had begun to feel her, and whenever she offended him, he would throw her down upon the floor, turn up her petticoats, and spank her.

When they were eighteen years of age, he took her maidenhead, and he continued to possess her whenever he felt inclined, for three years. Then he went to travel in Europe. He was away for a couple of years, and after his return he occasionally had further carnal relations with her.

When she was twenty-five years of age, she had got married to a quadroon man a few years older than herself, and from that time Randolph never touched her. But, as she pithily expressed it:

'Massa George had plenty ob odder gals in de house.'

When Randolph was thirty, his father and mother died within a short time of each other, and he became master of Woodlands. When that event occurred, Dinah was a widow, and was head parlourmaid, but after a time, Randolph made her housekeeper, and gave her a certain amount of authority over the other slave women, though he had never hesitated to whip her if she happened to displease him. It was, however, nearly two years since she had received a whipping.

Dinah, when once started, would have gone on chattering all night about Woodlands and its people, but as I was beginning to feel very sleepy, I sent her away and went to bed.

Chapter Fourteen

I learn something of Randolph's previous copulating proclivities –
I go for a ride and am rogered in my tight-fitting riding-dress –
Spanked and again rogered – I respond to his lunges and give the
Southern Bluebeard satisfaction.

Next morning, I received a letter from Randolph,
informing me that he would be home in three days' time, and
telling me to have a good dinner ready for him at the usual
hour, with gumbo soup, stewed terrapin, and roasted canvas-
back ducks. He was very fond of those three things, two of
which: gumbo soup and stewed terrapin, can only be got in
perfection in the Southern States.

Sending for Dinah, I told her that her master was coming
back, and gave her orders about the dinner, also telling her to
warn the cook and kitchen-women to be careful. Randolph,
being a great *gourmet*, was most particular about the cooking
of everything, and if a cook, through carelessness, spoilt a
dish, her bottom was generally made to smart.

After lunch on the day he was to return, I interviewed
Dinah, who told me that she had got the terrapin and the

canvas-back ducks, and that the cooks were preparing a very good dinner.

It was only two o'clock, and as I did not expect Randolph to be home until six o'clock, I thought I would go out for a ride. There would be plenty of time for me to have a long trot and afterwards to dress before he arrived. I knew he would scold me if he did not find me dressed for dinner, and waiting in the drawing-room to receive him. So after ordering my horse to be brought round to the terrace, I went up to my room, and assisted by Rosa, dressed in full riding costume, with a short chemise reaching to my knees, and a dark blue habit. On my head, I wore a soft felt hat of tan colour, and I had tan gauntlets on my hands. Rosa was always amused when helping me to dress in riding costume, and on this occasion, while buttoning my breeches round my broad hips, she laughed, saying:

'Oh, missis, how funny yo' does look in dem tight trousies. Dey does show de shape ob yo' figure, an' no mistake.'

However, when I was completely attired, the girl gazed admiringly at me, remarking that I looked 'real lubly.' And I think I may say without conceit, that I did look well in riding costume. I went downstairs, and out on the terrace, where one of the negro grooms was walking my horse up and down. He was getting old, but he was a very handsome creature, a thoroughbred, dark bay with black points; and he knew me well, as I used to visit him every day, giving him bits of bread, lumps of sugar, and slices of carrot, of which he was very fond. The groom put me up on the saddle, and then I trotted off alone. I never took a man with me.

It was a bright, cool day, the old horse was fresh, but perfectly under my control, and as he ambled with an easy action along the smooth, level road, the breeze fanned my cheeks, bringing an increased colour to them; my eyes began to sparkle and I felt in very good spirits. I rode seven miles to a farm-house, where I dismounted and had a glass of milk, while the old horse had a bucket of meal and water. Then after a short rest, I again mounted, and rode slowly back to Woodlands, arriving there at five o'clock.

The groom was waiting for me on the terrace, and as he helped me down from the saddle he told me that 'de massa' had been back about an hour. Hurrying into the house, I went straight to the drawing-room, where I found Randolph lying on the sofa.

'Oh, George!' I exclaimed; 'I am sorry I was not in when you returned: but I did not think you would be home until six o'clock.'

I expected he would be very cross with me for not having been waiting for him; but to my great relief, he was in a good humour.

'Never mind, Dolly,' he said; 'it doesn't matter.'

Then getting off the sofa, he lifted me up in his arms and kissed me on the forehead in a gentle affectionate way. He seldom kissed me, and when he did his kisses were coarse and sensual. I was surprised at his soft manner and tender kiss, and I thought to myself that if he would only treat me more as a woman and less as a subject for the gratification of his passions, I might get to like him a little.

But his soft mood did not last many moments. I saw the sensual look I knew so well come into his eyes as they roved over the curves of my bosom and the outlines of my hips, which were clearly defined by my tightly-fitting habit.

After a moment, he said:

'You are looking very fresh and rosy, and your habit does show off your figure to perfection. In fact you look so nice that I am going to "have" you this minute just as you stand.'

'Oh!' I exclaimed, rather taken aback, 'that will be very uncomfortable. I've got on breeches and boots. Come to my room and let me take them off.'

'No, I won't go to your room,' he said laughing; 'I intend to keep you here, and poke you just as you are. I've "had" women in all sorts of dress and undress, but I've never "had" one in full riding costume. It will be a decided novelty, therefore my pleasure will be increased. I've not touched a women since I left you. Now take off your hat and gloves, but don't remove anything else.'

When I had first seen him that afternoon, I was not

disinclined for a poke, after three weeks abstinence, and if he had taken me quietly upstairs to my room, let me undress, and then poked me properly on the bed, I should have been pleased. But now I was annoyed by the coarse way he had spoken, and I disliked having to submit to his embraces while dressed as I was.

However, I knew it would be useless to remonstrate, so taking off my hat and gloves I waited for his next move. He took off his coat and waistcoat, and then made me lean over the back of a low, broad armchair with my hands resting on the seat. I was not surprised, as he had often placed me over a chair before. He next rolled up the skirt of my habit to my shoulders, and as my body was curved by the position in which I was leaning, my bottom was well stuck out and my breeches tightly stretched. After a little fumbling under my corset, he unbuttoned the breeches, and with some difficulty pulled them down to the tops of my boots, then carefully tucking up my chemise, leaving me bare to the attack. He was always fond of looking at me, and feeling my bottom, so he stroked it, saying:

'Why, Dolly, your bottom seems to be plumper, prettier, and whiter than ever, but I am going to redden it a little with a spanking.'

When I heard him say that, I was frightened. He had never offered to do such a thing to me before. Raising my head, and looking over my shoulder, I said in a pleading tone:

'Oh, don't spank me, I can't bear pain.'

But I did not attempt to move from the position he had placed me in. Somehow or other, I never could resist his will.

'I won't hurt you,' he said, 'I'll only make you feel a pleasant tingling sensation.'

He then began to spank me; not with much force, but yet sufficiently hard to cause my skin to tingle more than I liked, and he applied the slaps to one side of my bottom only, leaving the other side quite untouched.

When he had spanked the whole surface from the upper part down to the thigh, he stopped, saying with a laugh:

'There, Dolly; one cheek is as pink as a rose, and the other

139

is as white as a lily. The contrast between the two is charming. It is a pity you cannot see your bottom at this moment.'

Then going to work again, he spanked the white cheek till is also turned a rosy pink colour, but I can't say that I only felt a pleasant tingling sensation; in point of fact my bottom decidedly smarted. But strange to say, the slight spanking had excited a voluptuous feeling in me, and I was anxious to receive the stroke. He unbuttoned his trousers, and then making me separate my legs slightly, he clasped his arms round my body, as stooping a little, he thrust his 'thing' into the 'spot' between the cleft of the thighs. Holding me in a close embrace with his belly pressed against my bottom, he began to lunge at me strongly, giving me the full length of his member, while I, pressing my thighs together, clipped the weapon tightly in the sheath, at the same time moving my loins briskly backwards and forwards to meet his powerful thrusts. He worked away in fine style, and I gave him every assistance, so in a few seconds the supreme crisis arrived. He discharged copiously, while I squirmed and twisted myself about, wriggling my bottom in the voluptuous spasm until all was over. Then my knees gave way under me and I should have fallen had he not held me up. He put me on my feet.

'That was a good one, Dolly, wasn't it? And you did your part very well,' he remarked.

I smiled, and pulling up my breeches, buttoned them round my waist; while he fastened the front of his trousers and put on his coat and waistcoat. I do not know whether during his absence he had touched a woman or not, but anyhow the poke he gave me that day was the most vigorous one I had ever received from him.

I had liked it, but I would rather have had it properly done to me on a bed. Since that time, I have learnt by experience that all men are fanciful; they like change, and are fond of 'making love' to women in all sorts of ways. But women do not care to be 'had' in fancy positions with their clothes on; they prefer to be embraced in the old-fashioned way, lying on their backs in or on a comfortable bed, with nothing on but a chemise or a nightdress.

We went to our respective rooms and dressed for dinner, meeting each other at table at seven o'clock. It was an excellent dinner; the cooks had done their best, and the gumbo soup, stewed terrapin, roast canvas-back ducks, and all the other things, were cooked to perfection, and as we were both hungry, we did full justice to the various dishes, also to the champagne, and other wines. He asked me how the women had behaved during his absence, and I replied that they had not given me the least trouble. Then I told him how I had spanked the two children for killing the kitten. He was very much amused, laughing heartily at my description of the affair, and he said that I was such a meek little creature that he did not think I would have had the courage to whip the children single-handed.

Chapter Fifteen

'Spoon fashion' – The irony of woman's destiny – I am futtered in the place where, when a virgin, I defended my honour – The calm is broken – Dinah receives an awful spanking – Her majestic bottom.

After dinner, when we were in the drawing-room, he told me that he had great trouble with his business matters, owing to the unsettled state of affairs between North and South. Randolph, like all Southerners at that period, hated the Northerners, speaking of them most contemptuously, and calling them 'damned Yankees.' He also said that he did not think they would dare to push matters to extremes with the South.

Being a Yankee myself, I did not like to hear Yankees spoken of with contempt, and I felt convinced in my own mind that they would be quite able to hold their own with the Southerners. However, I did not argue the point. I had long given up trying to argue with Randolph, for whenever I attempted to hold an opinion different to his, he always told me that I did not know what I was talking about, and to 'shut up.'

The evening passed, and at eleven o'clock we went to bed; but before going to sleep, he made me lie on my side, while he also on his side, lay behind me, with his arms round me, and his bare belly pressed close against my naked bottom, so that his stiff member passed between my thighs into its place. Then, grasping one of my titties in each of his hands, he poked me. This was rather a favourite position of his, when we were in bed, and he used to call it 'spoon fashion.' Next morning after breakfast, he went out to make an inspection of the plantation, to see how things had been carried on during his absence. He found everything in fair order, so he came back in a good humour to lunch, and when it was over ordered the two-horse buggy, and we went for a drive. It was a bright, hot afternoon, so he drove through the shadiest lanes, and we happened to pass the little dell where he made the assault on me.

He pulled up the horses, and pointing with his whip to the spot, said, with a laugh:

'Do you remember this place, Dolly?'

I did remember it well! and I thought of the long and desperate struggle I had made to keep my maidenhead, which I had to surrender to him after all.

'Oh, I remember the place very well,' I replied. 'Do you think I could possibly forget it?'

He again laughed, saying:

'How you did kick, and scream, and fight; you quite astonished me. I would not have believed that a little woman like you could have made such a strong resistance. It was an exciting struggle, and the thought of it has given me an erection, so I intend to have a roll on the grass with you.'

I said nothing, but I thought a great deal. I was going to be rogered by him on the very spot where I had once successfully resisted his assault. It was surely the very irony of fate.

He got out of the buggy, and hitched the horses to a tree; then lifting me down, he carried me to the little hollow, and laid me on the grass. Then after some amorous dalliance, he placed me in position, turned up my petticoats, and poked me strongly, making me bounce under him.

'Ah, Dolly,' he remarked when all was over, 'if you had let me get on the top of you that day, you would not have had your bottom whipped by the lynchers, nor would you have ridden the rail.'

I made no answer, but arranged my somewhat disordered attire; then we got into the buggy again, and continued our interrupted drive, not returning home until it was time to dress for dinner.

The days passed, and everything went on smoothly in the establishment. The women gave very little trouble: their conduct being so good that not a single one of them had had her petticoats turned up since Randolph's return. I mean turned up for a whipping, as I have no doubt that most of them, if not all, had their petticoats turned up for a poke in the evenings. Plenty of lovemaking went on, as a certain number of the women and girls, in turns, were allowed to be out every night till half-past ten o'clock. Anyone who was late in returning to the house was brought by Dinah next morning before Randolph, who either whipped the offender himself, or sent her to the overseer. She was also further punished by not being allowed out of the house at night for a month. So it was very seldom that a woman stayed out beyond the hour fixed for her return.

But the calm that had lasted for so many days was one afternoon ruffled by a breeze. I think something had gone wrong on the plantation; I don't know what it was, but anyhow Randolph, who had been out for a couple of hours, came back to the house in a vile temper. He blew me up because I happened to be wearing a pair of easy slippers without heels, asking me what the devil I meant by going about slipshod, 'like an untidy nigger wench!' When he had quieted down a little, he informed me that he had a business appointment with a gentleman – one of the neighbouring planters – and that they were to meet each other in an hour and a half's time at a certain cross-road, a few miles from Woodlands. He was then going to ring the bell, to give orders for his horse to be saddled, when Dinah happened to come into the room to ask me a question about dinner.

I answered her question, and as she was leaving the room, Randolph told her to order his horse to be brought round at once. He then went up to dress, returning in about half an hour's time, in riding costume. The groom, however, had not made his appearance with the horse, so Randolph kept walking up and down the room, fuming with impatience, constantly glancing at his watch, and every now and then looking out of the window, wondering why the horse had not been brought, saying that he would most likely miss his appointment, and vowing that if he did, he would have the groom cowhided by the overseer.

At last he rang the bell furiously, telling the parlourmaid who answered it to send Dinah up, and when the girl had left the room, he turned to me, saying:

'I think that confounded woman must have forgotten to send word to the stables.'

Presently Dinah, looking calm and placid, came into the room.

'Did you order my horse?' shouted Randolph, in an angry voice.

A frightened expression at once appeared on the woman's face.

'No sah, I didn't. I quite forgot dat yo' tole me to order de hoss',' she answered, in a faint voice, glancing deprecatingly at her angry master.

He flew into a violent passion – he was a most violent man – the veins of his forehead swelling, and his eyes gleaming with rage.

'Oh, you forgot, did you!' he exclaimed. 'I'll teach you to forget my orders.'

Rushing at Dinah, who stood cowering, he seized her, and sitting down on the end of the sofa, threw the great big woman across his knees, just as if she had been a little girl.

I could see by her astonished face that she was utterly taken aback, but she did not struggle. Ejaculating once: 'Oh massa!' she lay quietly over Randolph's thighs, with her hands resting on the floor at one side of him, and her feet on the other.

With one sweep of his arm he threw her petticoats up over her head, completely hiding her face, and laying her bare from her waist to her garters.

Dinah, being a tall, strapping woman, had large posteriors; her bottom was really a splendid one: broad, deep, and very plump, and as she was lying in a much curved position, the great half moons were raised high on Randolph's lap. She had large, round, muscular thighs, and the plump calves of her big legs seemed ready to burst through her tight, white cotton stockings. Her dusky olive skin was smooth and wholesome-looking, and all her drapery was clean. Holding her firmly in position, with his left arm over her naked loins, and with his right leg over the back of the lower part of her thighs, he began to spank the woman, raising his hand as high as he could in the air, and laying on the strokes with his full force. Each time his hand fell on her big bottom, a loud 'smack' echoed through the room, and the red prints of his fingers and thumb instantly showed on her skin. Dinah winced under the stinging slaps, her plump flesh twitching and quivering, but she did not utter a sound, nor did she attempt to put her hands behind her. He went on spanking her ruthlessly, and after a moment, she shook her head clear of her petticoats, and looked round at her master with a pleading expression in her great, brown, ox-like eyes. Her cap had fallen off, her hair had come loose, her lips were quivering, tears were rolling down her cheeks, and she writhed and twisted her loins in pain, but still she was silent.

He continued to rain down the shower of slaps, the red marks of his fingers spreading all over her bottom till not a part of it was left unmarked. Dinah's fortitude at last gave way, she began to utter little shrieks, and to kick her legs about, while she jerked her hips from side to side, and putting her hands over her bottom, tried in vain to shield it from the tremendous spanking, at the same time gasping out entreaties to her master to stop.

At last he did so, and pushed the woman off his knees on to the floor, where she lay crying, with her petticoats still up to

146

her waist, so that her great red bottom remained exposed. After a moment or two, she got on her feet, wiping the tears from her hot, flushed face with her apron, and then she twisted up her hair, picked up her cap, put it on her head, but not very straight, she shook her petticoats into their places, and stood sobbing before her master.

'There, you careless hussy,' he said, 'I think you'll remember my orders in future. Go away.'

Dinah, holding her apron to her eyes, walked rather stiffly out of the room. Randolph rubbed the palm of his hand, saying:

'Damn the thing, I have made my hand quite sore on the woman's bottom; her flesh is very firm, and I felt as if I were spanking a board. I ought to have used the switch and saved my fingers. But,' he added: 'if my palm is so sore, what must her bottom be? I fancy she won't forget that spanking in a hurry.'

'I think it was a shame of you to spank Dinah at all;' I observed.

The laughing expression instantly left his face, and he glared furiously at me, saying in a loud angry tone:

'You had better keep what you think to yourself. It is no business of yours what I do to my slaves. Why, damn it,' he exclaimed with increased anger: 'no one has ever dared to make such a remark to me before. I have a great mind to take you across my knees and give you a smart spanking too.'

My blood ran cold, and a lump came into my throat. He was quite capable of doing what he said.

'Oh, I beg your pardon. I am very sorry I spoke,' I said earnestly.

'So you ought to be. I thought you knew by this time that I will stand no interference;' he said, scowling at me.

He then left the room, much to my relief, and shortly afterwards I saw him canter down the avenue. I was very sorry for poor Dinah; she had always been most attentive to me, and I liked her very much. I wondered how Randolph had the heart to expose and whip so severely the woman who had been his foster-sister; had lived all her life in the house

147

with him, and had also been the toy of his passions. Feeling rather upset by the scene I had witnessed, and also by my narrow escape from a spanking, I went up to my room, and ringing for Rosa, told her to take down my hair and give it a good brushing, a thing which always has a soothing effect upon me. The news that Dinah had been spanked had already got about the house; she was not liked by her fellow slaves, because, as housekeeper, she kept them in order, reporting any woman or girl who misbehaved, or neglected her work.

Rosa brushed away at my hair for a few moments in silence, but I could see that she was bursting to say something, and at last she said:

'All de women is glad dat Dinah got a good spankin' from de massa. She tinks too much of herself. An' she always tells on a gal if she don't do exactly right, an' gets her a whippin'.'

'Dinah only does her duty,' I remarked. 'If the women and girls always behaved as well as they have been doing lately, Dinah would not have to tell of them.'

Rosa tossed her head, but made no further remarks, and when she had brushed my hair well, and re-arranged it, I sent her away, telling her to send Dinah up to me. I was rather curious to see how she was after her terrible spanking. In a short time she came into the room looking as smart and tidy as ever. Her hair was neatly arranged under a clean cap, and she had put on a clean apron, collar, and cuffs; her face wore its usual placid look, but her eyelids were red and rather swollen.

'I am sorry for you, Dinah,' I said. 'Your master spanked you so very severely.'

She seemed to be a little surprised at my expressing sympathy, but she was very grateful for it and she thanked me. Then she said:

'I'se had plenty ob spankins' an' whippins' in my life, but I never thought dat I'd come to be spanked again like a little gal. Why, missis, I ain't had such a ting done to me since I was thirteen years ole. But, oh my! dis one was a spankin'! It hurt most dreful. De massa laid on powerful heavy, an' his hand is bery hard. I'se been paddled twice, but I tink de Massa's hand hurt me to-day, near as much as de paddle did. My bottom is bery sore an' bruised, an' it'll be black an' blue all ober to-morrow.'

Dinah had spoken without emotion. She evidently did not think it strange that a woman of her age should have been whipped in such an ignominious way, and did not appear to bear her master the least malice. She was his slave; her body belonged to him, therefore he could do what he liked with it. Such was the degrading effect of slavery on the minds of the human chattels.

I sent her away and dressed for dinner, putting on a new frock which I had lately received from the dressmaker in Richmond. Then I went down to the dining-room, where I found Randolph, and as the dinner was ready, we sat down to table. He had missed his appointment he said, which was an important one, consequently he was very cross and snappish; but after he had eaten a good dinner, drunk a bottle of champagne, and smoked a cigar, he got into better humour.

When we went into the drawing-room, he seated himself in an easy chair, saying to me waggishly:

'Come here, Dolly, and let me see if you have taken off those beastly slippers you were wearing this afternoon.'

I went to him, and held my skirts above my knees, while he looked at my feet and legs. I had on a pretty pair of high-heeled boots and pale blue silk stockings, fastened with silver-buckled pink satin garters.

'Ah, this is something I like,' he observed; running his hand up and down my legs and ankles.

Then he put his hand higher up under my drapery, and opening the slit of my drawers felt my bottom.

'You are looking very pretty to-night, Dolly, and that new frock becomes you,' he said, drawing me closer to him while his eyes began to sparkle.

I knew what he was going to do! Taking me up in his arms, he carried me to the sofa and laid me down upon it, then he turned up my garments one by one, looking at my fine white petticoats deeply flounced with lace, my prettily-trimmed

149

drawers, and my filmy chemise; as he always made me wear the daintiest under garments in the evening.

When everything had been turned up, and my drawers had been taken down, he stretched my legs widely apart, and gazed for a moment or two at the 'spot;' then inserting his finger he tickled the sensitive little 'point' till it distilled a few drops of moisture, while I squirmed and kicked up my legs. He seemed to be very much excited, kissing me hotly on the lips, eyes, and cheeks several times, then throwing himself upon me he pressed his lips upon mine, and thrust his tongue into my mouth, as putting his hands under me and grasping the cheeks of my bottom, he fixed his weapon deeply in the sheath, and 'sworded' me vigorously.

When all was over and we had made ourselves tidy, he rang the bell, and ordered the parlourmaid to bring a bottle of champagne, and when the girl had brought the wine, we soon disposed of it, as our exciting combat had made us both thirsty. Randolph was pleased with himself and he was also pleased with me, so he was in very good humour. We had a long conversation on various subjects, and as he did not snub me when I differed with him, I passed a more pleasant evening than usual. At half-past eleven o'clock we went to bed.

Chapter Sixteen

After four months – The 'spirit of unrest' – My sympathies are with the North – An escaped Negress taken and flogged – A most awful flagellation – 'Paddling' described – A blistered bottom.

I will now pass over a period of four months. During that time, events had been marching rapidly, and stirring things had happened. The slave States had seceded from the Union. Jeff Davis had been elected President of the Southern Confederacy. Fort Sumter had been taken, and the war had begun. All those events are matters of history, so I need not enter into details of them, but I will confine myself to relating the things that were connected with Woodlands, and with my own fortunes.

The work on the plantation was carried on as usual, notwithstanding the very unsettled state of affairs, but there was a spirit of unrest among all the field-hands, and they were inclined to be insubordinate, so Randolph and his four overseers always went about armed with revolvers, and whippings were of more frequent occurrence than ever. The overseers in all cases inflicted the punishments, the male slaves being tied to the whipping-post and cowhided, while the females were stretched upon a bench, and either switched or paddled. By these severe means, discipline had so far been thoroughly maintained. Even the women in the house, with a few exceptions, became very troublesome, but here again Randolph would stand no nonsense. He became stricter with them than before, and whenever a woman or a girl had misbehaved in the least, Dinah, and another stalwart woman named Milly, were sent for, and the offender was taken up and prepared for punishment. Then in a few seconds, she would be squealing, writhing, kicking up her heels, and promising amendment, while Randolph, wielding the switch with vigorous arm, striped her bottom with red weals, and in some cases of grave misconduct he would draw blood. This treatment reduced to order all the women who were inclined to be unruly, and they soon returned to their ordinary behaviour.

For some time past, business in the State had been almost at a standstill, therefore Randolph could not dispose of his cotton, which had accumulated in the sheds, which were full to overflowing. He was a rich man, but most of his income was derived from the sale of his cotton, and now that there was no market for it, while at the same time the great expenses in keeping up the plantation were going on, he became very much pressed for ready money. However, he thought it would only be a temporary inconvenience, as he was quite convinced in his own mind that the South would eventually prove victorious in the war.

My sympathies, of course, were with the Northerners, and I wished them speedy success, but I dared not express my sentiments. I really don't know what Randolph would have done to me if I had said what I thought. He rarely left the plantation, and he never gave any dinner parties, as all his friends had either left the State, or joined the Confederate Army. He would have done so himself, only that he was too old to go as a private soldier, and he was unable to get a commission as an officer, owing to his having no knowledge of military affairs: but he had been elected a member of

Congress for the Southern Confederacy. As he would not leave Woodlands, he was obliged to fall back upon my society, and he seemed glad to have it; he also seemed to appreciate it. His manner became a little more tender; he did not speak to me so coarsely as he had often been in the habit of doing, and he treated me with less indecency. But with his slaves, both outdoor and indoor, he was more strict than ever. Since the breaking out of the war, several of the field-hands had run away, and had managed to get clear off, although the 'underground stations' had been closed. Randolph had offered two hundred dollars reward for the capture of each runaway, but strange to say, not one of them had been brought back. These losses had vexed him very much, the runaways having been some of his strongest and finest young men and women, each of whom was worth from fifteen hundred to two thousand dollars. So far none of the house-women had run away, but at last one of them did. One morning, when Randolph and I were at breakfast, Dinah came in and told her master that one of the women named Sophy, who had been out the previous night, had not returned to the house, and it had been found out that she had taken away some of her clothes. Sophy was one of the kitchen-maids, a fine, big, healthy young mulatto woman, twenty-six years of age, and worth about eighteen hundred dollars. There was no doubt that she had run away, so Randolph at once wrote out copies of advertisements, describing the woman, and offering the large reward of four hundred dollars to anyone bringing her back to Woodlands, or lodging her in a goal. He sent the advertisement to all the local newspapers, and also ordered bills to be printed and posted up in various places. Several days passed, the advertisements appeared in the papers, and the bills were stuck up all about the neighbourhood; but nothing was heard of the runaway. However, as all the white loafers were eager to secure the large reward, Randolph had hopes that the woman would be caught sooner or later. And so she was.

About five o'clock one evening, a couple of rough-looking white men drove up to the house in a ramshackle wagon, bringing with them the runaway, whom they had found concealed in the slave quarter of a plantation, twenty miles from Woodlands. The woman, whose wrists were tied together with a piece of rope, had evidently not suffered any privations during the time she had been absent. Her frock was clean, and she was in good condition bodily, but her face was looking very doleful, as she knew there was a severe whipping before her.

The men who had hunted her down received the four hundred dollars, and drove off in their wagon, while Sophy was taken away to the servants' quarters, and after she had been given something to eat, was locked up in a small bedroom by herself for the night.

Randolph was much pleased at having got the woman back, consequently he was in a very good humour all through the evening, so when we were in the drawing-room after dinner, I ventured to ask him what he intended to do to Sophy.

'Never you mind, Dolly,' he replied smiling. 'It's no business of yours. I've not quite made up my mind what I shall do to her, but anyhow, I intend to make the hussy smart to-morrow, and if you like, you can see the punishment.'

I asked no more questions, and he told me to come and sit on his knee. I did so. Then as a matter of course, the usual toyings took place, and in a very short time I found myself impaled as I sat on his lap. Afterwards, we talked about the war and I had to carefully conceal my real opinions. In due course we went to bed. Next morning at breakfast, he told me he had determined to make an example of Sophy, therefore he intended to whip her with the paddle, in the hall, before all the other women in the house.

I was sorry for Sophy – I was always sorry when a woman was whipped – but I dared not say a word, in fact, if I had said anything, it would only have irritated Randolph, and made him harder on the woman; moreover, it would have brought his wrath upon me. When he had finished his breakfast, and smoked a cigar, he left the room to make preparations for the punishment. In about twenty minutes he came back and said:

154

'Everything is ready now. You can come out to the hall if you would like to see a paddling.'

I had seen many women switched; some whipped with the strap, and several spanked, but I had never seen one paddled, and I was rather curious to see how the punishment was inflicted. I followed Randolph to the hall. I was sorry for the woman, as I have before said, but my curiosity overcame my pity. I had grown somewhat callous.

In the middle of the long wide hall, there was a machine I had never seen before, though I had heard of it. It was the whipping bench, a long, low, curved wooden structure about two feet broad, supported on four legs, each of which was furnished with buckled straps.

On the floor beside the bench was the paddle, a round flat piece of wood an eighth of an inch thick, and eight inches in diameter, fixed to a handle two feet and half long. It was very much dreaded by all the female slaves, as it caused great pain, bruising the flesh and blistering the skin, so that after a paddling the sufferer's bottom remained sore and tender longer than after a switching or a strapping.

All the women and grown-up girls in the house were present, and they were twenty-one in number, ten of them in a row at one side of the bench and ten of them at the other; Dinah stood by herself. Randolph ordered her and Milly – a strong black woman whom I have mentioned before – to go for the culprit. They went, returning in a couple of minutes with Sophy, who the moment she caught sight of the preparations for her paddling, burst into tears and hung back, so that the two women had to drag her up to the bench. Sophy was not a bad-looking woman, for a mulatto, and on ordinary occasions her yellow-tinted completion was clear, but at that moment, fear had turned her face a sort of dull grey colour.

'Oh, massa! massa!' she cried, stretching out her arms appealingly, with the tears running down her cheeks, 'don't paddle me. Whip me wid de switch or de strap, but don't, oh don't paddle me!'

'Put her on the bench,' said Randolph.

155

The woman, in an agony of fear, threw herself upon the floor. Dinah and Milly lifted her up, and then she began to struggle and kick, but in spite of her resistance, the two big, strong women soon had her stretched at full length on the bench, with her wrists and ankles securely fastened with the straps. Dinah then stripped her, and as her head and feet were lower than the middle of her body, which was raised by the curve of the bench, the part of her person to be operated upon was thrown well up.

She would have had a good figure, only that her bottom was out of all proportion. It was too big, but nevertheless it was fairly well-shaped, with well-rounded cheeks meeting each other closely; her thighs were large, and she had a sturdy pair of legs; her skin was smooth and of a clear yellow tint.

Randolph took up the paddle, and standing at the culprit's left side, said:

'Now, you bitch, I'll make your fat bottom smart. You've cost me four hundred dollars, and I intend to take the value out of your yellow hide.'

He raised the paddle high in the air over the trembling, crying woman, who in dread of the coming stroke, drew in the cheeks of her bottom until the division between them looked like a fine line.

Down came the paddle with great force, and with a resounding 'smack' on the upper part of the right cheek of her bottom; she gave a convulsive start, and gasped for breath, then she uttered a long shrill squeal, and at the same instant a great red blister-like patch, the exact size and shape of the blade of the paddle, sprang up on her yellow skin.

The second stroke fell on the left cheek, and again the loud sounding 'smack' was followed by a shriek, and another round patch showed red on her skin. He went on paddling her with great severity, laying the strokes alternately on the right and on the left side of her bottom, and striking a fresh place each time. She screamed and writhed, twisting herself about in agony, and jerking her tortured bottom from side to side on the bench as far as the straps binding her would allow; at one moment arching her loins, and at the next instant

156

flattening herself down with a shriek, as the paddle smacked horribly on the flesh.

She wriggled and squirmed, cried and screamed, and pleaded and prayed for mercy, but he gave her several more strokes; finishing up by applying two extra hard smacks, one to the upper part of each thigh, extracting from her two louder shrieks, and making her writhe more convulsively. It had been a most severe punishment, and her bottom had become a dark purple colour, while it was quite swollen and the skin had a puffy appearance.

Randolph threw down the paddle, telling Dinah to release the woman, and as soon as she was unstrapped, she rolled off the bench, and lay crying loudly. While she was being paddled, the other women had looked on in silence, the majority of them showing no signs of emotion, but some of the younger girls had tears in their eyes. They had all, with few exceptions, seen each other at various times receive a whipping, and everyone of them, without exception, had been whipped herself more or less frequently.

Randolph told Dinah and Milly to take Sophy away and attend to her. They lifted the sufferer up, and clasping their arms round her – she could hardly put one foot before the other – led her wailing out of the hall, to bathe her blistered bottom with cold water. He then ordered a couple of the women to take the bench and the paddle back to the shed where they were kept; the other women and girls he sent to their work, and I was left alone with him in the hall. Being well aware that whipping a woman always excited him, I felt pretty sure that I was going to be poked. I was not wrong. Putting his arm round my waist, he led me into the drawing-room, and made me lean over the high end of the sofa. Then he turned up my petticoats, let down my drawers, and gave me a strong poke from behind. He then went out, and I was off to my room to make myself tidy, as I was in rather a dishevelled state after his vigorous onslaught. When I had removed all traces of what had occurred, I rang for Rosa, and sent her to see how Sophy was getting on. When she came back she said:

'Dinah is bathin' Sophy's bottom with cold water. It looks drefful sore an' it's swelled up twice its size. I'se never seen such a bottom as dat woman's got. She won't be able to do no work for three or four days. I'se never had de paddle, an' I hopes I never shall. It's far wuss dan de switch.'

I sent Rosa away, and went into the garden, where I sat until Randolph came back to lunch. In the afternoon we went for a long ride together.

Chapter Seventeen

Defeat of the Federals – Randolph goes to Richmond – I am left in charge – Endeavours to stop the whipping of women – An eventful afternoon – The soldiers arrive – I meet Captain Franklin.

The weeks passed, and in their course, the tide of war flowed nearer to us at Woodlands. The Federal troops had entered Virginia, and many skirmishes had taken place with various results. Then came the battle of Bull's Run, in which as you know, the Federals were utterly defeated. When the news of the Confederate victory arrived at Woodlands, Randolph was jubilant, and he said to me that the damned Yankees would soon be driven out of Virginia. He gave the field-hands a couple of days' holiday, with an extra supply of food and liquor; the house-women also had a treat and were allowed to invite their sweethearts to a dance in the servants' quarters.

I was very sorry to hear of the defeat of the Federal troops, but I did not think that they would be driven out of Virginia.

A short time after the battle of Bull's Run, Randolph was

summoned to Richmond to attend the first meeting of the Congress of the Confederate States. As he expected to be away a considerable time, he gave me full instructions as to what he wished me to do with regard to affairs on the plantation during his absence; and told me I was to write twice a week, informing him exactly how things were going on. He went away a couple of days later, and I was for the second time left alone, but on this occasion I had full charge of everything at Woodlands. He had latterly been treating me with a little more consideration, and though I had not the least love for him, I missed his company a little at first. But I soon settled down contentedly to my solitary life and did what I could to keep up the usual routine of work on the plantation, my efforts being well assisted by the overseers, who had been told to take any orders I might give them. They were trustworthy men, and though rather rough creatures, were always civil to me. I determined that as long as I was mistress on the plantation, there should be as little whipping as possible, at least as far as the women were concerned. So I gave orders that no woman or girl was to be whipped in any way without my sanction. The overseers were very much surprised at my order, but I believe they obeyed it, and at any rate as far as I knew, no woman or girl was whipped during the time I was in charge of the estate. The days passed quietly and uneventfully on the plantation, but outside of it, everything was in a most disturbed state.

Fighting was always going on somewhere, the Federal troops were concentrating in force, and were pressing on Richmond: many of the neighbouring plantations had been occupied by parties of the Union soldiers, and I was daily expecting them to make their appearance at Woodlands. I wrote twice a week to Randolph, giving him particulars of everything that happened, and he wrote to me once a week, his letters always being business ones without a word of love.

At last 'the boys in blue' did come. One afternoon about four o'clock, I happened to be looking out of one of the drawing-room windows, when I saw a party of soldiers led by an officer, and accompanied by an army waggon, coming up the avenue towards the house.

In a few minutes they halted on the terrace, piled their arms, and unpacked the waggon, which contained blankets and other things belonging to the soldiers. My heart began to beat with excitement, and I sat down on the sofa to await the *dénouement* of the affair. In a minute or two, Dinah ushered in the officer, who saluting me politely, said:

'Madam, I have been ordered to occupy this plantation, but I assure you that you shall not be interfered with in any way. I will put my men in the slaves' quarters, but I must ask you to give me a room in the house.'

I rose to my feet, smiling. It did my heart good to see the dear old blue uniform again.

'I am very glad to see you, and your men, sir,' I said. 'I am a Northern woman, and all my sympathies are with you. Take a seat, and I will have a room prepared for you at once.'

He took a chair, looking very much surprised. Then I rang the bell for Dinah, and gave her the requisite orders. The officer was about twenty-seven years of age, a tall, handsome, fair man, with a bronzed face, clear grey eyes, and a long silky blonde moustache. His uniform was a little worn, but it fitted him to perfection, and he was evidently a well-bred gentleman. We entered into conversation, and as there was already a bond of sympathy between us, we were soon chatting and laughing as if we had been old friends. He told me he was a captain in the United States Army, that his name was Franklin, and how he came from Pennsylvania – my own State. This fact made me feel even more friendly towards him, and I informed him that I also was a Pennsylvanian. Then we laughed and shook hands. I could see that it puzzled him how it happened that a Northern woman, and one who openly expressed her sympathy with the Union soldiers, should be apparently the mistress of a Southern plantation. But he was too well-bred to ask questions, and I did not volunteer any explanations. I could not tell my own shame. After talking for some time, he rose from his seat, saying that he must go and see to the quartering of his men. I told him that dinner would be ready at seven o'clock: then he bowed and left the room.

I sent for Dinah, and asked her if she had seen that everything had been got ready for the officer. She replied that she had seen to everything, and had had his valise taken up to the room. I then told her that now the United States troops had come, she and all the other slaves would soon be set free.

'Oh, missis! is dat a fac'?' she exclaimed, showing her white teeth in a broad smile.

'Yes,' I replied.

'Den I'll look after de ossifer myself. He is a fine-looking young gentleman,' she said, bustling away.

I went to my room, dressed for dinner, putting on one of my prettiest frocks, and then I went down to the drawing-room to wait for Captain Franklin. Presently he came in, and after making me a bow, thanked me for the comfortable chamber I had allotted him. I think he was rather surprised to find me in full evening toilette with bare arms and shoulders. He had changed his rather warworn uniform, for an undress jacket and braided pantaloons, and he looked smart, soldierly, and very handsome. Dinner was announced and we went into the dining-room. The meal was a good one, and I had ordered Dinah to get out some champagne, as well as claret and sherry. As Captain Franklin had been campaigning in a very rough way for six months, he thoroughly appreciated the dainty well-cooked dishes and the good wine, and said with a smile, that he was a most fortunate man in having been detailed to occupy Woodlands, instead of having to live in a damp muddy tent, and fare on tough ration beef and hard biscuit. I laughed, saying that I was glad to hear he liked his quarters. Then we talked about all sorts of things, and I thoroughly enjoyed the conversation, finding that I had plenty to say, and was quite able to hold my own in an argument when not snubbed. He was polite and agreeable, treating my opinions with consideration, and never contradicting me. When we went into the drawing-room, he bade me good night, saying that he had to visit his men and mount a guard. He then went away, and I felt quite lonely. His coming to the house had excited me, and I found that I could not settle down quietly to anything that evening, so I went upstairs to my room and got Rosa to brush my hair for half an hour, and then I went to bed.

Some days passed, and I soon found that the presence of the soldiers had caused nearly all the work on the plantation to come to a stand-still. The field hands did pretty much as they pleased, although as yet they were slaves, the proclamation of their freedom not being made until some time afterwards. I had written to Randolph, making him fully acquainted with the state of affairs, and had received a letter in which he said that he would not come back to Woodlands just then. It would be no use, and would only annoy him to see his old home overrun by a lot of damned Yankees. He did not think he would be able to stand it quietly, and there would probably be trouble, which most likely would end in shooting. He also said that he was thinking of taking a house in Richmond, and if he did, he would at once send for me. He wanted me badly, as there was not a decent-looking woman to be had in the place. He wound up by saying that when I came away, I could leave everything in charge of the overseers; if there was anything left to take charge of.

The letter was typical of the man. It was utterly selfish; there was not a word of tenderness in it, and he had not even thought it necessary to be silent about his doings with other women. However, his unfaithfulness did not trouble me in the least, and I only smiled when I read that part of his letter. During the time that had passed, I had seen very little of the soldiers, as they kept well out of the way, but I was pretty well sure they were having a good time with the women and girls belonging to the plantation. I knew that Rosa had secured the sergeant for her beau, as I had seen her one afternoon in a summer-house with him in a rather suspicious attitude. But I did not care how many sweethearts the girl had, or what they did to her, as long as she was at my service whenever I wanted her. And she always was.

Captain Franklin had never obtruded his presence on me, but we met at meals, and he always used to spend an hour with me in the drawing-room after dinner. It was a most pleasant time to me, as he was always agreeable and amusing; moreover, we had many ideas in common, and our natures were sympathetic. I saw that he admired me, and before long I felt pretty sure, from the way he looked at me, and by various other little signs, that he had more than a mere liking for me, although I had but little doubt that he guessed the relations existing between me and the owner of Woodlands. But whether he had or not, he always treated me with respect, and I could not help contrasting his courteous, gentlemanly manner, with the coarse, and often brutal way, in which Randolph had nearly always treated me.

Chapter Eighteen

My first love – Captain Franklin's reserve – I employ the courtesan's art of seduction – Low-necked dress and violet perfume – Unwinding a skein of wool – I faint in Franklin's arms and what happened – The violence of his attack – Our mutual passion – The end of the romance.

From the day Captain Franklin came to the house, I liked him, and as I got to know him better, my feelings had gradually grown warmer, until at last I fell in love with him. It was the first time in my life that I had felt the passion. It took full possession of me, and I was always thinking of Franklin when he was not with me. Then I began to want to feel his kisses on my lips, and I longed to lie in his arms. I had not disliked being poked by Randolph, for whom I had not the slightest affection, therefore I thought how delightful it would be to be embraced by the man I loved. Randolph had never cared for me; he had not scrupled to tell me he was unfaithful to me, and above all he had possessed himself of me originally by most cruel means, therefore I did not consider that I was in the least way bound to be faithful to him.

He certainly had given me plenty of fine clothes, and a quantity of jewellery, but then – as he would probably have said himself – he had taken the value out of my body. Anyhow, I thought he had most fully. I became quite lovesick on account of Franklin, or to put it more truly, though in coarser language, I wanted to be well poked by him. But although he had plenty of opportunities, he never made love to me, even in the mildest manner, and yet I felt sure that he did love me. I could not make out whether his reserve was caused by shyness, or by a sense of honour that would not allow him to make advances to a defenceless woman who was quite in his power. Three or four more days passed without his showing more warmth, and as my 'love-sickness' was increasing, and as there was only one cure for it, I determined to make the first advance. Randolph had instructed me well in all the little artifices by which a woman may allure a man. I would try the effect of one or two of them on my cold lover. I remembered that Randolph had told me that if a man happened to be fond of perfume, the odour of it on a woman increased his sensual desire for her. Franklin liked the perfume of violets; so that night when I was dressing for dinner, I sprinkled my chemise and hair with the delicate but strong essence. I then put on my finest petticoats, and a pair of very dainty drawers, with deep frills of lace, drawn in at the knees with bows of pale blue satin ribbon. I then encased my legs in pink openwork silk stockings, and put on my feet a pretty pair of bronze leather high-heeled shoes, with silver buckles. I next made Rosa lace me tightly in my corset, and finally I put on a very low-necked frock. When I was fully dressed, I gazed at myself in the pier glass, feeling perfectly satisfied with my appearance. My dress fitted me to perfection, my cheeks were tinged with a faint pink colour, my eyes were bright, and my bare shoulders and arms looked very white and plump. I went down to the drawing-room, where I found Franklin, whom I had not seen all day, as he had been away on some military duty since early in the morning. We shook hands, and I let my hand linger in his,

166

but he did not press it, although I saw he noticed my more than usually elaborate toilette.

The dinner passed over quickly, and we were both in good spirits, chatting and laughing merrily. When we went into the drawing-room I began to exercise my arts. Seating myself on a foot-stool, just under the lamp, I asked him to hold a tangled skein of wool for me while I wound it. To do this, he would have to stand close to my knees and look down at my hands as I wound the wool. He took up his position in the very way I wanted, and while I moved my arms to and fro winding the wool, I at the same time, in an apparently unconscious manner, swayed my body so that he could if he chose, see the upper part of my bosom and the division between my titties. At first, he kept his eyes steadily fixed on my hands, but after a few moments his gaze was turned upon my half-naked bosom, and I saw his eyes begin to sparkle as he looked into the depths of my corset. I smiled inwardly, saying to myself that I had at last made him show some sign of feeling. Affecting a serene unconsciousness, I continued to show my titties and to wind the wool till it was all done. Then putting my hand to my forehead and closing my eyes, I complained of a sudden faintness, saying that I would lie down on the sofa for a few minutes.

He appeared to be very much concerned, and he asked me anxiously, if he could get me anything. I shook my head, then rising feebly to my feet, I stood swaying about as if I was on the point of fainting, and he, thinking I was going to fall, put his arm round my waist to hold me up. The moment he did so, I collapsed limply in his arms with my head against his breast, and my eyes closed. I ought to have turned pale, but I was not able to do that – however, it never struck him that it was strange I should have kept my colour all through my 'fainting fit.'

With an ejaculation of pity, he tenderly raised me in his arms, carried me to the sofa, and laid me down upon it. I pretended to be quite insensible, but I kept my eyes half-open, and I had managed to slyly raise my skirts nearly up to my knees, so that my feet and legs were exposed. He began to

167

chafe my hands, but I saw that his eyes were fixed on my legs, and I noticed that his face had become a little flushed. Opening my eyes, I said smiling:

'Oh, I am all right now. It was only a slight attack of giddiness and it has quite passed off.'

As I spoke I stretched myself, so as to show more of my legs, and bring into view the frills of my drawers. Still holding one of my hands, he sat down close beside me, looking in my face most tenderly and affectionately.

Taking my handkerchief from my pocket, I passed it over my forehead, and then I let my hand drop, as if by accident, on the upper part of his thighs. I felt him start, and I saw a soft light shining in his eyes, which were again fixed upon my legs. I pressed his thighs with my fingers. Then all his reserve disappeared; he bent down and kissing me on the lips, said in a tone of passion:

'Oh, my darling girl I love you! and have loved you, from the first day I came here.'

His kiss was a fervent one, but tender. It was a kiss of love; the first I had ever received; and it made me thrill with a delicious sensation from head to foot.

Throwing my arms round his neck, I exclaimed:

'And I love you too. Give me another nice kiss.'

Again he kissed me on the mouth, then pressing his lips upon my bosom just above the edge of my dress, he inhaled the violet perfume, saying: 'How sweet you are dearest! Violet is my favourite scent.'

I again closed my eyes, and settled myself well down upon the sofa, feeling pretty sure that I would soon have my desire gratified. It was! Now that the ice had been broken, Franklin was no 'laggard in love.' He felt my legs, praising their shape, admiring my pretty shoes and stockings, and also the dainty lace frills of my drawers. But he soon put his hands up my petticoats, and untying the strings of my drawers, pulled them down, then his hands roved all over my bottom, and he did not neglect the 'spot' between my thighs. However, he did not waste much time in dalliance. In a moment or two, he prepared himself, then raising my petticoats, he stretched out my legs, and opening the way with his fingers, inserted the tip of his member in the 'spot' which was ready to receive it. Clasping me in his arms, and pressing his lips upon my mouth, he gently but firmly forced the dart deeply into my body, with a few strong movements of his loins, and then he began to poke me in the most powerful way. He was eight years younger than Randolph, larger made, and much more vigorous.

The force of the attack almost took my breath away, while the size of the weapon stretched the sheath to its utmost extent, but I only felt a sensation of intense pleasure at being at last embraced by the man I loved. All my voluptuous feelings were excited to a high pitch by the friction of his large member in the folds of the sensitive 'spot,' so I was not backwards in the amorous combat. Pressing him to my bosom, and throwing my legs round his loins, I met each of his strong down-thrusts with a brisk upward heave of my bottom. He increased the length of his strokes, his member seemed to go deeper into me, and as the end approached his movements became quicker and quicker, while I bounded under him, arching my loins, and sighing and groaning in an ecstasy of voluptuous pain. At last, with a final tremendous dig, he 'spent,' while I wriggled my bottom convulsively, and squirmed till I had received every drop of my lover's offering. Then heaving a deep sigh of gratified desire, I lay quietly in his arms, while he kissed and petted me. It had been a most delightful embrace. I had never before so thoroughly enjoyed being poked. I think that a man always enjoys poking a woman whether he loves her or not: but I am sure that a woman never really enjoys a man's embrace unless she loves him.

After a moment or two of kissing and soft words, he withdrew his still half-stiff member from the clinging lips which were loath to let it go, and then he pulled down my clothes, and buttoned up his trousers. I got off the sofa, and after arranging my disordered attire, I sat in an easy chair, and looked with a smile at my stalwart lover. He smiled lovingly back, and coming to me lifted me out of the chair;

but sitting down in it himself, he took me on his knees, and putting his arms around my waist, held me, while I nestled close up to him with my head on his breast.

After a little love talk, I told him why I had originally come to Virginia, afterwards relating what had been done to me, and how I had been forced by torture to come to Woodlands. He was moved by my story, and when I had finished it, he kissed me and sympathized with me. Then he said;

'I am not a rich man, so I cannot offer you a house and luxuries such as you have here. But I love you, and when the war is over, I will gladly take you to live with me, if you will come.'

'Oh, I shall be only too delighted to go to you,' I replied earnestly. 'But are you sure you really love me?'

'I do really love you,' he answered, kissing me affectionately on the forehead.

It delighted me to hear him say those words, and I made him repeat them. Nestling closer up to him, I returned his kisses with interest, and as my desire was not yet satisfied, I unbuttoned his trousers and let out the thing I wanted. He laughed, and after a little play with my bottom, was ready for action. He then again laid me on the sofa, and gave me another delicious poke, followed by a long chat, sitting side by side on the sofa. When it was bedtime, he wanted to come to my room and sleep with me, but I would not let him, as I did not want the women to know anything about my doings. So after a long and loving kiss we parted for the night. I must say though that I should have very much liked to have cuddled up to him all night 'spoon fashion.'

Next morning we met in the dining-room, both of us bright and cheerful, and after kissing each other affectionately we sat down to breakfast with good appetites. When the meal was over, I took my sweetheart to my favourite little arbour which was an ideal place for love-making, and in a short time I was sighing in his arms. Then there passed several days of quiet happiness. Franklin was constantly with me; we wandered about the garden together, or sat in the arbours with our arms round each other's waists like the fondest of lovers. And we *were* lovers. I think he really did love me, and I know I did love him. He rogered me every day, some time or other, and I seemed to get fonder and fonder of his embraces. They were done so vigorously and yet so decently. He always had me in the one position – lying on my back – and he never exposed my person more than was absolutely necessary. **I think a man copulates with the woman he loves differently to the way he pokes the woman he merely lusts for**. We used to talk and make plans as to what we would do in the future, when the war was over, and we were back in Pennsylvania. It was all very nice, and we both hoped that the fighting would soon cease, so that we might live together.

In the meantime I would have to remain at Woodlands. But our love-making was suddenly put an end to by Franklin receiving orders to withdraw his detachment, and return to the headquarters of his regiment. I was deeply grieved at his having to go, and he was equally grieved at having to leave me, but as we had both known that the order was bound to come sooner or later, we made the best of it, and cheered each other up.

Next morning when we had finished breakfast, he laid me on the sofa and gave me a farewell 'visit.' Then after bidding me good-bye, and promising to write to me, he kissed me tenderly and left the house. I stood at the window, with tears in my eyes, watching my lover at the head of his men marching down the avenue, and when they reached the bend leading to the gate, Franklin turned round, and waved his sword to me in a parting salute.

And so ended my little romance. It had not lasted long, and I have never had another in my life so far.

I may as well here tell you that I never saw my soldier lover again, as he was killed a year afterwards at the battle of Cedar Mountain. At that time, I was living in New York, but I mourned for him sincerely, as I had never ceased to love him, and I still keep the letters he wrote to me, and also a lock of his hair that he gave me the day he parted.

Chapter Nineteen

The country is occupied by the Federals – The slaves demoralized – Randolph instructs me to join him at Richmond – 'Bushwackers' and their depredations.

But to resume. A fortnight passed, and a very wretched time it was to me in every way. I missed my lover; the slaves on the plantation were very insubordinate; and I was troubled at the idea of having again to live with Randolph.

I had written to tell him that the soldiers had left Woodlands, and asking him when he intended to return. He answered saying that he had not made up his mind what to do, whether to come back or to send for me, but he would let me know in due course. Meanwhile I was to see that the affairs on the plantation were carried on as usual. I was so vexed at his letter that I sat down and cried. It was very easy for him, amusing himself in Richmond to tell me to see to his affairs, but things had got into such an utterly disorganized state, that it was quite impossible for me to keep order. I was only a girl, not twenty-two years of age. All work on the plantation had come to an end, as the whole country for miles round was occupied by the Federal troops, and the slaves, knowing that their freedom was at hand, would hardly do anything, while the overseers, under the circumstances, no longer dared to enforce the discipline by their usual methods. Many of the field-hands had run away and no attempt to capture them could be made, while others had openly joined the negro regiments which were being raised by the United States authorities. The majority of the house-women too, had become utterly demoralized, and several of them had gone off, but others, among whom were Dinah and Rosa, had remained faithful. After a few more days, I wrote again to Randolph, telling him that things were getting worse and worse, and saying that I was afraid to remain any longer by myself at Woodlands. This time, I received a letter saying: That as things at the moment were in such a bad state in Virginia, it was no use his trying to keep the plantation going any longer. I was, however, to tell the overseers that he would continue to pay them their salaries if they would remain on the estate and do the best they could for him. He had taken a furnished house, and I was to go to him as soon as possible. The house at Woodlands was to be shut up, and left in charge of Dinah and the other women who had remained.

I was glad to get at last some definitive instructions; for the strain on me had been almost more than I could bear, and I had got into a low nervous state.

Sending for the faithful Dinah, I told her that I was going to join her master in Richmond, and that I intended to start in three days' time. I also informed her that she was to take charge of the house, and I gave her instructions about shutting up. Then I wrote to Randolph, telling him when to expect me.

Next day, I saw the overseers, and gave them their employer's message. The men said they would remain on the plantation and do the best they could to prevent things going to ruin, but they added that there was no chance of getting the slaves to do much work as long as the Federal troops were in the neighbourhood. I spent the following day in packing my trunks, and settling affairs, as far as I could, with Dinah and the other women. They were all sorry that I was about to leave them, though delighted at the idea of being left alone in the house to do as they pleased without fear of a whipping.

The only way for me to get to Richmond – which was thirty-two miles distant – was by driving, and I intended to start at four o'clock in the afternoon, so as to arrive at my destination about eight o'clock. I chose four o'clock as the hour of starting in order that I might escape the heat of the day. All the horses were still in the stables, and some of the grooms had remained; one of them being an old and faithful negro coachman, named Jim, who had taught me to ride, and in whom I had perfect confidence. I sent for him and told him that I wanted him to drive me to Richmond next day, and that he was to have the pair-horse buggy ready at four o'clock.

'Very well, missis,' he said. 'I'll put yo' through all right if I kin. But don't yo' take no money or joolery along with yo'; 'cos de road nowdays is 'fested wid dem low down cusses ob bush-wackers; an' if we was ter come across any ob dem, dey would most sholy rob yo'.'

It had never struck me that there would be any danger in the drive to Richmond, but now that Jim had mentioned the bushwhackers, I remembered that I had lately heard several stories of the lawless doings of these men. 'Bush-whackers,' I must tell you, were low white loafers, who, while pretending to act as guerillas against the Federal troops, were in reality highwaymen, who robbed and sometimes murdered defenceless people, whether they were Northerners or Southerners. Bands of these ruffians infested the Southern States during the war.

I sent Jim away, but I thought I would follow his advice; so going upstairs, I opened my trunks, and taking out all my jewellery, locked the articles up in a safe that was built in the wall of Randolph's bedroom.

The rest of the day wore slowly away; I was restless and nervous; I could not eat my dinner, and I went to bed early.

Chapter Twenty

Farewell to the plantation – On the road – Stopped by the 'bushwhackers' – Robbed, kidnapped, and the awful consequences.

I had a good night's rest and got up next morning feeling well and also much calmer in my mind. After breakfast, I made a few final arrangements, and at four o'clock the buggy, with a fine pair of horses, was driven round to the terrace by Jim. The two trunks I intended taking with me were brought down, and put into the vehicle. I shook hands with Dinah and Rosa, my two favourites, bidding them good-bye and telling them to take care of everything in the house as well as they could. Then climbing up into my seat, I waved a general farewell to all the other women who had come out to the terrace to see me off; and they shouted in shrill chorus: 'Good-bye, missis!'

Then Jim touched the horses with the whip, and we started on our journey. It was a beautiful afternoon, but very hot, though there was a faint breeze stirring; however, as I was lightly clad, I did not feel the heat oppressive. We were soon out of the avenue, and as the comfortable buggy rolled smoothly and quickly along the road, the rapid motion caused the warm, scented air to lightly kiss my cheeks; my spirits rose, and I had a feeling of exhilaration such as had long been a stranger to me. I was not looking forward to seeing Randolph, but I felt glad because I was at last free from the load of care that had been weighing me down during the past few weeks at Woodlands. The road we were travelling was a good one, and, before the war, there had always been a great deal of traffic on it, but now it was almost deserted, so we did not meet a single vehicle until we had gone several miles, and there were very few pedestrians. To pass the time, I talked to Jim and was rather amused by his quaint but shrewd remarks on things in general. When I told him that most likely all the slaves in the South would soon be set free, he remarked in his own jargon, that no doubt it would be very nice to be free, but that, after all, freedom would not fill his belly, and that he would not be able to make a living if Mr Randolph did not keep him. Old Jim had been born at Woodlands, and had never been out of Virginia.

As there was no necessity for hurry; I told him not to press the horses, so we trotted along at an easy pace, and by six o'clock had completed half our journey. We then reached the top of a very steep hill, and entered a long stretch of road running through a thick wood. Jim had just pulled up the horses to give them a short rest, when four rough-looking men suddenly appeared from the bushes, and covered us with their revolvers.

'Drop the reins and hold up your hands, you nigger!' shouted one of the men.

Exclaiming in a low tone: 'By gosh, missis, de bushwhackers has got us!' Jim held up his hands, while I, dreadfully frightened, uttered a shriek, and cowering down, averted my eyes from the threatening muzzles of the pistols. Two of the men lowered their weapons, and came to the side of the buggy, while the other two kept their revolvers levelled at us. Then one of the bushwhackers, a burly, black-bearded ruffian, said with an oath:

176

'Get out of the buggy, the pair of you; but don't attempt to run away, or you'll both git holes bored in you.'

We got out, and stood on the road, side by side. Jim was quite unmoved, and though I had been alarmed at first, I was beginning to feel less frightened. I thought the men would merely take everything they wanted, and then let us go on. Seeing that we had no idea of attempting to escape, the bushwhackers returned their pistols to their belts, and began their work of pillage. The traces of the horses were cut; then one of the men mounted one of the animals and, leading the other, rode off at a brisk trot down the road. It had never struck me that they would take the horses, and I wondered how I was to get to Richmond. The three men who remained threw my trunks on the road, and breaking them open, tossed out all my dresses and linen, searching for articles of more value to them than woman's clothing. But finding nothing, they broke into loud curses and kicked my things all over the road. The blackbearded man, who appeared to be the leader, then told me to hand over my purse.

I did so, but as there was only five dollars in it, he gave vent to his feelings of disappointment in a fresh volley of oaths that made me shiver. The men then going a short distance away, talked with each other in low tones, occasionally bursting out laughing, while I stood in suspense, wondering what was going to happen next. After a minute or two, the leader came back to us and addressing Jim, said:

'See here now, old darkie, I know whar you come from, so jest you start off and go straight back to Woodlands, and don't as much as look back or it'll be the worse for you. Now git!'

Jim gazed at me for a moment, with a dog-like expression of faithfulness in his eyes and a resolute look on his rugged black face, then turning to the man, said firmly:

'No, sah, I'll not leave my missis.'

The man drew his revolver, and pointing it at Jim, said savagely:

'You damned nigger! we'll take care of your mistress, and if you don't start right away, I'll put a bullet through your woolly head.'

Jim never flinched, but stood quite still, looking steadily at the man. I am a coward, but at that moment I felt brave. I could not allow Jim to sacrifice his life uselessly. It struck me that the men meant to keep me prisoner to extract money for my ransom, so I said:

'It will be no use your remaining with me, Jim. So you had better go back to the house.'

'Oh, missis,' he said, 'I don't like to leave yo', but if yo' tink it ain't no good my stayin' I'll go, an' praps I may be able to do sumthin' for yo'.'

He then walked slowly away, turning round every now and then to look back at me. I watched the faithful old negro, who I know would have sacrificed his life for me, till he had passed out of my sight down the slope of the hill, then I burst into tears, feeling utterly forlorn. Two of the men picked up some of my things, and made them in a bundle, while the leader said to me, in a quiet tone:

'Now come along with us, and we'll put you up for the night in our shanty, and to-morrow I daresay you'll be able to get a lift on to Richmond, if you want to go there.'

Then taking me by the arm, he led me through the bushes at the side of the road into a path. The other two men followed, and we walked through the gloomy wood for about a mile, until at last we came to a small shanty. They took me in, and as it was quite dark, one of the men lighted a rude lamp, which enabled me to see the place in which I was to pass the night. It was a squalid-looking place: the floor was the earth, the walls were of squared logs, and the ceiling was made of shingles. The furniture consisted of an unpainted wooden table, three or four benches and stools, a couple of tin buckets holding water, and three rough-looking beds covered with deerskin. On the open hearth a fire of logs was smouldering, and there were a few cooking utensils scattered about.

Chapter Twenty-one

In Bill Jackson's gang – The supper in the shanty – I am violated by the three ruffians – 'Spread-eagled' and stark-naked – observations on the difference in the members of the ruthless scoundrels.

I had been a little relieved at hearing that I was to be allowed to go in the morning, but I did not like the prospect of spending the night in the dirty shanty with the three men. One of them threw some fresh logs on the fire, and when it had burnt up, he fried some bacon, which he put on the table in the frying-pan along with a piece of corn bread, a bottle of whiskey, and some tin plates and pannikins. The men, each one drawing his sheath knife, sat down to the rough supper, and they offered me some, but I could not eat a morsel, though I drank some water. Then sitting down wearily on a stool at the far end of the room, I watched my captors as they devoured their food. All three were coarse-looking fellows; the black-bearded man, who was called by his companions Bill Jackson, was about forty years of age; the other two men, who addressed each other as Frank and Tom, were respectively about thirty and thirty-five years old. While the meal was in progress, they did not talk to each other, nor did they speak to me, but every now and then, one of them would glance at me with a smile on his face. And yet, strange to say, it did not strike me that my person was in danger. When they had finished eating, they smoked corn-cob pipes, chatting a little, and passing round the bottle of whiskey till it was finished, but they were all perfectly sober.

Then the man Jackson rose from his seat, and coming over to me, said with a coarse laugh:

'We've been greatly disappointed at not havin' found anything in your trunks wuth a dollar to us. Now we ain't men who works for nothin', so we're bound to git sumthin' out of you.'

'Oh,' I exclaimed eagerly; 'I shall be glad to give you anything you want. If one of you will come to Richmond with me tomorrow, my husband, Mr Randolph, will pay you the money.'

I called him my 'husband,' thinking to impress the men. But they burst out laughing, and Jackson said:

'We know better than that. Randolph is not your husband an' I guess he would not pay much for you: but whether he would, or not, nary one of us 'ull go to Richmond to see. There is rather a prejudice agin us in the city, and if we was to go there we would never get away again. So as it is impossible for us to make any money out of you, we intend to make you pay us in another way. We are going to fuck you.'

To adequately describe the horrible events of that night I shall have to use the words the ruffians used. Aghast and utterly horrified, I sprung to my feet, and bursting into tears, exclaimed in a choking voice:

'Oh, don't do such a thing to a defenceless woman! I will send you any money you like if you will not touch me. Oh! Let me go!'

They laughed. Then my terror changed to anger, and I threatened them with the consequences that would follow if they dared to outrage me. But they only laughed more. Then I tried to wheedle them and coax them into letting me go, but

180

without effect, and then again I begged and prayed them to spare me, as the story of poor Peachie came back vividly to my agonized brain. But all my tears, threats, coaxings and entreaties were useless – in fact, my abject fear and intense misery seemed highly to amuse the wretches – and Jackson said:

'Now see here, young woman; you may jest as well shut up. We are going to fuck you. Will you take the fucking quietly or will you not?'

'No! No! no!' I cried. 'I will not let you do it to me! You shan't do it to me! Oh, you miserable cowards! Don't dare to touch me! Oh, you beasts! you wretches!'

The more I raved in my rage and fear, the more they laughed.

'Well,' said Jackson, 'if you won't take it quietly, you'll have to take it fighting. Now lads, let's strip the little bitch and "spread-eagle" her.'

The three then seized me, and I fought, kicked, scratched, and tried to bite, at the same time uttering loud shrieks, but, in spite of my frantic struggles, the men easily carried me to one of the beds and laid me on it. Then, holding me down, they began to strip me, turning me over and over, wrenching off the buttons, breaking the strings of my garments and pulling them off roughly, until I was stark naked, except for my shoes and stockings, while I resisted with all my strength, screaming, crying and begging them not to 'do it' to me.

Laying me on my back, they stretched out my arms and legs as widely as possible, fastening my wrists and ankles with ropes to the side of the bed. I was thus 'spread-eagled', and entirely at their mercy. Standing beside the bed, they looked down upon me, their eyes gleaming with lust as they scanned every part of my naked body, while at the same time they made admiring remarks on my shape, the whiteness of my skin, and the golden colour of the hair shading the 'spot.' From words they proceeded to deeds. They began to feel me, and I had three pairs of hands on my body at the same time. While one was squeezing my titties, and pinching the nipples, another was pulling the hair on the 'spot,' and tickling the lips with his finger, while the third was feeling my thighs and bottom.

Then they would change about, so that at last everyone had felt my shrinking body from head to foot. They touched me roughly, their hands were coarse and hard, I was sick with disgust, and I cried and trembled, but I had given up screaming. When the wretches had felt me to their hearts' content, a difficulty arose. Each man wanted to be the first to 'have' me, and so they came to high words, but no one would give way. At last one of them suggested that they should settle the matter by cutting a pack of cards, the man who cut the highest being allowed to poke me first, and the next highest to follow. This was agreed to. Then a dirty pack of cards was produced, and cut by the men in turn. The youngest man cut a knave, the man Jackson came next with a ten, and the third man cut a seven. You can imagine what I felt while my body was being disposed of in such a way. It had been intensely revolting to me to be pawed all over by three men simultaneously, but it would be still more revolting to be poked by three coarse ruffians, in succession. The thought was maddening, and I lay writhing in my bonds, my bosom heaving, my heart swelling, and the scalding tears running down my scarlet cheeks.

The man who was to 'have' me first, unbuttoned his trousers, letting out his member, which stood stiffly erect, and I could not help looking at it with a sort of fascination, noticing that it was long but not very thick. Saying:

'Here goes for the fust fuck,' he threw himself upon me like a tiger seizing its prey, and clasping my naked body in his arms, tried to get the weapon into the sheath.

But at first he could not succeed, for although my extremities were tightly secured; I could move my loins, and so I twisted about as much as was possible, thus for some time preventing his entering me.

The other men meanwhile stood looking on, laughing and jeering at their companion's vain efforts, and telling him that he didn't know how to get into a woman. The struggle lasted for some time, but at last I became exhausted and lay still for a moment. Then before I could recover my breath and renew the fight, the man got his long 'thing' into me, up to the roots, and began to poke me furiously, at the same time pressing his lips to mine with loathsome kisses.

Filled with disgust, I lay shuddering under him while he worked away at me, but as he was highly excited, the end soon arrived, and though I could not help receiving his copious discharge, and though nature forced me to 'come,' I had no feeling but one of loathing, so I never moved at the supreme spasm.

He got off me, saying in a tone of vexation:

'She is a damned bad poke! I thought my prick was long enough to have stirred her up, but the bitch had no more life in her than a log of wood.'

The brutes laughed. The man Jackson then made ready for the assault, displaying to my horrified eyes a tremendous weapon, which he shook up and down, saying with a horrid laugh:

'I'll bet this yer little thing will make her squeak if it does nothing else.' He added: 'This'll be the first time, to my knowledge, that I've ever "had" a buttered bun.'

He then got on the bed between my widely-stretched legs, but he did not at once attack me like his predecessor. Turning to the other two men, who were looking on grinning, he said:

'I always take my time over a job of this sort, and I like to play with a woman before fucking her.'

Then he played with me, feeling my titties with both his hands, and also sucking the nipples one after the other. He then passed his hands over every part of my body, stroking my thighs, pinching my bottom, and pulling the hair on the 'spot,' and finally he thrust his finger deeply in, hurting me dreadfully, and making me utter a shriek, while my body quivered all over, and I entreated him not to torture me in such a way. Removing his finger, he inserted his member – I made no useless resistance this time – and with some difficulty forced the great thing into its place. Then gripping me firmly, with his hands under my bottom, he began to poke me slowly with long thrusts, each time drawing the dart out till only the tip was left between the lips, then driving it in again with great force, each tremendous dig shaking me all over and making me wince, and as the parts were stretched to the utmost by the great size of the column as it was worked up and down in me, I suffered considerably and uttered cries of pain. He spun the affair out as long as he possibly could, while I lay groaning in misery under the terrible battering, and trying to hold myself back, but again nature obliged me to 'come' before he did. Oh! it was horrible! At last he quickened his movements, then in a few seconds he 'spent' and the jets of fluid spurted up me, while I heaved a sigh of relief when I felt his great 'thing' shrink in size inside the folds of my 'spot,' but I never moved my bottom. My disgust was increasing.

He withdrew, saying:

'Well, she certainly ain't much as a poke, but she's got a nice little c....t, and my big p....k made her squeak, as I said it would.' Then turning to the third man, he said laughing: 'But you'll be able to get into her easy enough, Tom, as her tight slit is well greased by this time.'

The man laughed, saying, 'Yes, her c....t is well buttered.'

He then prepared himself, and I saw that he was the smallest of the three, though the instrument he displayed was in full erection. He lost no time in preliminaries, but at once laid himself down on me and with his two forefingers separated me without the least difficulty, and began to poke me quietly, but with plenty of vigour, so that in a few seconds I was for the third time deluged with hot sperm, and for the third time I received the discharge without stirring, but with a sickening sensation of disgust. He then got off me without making any remark, and I thought the horrible ordeal was over, and that they would release me. But to my horror, they did not, though I begged them piteously to let me go.

'We've not done with you, my girl,' said Jackson.

Leaving me tied up on the bed, weeping and shivering with shame and despair, the men filled their pipes, and sitting down on stools, chatted coolly with each other about me and the way I had behaved while being poked, and while they talked they gazed at my naked palpitating body. When they had smoked their pipes they came to the bedside again. Faint and sick with disgust, shame, fear and horror, I wailed pitifully, beseeching them to have mercy on me, and not to touch me again, saying that it would kill me. I might have spared my breath. They only laughed and Jackson observed that a woman could take twenty men without being a bit the worse. Again I begged and prayed them abjectly to let me go, but nothing moved the brutes. They had neither pity nor compassion.

However, I need not enter further into the details of my martyrdom; it will suffice to say that they all three poked me again one after the other, and when the last man had withdrawn his member from my quivering body, the receptacle was filled to overflowing by the six copious discharges it had received, so that the hair was covered with the horrid stuff, and it was also trickling in thick drops down my thighs. I was in a half fainting state; there was a cold sweat on my forehead, my flesh was bruised by the rough way I had been handled, and my whole body was jerking convulsively, while the unutterable disgust and loathing that overwhelmed me, caused me to have an intense feeling of nausea.

They unfastened my wrists and ankles which had red marks round them where the ropes had chafed the skin, and then Jackson threw a blanket over my naked body, telling me that I might go to sleep if I could, as they had got as much out of me as they wanted. Drawing the blanket over my head, I huddled myself up, crying miserably. The men took no further notice of me, but sat smoking and talking in low tones for about half an hour; then leaving the lamp burning, they threw themselves in their clothes upon the other beds, and in a short time I knew by their snoring that they were fast asleep.

My mouth was dreadfully parched, and the 'spot' was throbbing painfully. I wanted a drink so slipping quietly off the bed, I got a tin cup, and going to the bucket of water, quenched my thirst. I then bathed the red and swollen lips of the 'spot,' and washed off my body all outward traces of the

185

horrible pollution. I dressed myself in my tumbled garments, and lay down again on the bed, hoping to forget for a time in sleep the horrors through which I had passed. But though I was physically and mentally worn out, sleep would not come to me. I shall never forget the misery of the long night I spent in the shanty, tossing and turning on the dirty bed. I was feverish at one moment, and chilly the next, but all the time I felt sick with disgust, haunted moreover by a dreadful fear that the wretches might not let me go in the morning. I would have run away to the woods and tried to find my way back to the road, but the door was locked and the small window was closed by a heavy shutter. But if I had managed to get out of the shanty, I should have lost myself in the thick wood and been starved to death.

Chapter Twenty-two

Daybreak and breakfast – Renewed fears and forced kisses on the mouth – I am liberated – The friendly carrier – Arrival at Richmond and meeting with Randolph.

I don't think I ever lost consciousness during the weary hours, and I thought the morning would never come, but at last I saw the welcome daylight showing through the chinks in the shutter. Presently the men woke, and getting off the beds, stood yawning and stretching themselves for a moment or two; then looking at me, they laughed, making remarks about my pale cheeks and red eyes, while I lay in dire suspense, fearing that one or another of the ruffians would take it into his head to poke me again. But to my intense relief no one touched me. The window was opened, and the fire was lighted, some bacon was fried and a pot of coffee made; then the men sat down to breakfast, ordering me to sit at the other side of the table and join them in their meal.

With downcast eyes and flaming cheeks, I seated myself opposite the three brutes who had outraged me so shamefully, and as I was very faint, I tried to eat a bit of bread, but it stuck in my throat. I managed however to drink a pannikin of the milkless coffee, which, bad as it was, refreshed me a little.

When the rough meal was over, and the men had lighted their pipes, I raised my eyes, and addressing Jackson, reminded him of his promise to let me go.

'Oh, do please let me go,' I pleaded earnestly, bursting into tears, and stretching my hands towards him, appealingly. 'You have nearly killed me. Surely you won't be so cruel as to keep me.'

He looked at me for a short time, and my heart seemed to stand still. At last he said:

'You are a pretty girl, and though you are a bad poke, you are better than nothing. We'd like to keep you for further fucking, but you'd be in our way, so we'll let you go. I'll put you through the woods to the road, and then you can either go back to Woodlands, or on to Richmond; both are the same distance away, about sixteen miles. You can come along at once if you like.'

A dreadful weight was lifted from my heart, and I rose from my seat eagerly.

'Oh, I am quite ready to start.'

He laughed.

'All right,' he said, 'but you must first shake hands with us, bid us good-bye and give us each a nice kiss on the lips.'

So I had to kiss each of the ruffians in turn, bidding him good-bye, and as I did so, each man put his hands up my clothes and felt the 'spot.' Jackson then left the shanty, and I followed him; he evidently wished to confuse me as to the exact position of the place, so he led me by devious paths through the woods for at least a couple of miles before bringing me out on to the road. Then, after pointing to the direction in which Richmond lay, and telling me that I could not miss my way, he disappeared in the bushes.

There was not a person in sight, and I sat down on a log at the side of the road, uncertain what to do, whether to go back to Woodlands, or on to Richmond. But I did not quite see how I was to get to either place, as I could not possibly have walked the distance. Under ordinary circumstances, I was a good walker, and would have thought very little of a walk of sixteen miles, but at that moment I was weak and faint, sore and stiff; every movement of my legs causing me pain. Not knowing what to do, I began to cry in sheer helplessness, thinking what a dreadfully unfortunate woman I was in every way. But a bit of luck came to me. I had been sitting by the roadside for about ten minutes, when I saw in the distance, a farm-wagon coming along the road in my direction, and when it had got close to me, I perceived it was being driven by a respectable-looking middle-aged man. Rising from my seat on the log, I tearfully asked him if he would kindly give me a lift towards Richmond.

He pulled up his horse at once, said he would, and then giving me his hand, helped me into the wagon and made me as comfortable as he could, looking rather curiously at me, but asking no questions. I gave him a short account of how I had been stopped on my journey and robbed by bushwhackers, but I was silent as to the other things that had been done to me.

He was full of sympathy for me, and anger against the bushwhackers in general, who he said ought all to be lynched. Then he added:

'I reckoned thar was suthin' wrong when I see a lady like you a settin' by the roadside cryin'. Dern this war! There's no law or order now in the whole state of Virginny. I wish I was out of it and back in Connecticut, whar I come from.'

I was glad to hear that he was a Northerner, the fact seemed to give me greater confidence in the man. I had got to be frightened and suspicious of all Southerners. I told him that I also came from the North, and heartily wished I was back there. On hearing that he insisted on shaking hands; then he informed me that he was going all the way to Richmond, and expected to get there in about three hours – it was then ten o'clock. The wagon was heavily laden, so we jogged along the road slowly, and almost in silence. He was a taciturn man, while I, as you may suppose, was not inclined to talk at that moment. In fact, it was as much as I could do to prevent myself crying.

When at length we reached the outskirts of the city, the man said most kindly that if I would give him my address, he would drive me to it.

I thanked him gratefully, telling him where to go, and in about half an hour we reached the house which Randolph had taken furnished. It was a comfortable-looking, three-storied, detached building standing in a garden, and situated in one of the best parts of Richmond.

The kind man got out of the wagon and helped me down; then I asked him to come into the house and see 'my husband,' who would like to thank him, and also reward him for the service he had rendered me. But the good fellow said he wanted no reward, and that he was glad he had been able to help a Northern lady in distress. Then he bade me good-bye, and drove off.

I knocked at the door, which was opened by a good-looking, smartly-dressed, white servant-girl, and I asked her if Mr Randolph was at home. She looked curiously at me for a moment, then asked civilly if I was the lady Mr Randolph had expected to arrive the previous night? I said that I was, and she at once asked me to come in, and then ushered me into a handsomely furnished dining-room, where I found Randolph seated at lunch.

He did not rise from his chair, but sat staring at me in surprise, noticing my pale face, red eyes, and generally draggled appearance, then he said in an aggrieved tone:

'Why, Dolly, what an object you are! Where on earth have you been? What has happened to you? I expected you at eight o'clock last night. Where is Jim and the buggy?'

I had not expected to be received with much show of affection, but his cold manner annoyed me very much. I was in need of sympathy and kindness at that moment.

'Oh, don't bother me with questions,' I said sharply. 'I have had hardly anything to eat for twenty-four hours, and I am faint with hunger, so I mean to have something to eat and drink before I tell you what has happened.'

He looked quite surprised at my unwonted display of

spirit, but drew a chair to the table for me, poured me out a glass of wine and helped me to a cutlet. I really was famishing, so I made a good meal, drank a couple of glasses of wine and had a cup of black coffee; then feeling much better, I sat down in a comfortable easy chair and told him something of what had occurred. How Jim and I had been stopped the previous night by bushwhackers who had taken the horses, broken open my trunks and robbed me of everything I had in my possession. But I could not bring myself to tell him that I had been outraged by the three men. He listened attentively to all I told him and when I had finished, he asked:

'Where did you pass the night, and how did you get here this morning?'

I had expected the questions and was ready with the answers.

'I stayed in the woods all night,' – so I had, in the shanty, – 'and this morning I met a man going by with a wagon and he brought me on to the city.'

I do not know whether Randolph thought I was keeping back something or not, but anyway he did not ask me a single awkward question. He was very much vexed at the loss of his two valuable horses, but he was rather amused at my description of the way the bushwhackers had kicked my clothes about in disgust.

'Damn the thing,' he said. 'I would not have sold those horses for less than eight hundred dollars, but we can easily replace your finery, Dolly. It was lucky you left your jewellery behind you. I will go to the police and give information, but I am pretty sure nothing can be done, as the whole country is in such a disturbed state. When you want to go to your room, ring the bell, and Clara, the girl who let you in, will attend to you.'

He then went away, and I remained reclining in the easy chair for a short time. Then I rang the bell, and when Clara came, I told her I wished to go to my room.

She showed me upstairs to a long, airy, prettily furnished bedroom, with a bathroom adjoining, and as soon as she had gone away, I stripped myself, and had a most refreshing bath, scrubbing myself all over with scented soap, till at last I felt that my body was thoroughly cleansed from all outward impurities. When I had dressed myself, the girl came back, and brushed my hair, and although she was quite aware that I was not Randolph's wife, her manner was respectful.

I put a few questions to her, and as she was by no means reticent, I soon found out that Randolph had been in the habit of poking her whenever he felt inclined. However, the knowledge of that fact neither surprised nor annoyed me. It was just what I had expected to hear, from the moment I had seen the girl's pretty face and neat figure.

After she had finished brushing my hair, and had left the room, I lay down upon the bed and fell into a profound sleep.

When I woke, I saw by the clock on the mantelpiece that it was seven. I had slept for four hours, and I felt quite fresh; the colour had come back to my cheeks, my eyes had lost their heavy look, and the illtreated 'spot' was feeling fairly easy. I was just about to get up and go downstairs, when Randolph entered the room, and coming to the bedside looked down upon me.

'Well, Dolly,' he said, 'I suppose you've had a good sleep? You're looking all right again, so I intend to have a poke, to give me an appetite for dinner. It will be as good as a cocktail for me, and I will make you "cock up your tail,"' he added laughing.

I loathed the very idea of being poked again, and I heartily wished there was not such a thing as a male organ in the world. Six times in less than twenty-four hours had the horrid weapons pierced my poor little 'spot' and now it was going to be transfixed for the seventh time. However, I knew that if I made any objection, it would only make him angry and excite his suspicions, so I did not say a word.

He proceeded to 'cock up my tail,' by laying me in a curved position over the side of the bed with my feet on the floor, then turning up my petticoats, and letting down my drawers, he took a long look at my bottom, then he stroked it, and spanked it harder than was pleasant, saying coolly:

'Well, Dolly, I must say that I have not seen a prettier

192

bottom than yours, or spanked a plumper one, since I came to Richmond.'

He then began to ram at me from behind, with evident pleasure to himself, but with pain to me, for though outwardly the 'spot' was apparently all right, the inner lips were excoriated; consequently I suffered a good deal and had to clench my teeth to keep myself from crying out. But to prevent him suspecting anything was wrong, I worked my bottom backwards to meet his thrusts, as if I had been really enjoying the embrace, and when he 'spent,' I wriggled myself briskly. But I was exceedingly glad when all was over and he had withdrawn his member from the sore 'spot'. However, he was pleased with me, and giving me a kiss, complimented me on the way I had done my share of the work. After the necessary ablutions, we went down to dinner, which was a good one, and also well cooked, the waiting being done by a neatly dressed, but rather elderly, white parlourmaid. All the servants in the establishment were white women, whom Randolph had taken over along with the house, the owner of which had gone to Europe with his wife and family at the outbreak of the war.

During the progress of dinner, Randolph and I talked about the state of affairs at Woodlands, and he asked me a number of questions, all of which I was able to answer fully and truthfully. Strange to say, he did not ask me a single question about the Federal officer, Captain Franklin. When dinner was over and we were in the drawing-room, we conversed about the war, and he said that most of the planters in the Southern States would be ruined if the Federals eventually proved victorious in the struggle. He further said that though he himself would be hard hit by the abolition of slavery, he had fortunately a large sum of money invested in foreign securities, so that whatever happened he would still be comparatively a rich man.

At eleven o'clock he told me to come to bed, adding that he wanted to have a good naked roll with me. I was glad to go to bed, but I did not look forward with pleasure to more love-making: however, I followed him meekly upstairs to the bedroom. After locking the door, he lit all the candles, so that the chamber was brilliantly illuminated. Then he made me take off all my clothes, doing the same himself, and when we were both stark naked, he put his arm round my waist, and waltzed round the room with me till I was quite out of breath, while all the time, his bare breast was pressed against my naked palpitating bosom, his stiff member rubbing against my belly, and he occasionally stimulated my flagging steps by applying a smart slap to my bottom. When he was tired of 'dancing,' he lifted me on to the bed, and then holding me in his arms, twining his legs round mine, he rolled over and over, clasping me in a tight embrace, finally finishing up by laying me on my back and sabring me lustily.

Then he allowed me to put on my chemise – I had no nightdress – and get between the sheets, where he soon followed me.

I thought he was done with me, but I was very much mistaken. He was in great form, so I got very little sleep, as he kept playing with me, at short intervals, all night, besides poking me thrice in a different position each time. It was late next morning when we got up, and it was noon before we had finished breakfast. He then left the house on some business or other, while I sent for my dressmaker and ordered a fresh stock of frocks, hats, and bonnets. I then went out shopping and bought a full supply of dainty undergarments, silk stockings and shoes. Randolph always liked me to be prettily dressed, and he never objected to pay the bills for the clothes that adorned me, but he did not give me much money to spend; in fact he was rather stingy. In a few days, I was completely fitted out again, and was able to go out with him, by day or night, wherever he wished me to accompany him.

Chapter Twenty-three

The battle of Fair Oaks – Departure for New York – No more sights of beaten slaves – Randolph's fresh 'amours' – He starts for Europe – My last spanking – The only reminiscence of 'tenderness' – I begin housekeeping.

A few weeks passed; Randolph paid a visit to Woodlands, and found that everything on the plantation was in a most neglected state, but the house had been kept in order by Dinah and the other women. When he came back, he brought me my jewellery.

A week after his return, the battle of Fair Oaks was fought, the Federal troops drew closer to Richmond, and everything in the city became more dull and wretched than ever. On my former visits I had liked the place well enough, as it had been brisk and lively, and there was always something to be seen, but now there were no amusements of any sort. The shadow of the war was over everything and everybody. It was a dreary place to live in. I was very tired of it, and I would much rather have been at Woodlands.

Randolph, also, had got very tired of Richmond, and of the

everlasting fighting that was going on all round, which never seemed to be decisive in any way, although hundreds of lives on both sides were sacrificed.

At last, he made up his mind to leave the South altogether, and go to New York, taking me with him. So he told me to pack up, and be ready to start in a week's time. I was delighted at receiving such an order, and I soon had everything in perfect readiness. The day of our departure arrived; we left Richmond, and in due course reached New York. And as it turned out, we left the city just in the nick of time, for a few days after our departure, the place was regularly infested by the United States troops, and after that event happened it became a difficult matter for persons, even if they were non-combatants, to pass through the Federal lines.

We put up at one of the best hotels in New York, and for a time I was as happy as a woman in my precarious position could be. I was away from the dreadful fighting; I could come and go as I liked without any fear of being whipped by lynchers, or outraged by bushwhackers. I had plenty of pretty clothes of all sorts, and also a considerable amount of jewellery. Randolph frequently took me to places of amusement, and I saw that I was always admired. He was fairly kind to me, and he gave me more money to spend than he had ever given me before. Moreover, I was delighted to have got away from the horrid slave States, and I was glad to know that I should never again see a poor slave woman writhing in agony, and shrieking for mercy while her naked bottom was being wealed by the switch, striped by the strap, or blistered by the paddle, wielded by a man. I had determined, whatever happened, never to go back to the South.

The weeks slipped by. Randolph had made a number of friends, both male and female, so I saw very little of him by day, and he very frequently stayed away from me all night.

I knew he went with other women – in fact he made no secret of his amours – but the knowledge of them did not trouble me in the least. I took a poke from him whenever he chose to give me one, but I never tried to get him to embrace me. I had a number of admirers myself, and could have had plenty of poking had I wished, but I was always faithful to Randolph, not from any feeling of honour towards him, but simply because I did not care for strange men.

At that time there was no necessity for me to allow myself to be poked if I did not wish to be. Captain Franklin was the only man who ever 'had' me, with my own consent, during the whole time I lived with Randolph.

As the days passed, I saw less and less of him, and even when he was with me he never touched me in any way, while his manner towards me became very cold, although he never was actually rude to me at that period. I guessed what it all meant. He had got tired of me, and I had a presentiment that he would soon turn me adrift. However, I had always known that our relations would come to an end, sooner or later, and that then I should have to do what many a woman has had to do when finding herself deserted by the man by whom she has been ruined. It was not long before Randolph gave me the news I had been expecting. One morning, after an absence of three days, he came to me and said he had something to tell me. My heart gave a jump. I knew what he was about to say, but I made no remark. He said:

'I am going to Europe with a party of friends, so I cannot take you with me. In fact, Dolly, the time has come for us to part altogether. But although I am leaving you, it is not through any fault of yours. You have always been a good-natured girl, and done whatever I asked you. Therefore I wish to do the best I can for you. I intend to buy you a little house, and furnish it well for you. I will also give you a sum of money to start with. You are only twenty-two years of age; you have a pretty face and a very good figure. You also have lots of good clothes and a quantity of jewellery. You will soon make friends, and I am quite sure you will manage to get on very well here in New York.'

It was a hard way of putting the matter before me and the tears rose to my eyes, but nevertheless I felt a certain amount of gratitude to him for what he intended doing for me. He had ruined me, but he might have cast me off with nothing at all. I thanked him, and he gave me a short kiss saying that he would take me out next day to look for a house. He then went away, leaving me to think over my future prospects. They did not seem to be very bright to me at that moment, but they might have been worse, so I made up my mind to face my position as bravely as I could. I did not see Randolph any more that day, or night, but next day, after lunch, he came for me and we looked at several houses in various parts of the city, but did not find one that was suitable. I need not, however, lengthen out my story by telling you of our house-hunting: it will suffice to say that eventually he bought this house, furnished it throughout, and engaged a couple of white female servants. I afterwards sent them away, and got two coloured women, who I have at this moment in my service. I find them much easier to get on with, and also far more faithful than white servants. .

When everything was in order, he brought me here one afternoon, handed me over the title deeds of the house, and gave me a thousand dollars. We then sat down and had a chat, while he drank a glass of wine and smoked a cigar. When he had finished, he rose from his seat, saying with a laugh:

'You know, Dolly, that I am fond of whipping a woman's bottom. Now I don't suppose I shall ever have a chance of doing such a thing in Europe, so you must let me give you a farewell spanking, a real smart one.'

I did not like the idea at all, and a cold shiver ran down my back, as I knew he would hurt me dreadfully, but I had not the strength of mind to refuse his farewell request, so in a rather faint voice, I said:

'I will let you spank me, but do not be too hard upon me. You know that I cannot bear pain.'

Taking a handkerchief from his pocket, he tied my wrists together, a proceeding that alarmed me.

'Oh, don't tie me!' I exclaimed.

He laughed, saying:

'I am going to whip you as if you were a naughty slave girl, so your hands must be tied to prevent you putting them over

198

your bottom during the spanking.'

Thoroughly frightened, I made some feeble remonstrances, but he seized me, and sitting down on a chair, placed me in the orthodox position across his knees: then he turned up my petticoats and took down my drawers.

'Now,' he said, stroking my bottom, 'don't make too much noise, or the servants will hear you.'

Then holding me firmly down, he began to spank me very severely. Oh, how hard his hand was, and how it did sting!

I burst into tears, wriggling and squirming about on his thighs, and as I did so, I could distinctly feel his stiff member pressing against my belly. Clenching my teeth and holding my breath, I kept down, for a short time, the cries that rose to my lips, but at last the stinging pain became so intense that I began to squeal shrilly, kicking my legs about in anguish, and begging him to stop.

But he went on spanking me till my bottom burned and throbbed in a most agonizing way, and I screamed out as loudly as I could.

Then he stopped, and laying me in a stooping position over the end of the sofa, poked me while I was still crying and smarting with the pain of the horrid spanking.

When all was over, he untied my wrists and laid me on the sofa, while he stood beside it, looking down at me, with a smile on his face, as I lay with the tears trickling down my cheeks, all my clothes rumpled, and my drawers hanging about my ankles. My face was red, but I am sure that my poor bottom must have been much redder, judging from the way it was throbbing and tingling. It was black and blue the next day. Bending down, he gave me a kiss, saying laughingly:

'There, Dolly, that is the last spanking, and the last poke you will ever get from me!'

'It was very cruel of you to have spanked me so severely,' I said tearfully. 'I cannot understand why you should have taken pleasure in giving me such dreadful pain.'

He was not a bit sorry for having whipped me with such wanton severity, but said:

'Oh, you will soon find that many other men besides me are

fond of spanking a woman till she squeals.'

I have since found out that such is the case: many men are very fond of taking a woman across their knees. I have often been asked to allow myself to be spanked, but I have never consented. Randolph is the only man who has ever taken me on his knees, for a spanking. He went on laughing at his own poor joke:

'You know, Dolly, that when a man sets up a new establishment, he generally gives a housewarming. Well, I have given you a bottom-warming instead. I have always admired your bottom, and I shall always have a pleasing recollection of it as it appeared to-day. It looked very pretty while the plump white cheeks were blushing at the touch of my hand.'

He then again kissed me on my tear-bedabbled face, bade me good-bye and calmly left the house, leaving me lying on the sofa, sore, angry, and indignant. Fortunately, the servants had not heard the shrieks I had uttered while being spanked. I lay quietly until the intense smarting pain of my bottom had somewhat subsided; then I fastened up my drawers, and going into the bedroom, bathed my flushed face, thinking to myself what an utterly heartless man Randolph was. There certainly had never been any sentiment in the relations between us: but I thought he might have parted with me in a more tender way. However, I had no tender feeling for him after the way he had treated me, and so the only 'tenderness' there was about our parting was the 'tenderness' of my sorely spanked bottom.

Chapter Twenty-four

*The last of my tyrant – I make other friends – How my present life
began – Hate of the Southerners justified.*

He sailed for Europe next day, and I have never seen him
or heard from him since, but I know that he remained abroad
until the war was over, and then he returned to Woodlands,
where I believe he is now.

As soon as I had got fairly settled in my new home, I put
five hundred dollars in the bank, and went on keeping house
with the remainder of the money.

At first, I did nothing but amuse myself, and I thoroughly
enjoyed being mistress of a house of my own, doing just what
I liked, without anyone to bother me. But after a time, as
money was constantly going out and none was coming in, and
as I had determined not to touch the five hundred dollars in
the bank except in case of absolute necessity, I saw that I
should have to replenish my purse. And there was only one
way for me to do it.

I did not like having to adopt the life, for notwithstanding
all I had gone through, I was still a modest woman to a certain

extent. But I made the plunge, and as I had a pretty face, a well-shaped figure, good clothes and handsome jewellery, I attracted admiration and soon made a number of friends. I hated the life at first, and I dislike it still, but have got accustomed to it – like other women in the same position. Nearly four years have passed since that time, and I have done well in the 'profession.' I have many good friends, some of whom are rich and liberal. I have saved money and am still saving, and I have had a couple of offers of marriage.

Perhaps I will get married some day, if I get an offer from a man whom I could love, for although I am what I am, I will never marry a man unless I love him.

About a year ago, I paid a visit of a couple of days to Philadelphia and while there, I heard that Miss Dean was still unmarried, and was as charitable as ever. It had never got to be known that she had been shamefully whipped during her stay in the South. I need hardly tell you that I did not call upon her, though I should have liked to have seen and spoken to the sweet woman again.

My story is finished, and now you know why I said I hated Southerners. Don't you think I have good reason to hate them? They were the cause of all my misfortunes. If they had not whipped me and ridden me on a rail, I should not have been outraged by three ruffians, nor been compelled to adopt my present life.

Conclusion

I remained in New York for three weeks after Dolly had related her story to me, and I frequently paid her a visit, not only because she was a pretty little woman and a splendid poke, but because I had got to like her, and I also pitied her very much. She certainly had been hardly dealt with by men while she was in the South.

On the day I bade her good-bye, I gave her my address, and told her that I should like to hear from her if ever she felt inclined to write to me.

I think she was a little sorry to part with me; for there were tears in her eyes, and her voice shook, when she wished me good-bye.

Next day, I sailed from New York in the Scotia, and after a rather rough passage arrived in Liverpool, from which place I went straight home and settled down to my usual life.

Six months afterwards, I received a letter from Dolly, telling me that she was going to be married to a man in a good way of business, a few years older than herself, who loved her, and whom she really loved.

I was glad to hear the news. She was a good-tempered, amiable young woman, who although weak in many respects, would, I was convinced, make a good and faithful wife to the man she loved.

I wrote her a letter of congratulation, and sent her a wedding present, which she acknowledged in a nicely-worded letter. Our correspondence was never renewed, but I hope she is a happy wife.

The poor little woman, who had suffered so much from no fault of her own, deserved to have some luck after all her troubles.